PRAISE FOR
WORRY

"Fabulously revealing . . . The novel runs on an engine that relentlessly converts suffering, usually of the inner-turmoil variety, into comedic relief. . . . Some stories give you the unvarnished truth, some the varnished one. *Worry* is generous and wise enough to give both."

—*The New York Times Book Review*

"A bitingly funny, extremely online novel about sisterhood."

—*The Washington Post*

"*Worry* is exacting and hilarious, the startling, familiar shock of seeing your own slightly warped face reflected back to you when your iPhone dies from hours of scrolling. . . . But at its core, *Worry* is a novel about sisters and the love they share despite being given access to each other's emotional nuclear codes."

—*Nylon*

" [A] mordant debut . . . comical and savage . . . With unflinching honesty, Tanner captures the claustrophobia of twenty-first-century young adulthood."

—*Publishers Weekly* (starred review)

"Smart . . . Vivid . . . Oppressively visceral."

—*Air Mail*

"Alert: A genuinely funny book has entered the chat. . . . This debut novel's observations about life in 2019—and in your twenties—are darkly hilarious and almost too spot-on."

—*theSkimm*

"If a Big Sister Manifesto did exist, one that captured the hypocrisies of the role along with the heroism, the joy along with the pain, then Alexandra Tanner has come as close as it gets with her debut novel, *Worry*. . . . Like Ferrante and Heti before her, Tanner has constructed a layered *Künstlerroman*, an artist's novel about two artists coming to maturity."

—*Los Angeles Review of Books*

"Dark, funny . . . a haunting snapshot of contemporary life."

—*Minneapolis Star-Tribune*

"Reading this feels a lot like hanging out with a sister . . . like looking in a fun house mirror at times, sometimes to my horror, but always to my entertainment."

—*Condé Nast Traveler*

"Limning the absurdity of our internet-addled, dread-filled moment, Tanner establishes herself as a formidable novelist."

—*The Millions*

contains both the chaos of Lena Dunham's *Girls* and the neurotic humor of *Curb Your Enthusiasm*."

—*Chicago Review of Books*

"Alexandra Tanner is an author to watch: she's both funny and serious, snarky and sweet, and gives us that rare, realistic window into recognizable life."

—*Literary Hub*

"A portrait of contemporary life that is equal parts hilarious, brutal, and affecting."

—*Lilith*

"Existential, absurd, and deeply funny."

—*Our Culture*

"I've spent my whole life desperately trying not to say the stuff that comes out of these characters' mouths."

—Tony Tulathimutte, author of *Rejection*

"Disturbingly relatable."

—*Jezebel*

"Fans of Jen Beagin and Melissa Broder will appreciate Tanner's style. . . . A stinging yet joyful story about life playing out online or nowhere."

—*Booklist*

"A dark and laugh-out-loud-funny debut about sisterhood, internet poisoning, and suspecting that there is something incurably wrong with you but not wanting to know what it is (relatable!)."

—Ruth Madievsky, author of *All-Night Pharmacy*

"This book is like popping an Adderall and discovering the beauty of your food processor.

—Beth Morgan, author of *A Touch of Jen*

"Gorgeous, hilarious, disturbing . . . If you have a sister, are a sister, or wish you had a sister, read *Worry*."

—Jenny Mustard, author of *Okay Days*

"One of the most exciting literary debuts—and just one of the flat-out best novels—in memory."

—David Burr Gerrard, author of *The Epiphany Machine*

WORRY

A NOVEL

ALEXANDRA TANNER

SCRIBNER

NEW YORK   AMSTERDAM/ANTWERP   LONDON

TORONTO   SYDNEY/MELBOURNE   NEW DELHI

Scribner
An Imprint of Simon & Schuster, LLC
1230 Avenue of the Americas
New York, NY 10020

This book is a work of fiction. Any references to historical events, real people, or real places are used fictitiously. Other names, characters, places, and events are products of the author's imagination, and any resemblance to actual events or places or persons, living or dead, is entirely coincidental.

First Scribner trade paperback edition April 2025

SCRIBNER and design are trademarks of Simon & Schuster, LLC

Simon & Schuster strongly believes in freedom of expression and stands against censorship in all its forms. For more information, visit BooksBelong.com.

For information about special discounts for bulk purchases, please contact Simon & Schuster Special Sales at 1-866-506-1949 or business@simonandschuster.com.

The Simon & Schuster Speakers Bureau can bring authors to your live event. For more information or to book an event, contact the Simon & Schuster Speakers Bureau at 1-866-248-3049 or visit our website at www.simonspeakers.com.

Interior design by Hope Herr-Cardillo

Manufactured in the United States of America

10 9 8 7 6 5 4 3 2 1

Library of Congress Control Number: 2023029360

ISBN 978-1-6680-1861-3
ISBN 978-1-6680-1862-0 (pbk)
ISBN 978-1-6680-1863-7 (ebook)

For Jess

My sister Poppy arrives on a wet Thursday, dressed ugly and covered in hives.

"I started flaring a little in security," she says, dropping her bags, toeing off her salt-streaked boots, unwrapping a chunky gray scarf I gave her six years ago after realizing it signaled nothing about me at all. Beneath the scarf, Poppy's neck is doppled with welts, some pinker and fresher than others.

She closes her right eye and blinks her left rapidly, like something's stuck in it, while she fills me in on her trip.

"Leaving Florida, there were—you know how there's always that old, old couple in line at security who don't take off their belts, don't take out their iPads, then they have, like, soup with them, and things of lotion, and they go through probably eight times? I was behind those people. The whole thing was chaos. And I had to steal a water bottle at the little store because

I

there was no one at the register." Now I notice a huge Evian sticking out of her tote.

To save fifty bucks on airfare, Poppy flew from the Palm Beach airport not to JFK or LaGuardia or even Newark but to MacArthur, on Frontier, then rode a shuttle from the airport to Ronkonkoma to catch the LIRR, then took a two-hour train that ended up taking three hours because someone jumped onto the tracks and died as it was pulling into Jamaica.

"I saw the *fucking* body bag," Poppy says. She claws at her throat. Her fingernails, overlong as always, leave red slashes. If she scratches too much, the hives will bleed, become infected, refuse to heal. Her body is a log of all the times she couldn't be good and patient and just wait for the swelling to go down.

"Don't itch," I say, swatting at her hand. "I've seen body bags. You'll see more if you move here. Do you have your EpiPen with you?"

"Yeah," Poppy says. "But it's not that bad, it'll go down in a minute. I just need to let it breathe." She sounds uncertain. "I haven't had a real flare in forever," she continues; "I don't know if this is really even a flare, it's probably like normal-people hives, I'm just not used to wearing a scarf for this long. And air travel is stressful, you know? So I don't think it's *hives*-hives. Also, I *am* moving here. That's why I have all this shit with me."

"We'll see," I say. "Should you use it?"

"Use what?" She throws herself down on the couch and fans her neck.

"Your EpiPen?"

Poppy looks at the floor, then back at me. "I don't have one right now. They doubled the price, and Mommy and Daddy's insurance doesn't cover it anymore, and I've been on the phone with this company five, or, like, maybe four times this month, and I just don't want to pay them seven hundred dollars or whatever they want for it. Like, I could, but I shouldn't have to. It's burglary, it's criminal. My throat could close up and they want me to pay seven hundred dollars to have, like, a *chance* to stop it? Fuck Blue Cross Blue Shield," she says, pushing her knuckles into her eyes, "fuck health care, fuck America."

"Okay," I say, "but what if your throat, like, does close up—"

"You know I've never had my throat close up, oh my god, that's not the point," Poppy says, pinching at her lashes to tug her lids away from her eyeballs, a thing she knows I hate.

"Stop that."

"Oh my *god,*" she says again, "you stop," and she stomps into the bathroom and shuts the door. I hear her peeing. After a moment she calls to me, sheepish, and asks me to bring over her phone, which, she tells me, is in the pocket of her coat: a monstrous and woolly wine-red robe-wrap kind of thing that I recognize as a hand-me-down from our mother. I take Poppy her phone—"I couldn't poop on the plane," she says as I hand it over, "it was so bumpy, plus, oh my god, have you heard this? That you're not even supposed to wash your hands with the water from the airplane bathroom because it's so filthy?"—and then I shut the door on her and try on her coat in the living room mirror. It goes better with my eyes than hers, and since I'm two inches taller than she is, it hits my legs in the right place. On me, it's not so terrible. Now I'm wondering how I can get her to give it to me. Maybe I'll tell Poppy I think the coat's disgusting, and once she stops wearing it out of shame, I'll take it—but then how would I explain wanting something I'd insulted? To avoid a whole fight I'd have to wait, probably until Poppy moved out of the apartment, maybe even until she left the city for good; but considering she's just landed and has three job interviews and five apartment viewings lined up for later this week, and considering all Poppy has ever wanted is to come live in New York, and considering I should be supportive of her sole desire, maybe her departure isn't something I should hope for. Poppy wants to stay, and I'm supposed to want to help her stay. Maybe I'll just let her keep the coat.

In the bathroom, Poppy shits. I hear it hit the water. I carry her things across the apartment into the office, two trips, and each time I edge close to the bathroom, I can make out the voice of Donald Trump leaking from her phone.

"You motherfucker," Poppy says. She opens the door and calls to me. "I hate that he's, like, the funniest person in the world. Don't you hate how fucking funny he is?" She closes the door before I can answer. Then she opens it again. "Oh, and on top of it all, I literally just got my period."

"It turns me into an animal," Poppy tells me on our way to the park. A walk, she says, dulls cramps, if you can get yourself out the door. "A few days before it comes I'll get itchy. I can feel every hair on my head, all the necks of my shirts start bothering me, things like that. Sometimes I flare. Everything's loud, everything smells. All my senses are heightened. Except vision. My vision gets so much blurrier than normal, like to the point where I can't even see across the room. Even right now it's like—I don't know, like everything has an aura."

I'm jealous of the way Poppy still thinks that everything she's ever experienced is special.

She keeps going. "You know what I'm talking about. Your periods are really crazy, too, right?"

I wouldn't describe my periods as "really crazy." "Yeah," I say anyway. "It can be an intense time."

"What happens to you?" Poppy can never just let me agree with her and move on.

"Um," I say. "My lymph nodes feel big sometimes."

Poppy frowns. "That's not a period thing."

Suddenly my neck's sweaty. "It is for me. Don't invalidate my experience. I've been menstruating longer than you, I know how I menstruate."

"But I started menstruating earlier in the timeline of my life than you did. I started menstruating in *grade* school. So I don't think you *have* been menstruating longer than me in years *total*."

I frown at her. "That doesn't make sense."

"It does. You just can't do basic math." Poppy starts walking faster than me, staring at the ground. Now we're fighting about nothing, about a detail I made up to pacify her. I often find myself in spots like this with Poppy, getting all mixed up trying to pretend we're more alike than we are.

"Do you think it's normal if my lymph nodes *do* feel big sometimes?"

Poppy huffs. "I'm sure it's normal," she says.

"Because I saw this thing online where a girl thought she just had big lymph nodes but it was actually lymphoma, and her friends made her a GoFundMe, but they put up these pictures of her where it was, like, obvious this girl is *not* making it—"

"You don't have lymphoma," Poppy says. "You're the healthy one."

"I get really bad strep every sixteen months like *clockwork*. What makes you get strep every sixteen months?"

"Being alive," Poppy says. "Getting strep is part of being alive."

At the park, a few trees are trying to bloom. Wet sleet falls, patching the grass with blackening slush. Some cold-looking children, flush-cheeked and hunched, play soccer in long pants. Poppy tells a story about a friend of hers who used to coach coed youth soccer on weekends. Her friend's team of six-year-olds had decided to call themselves "The Mommies and the Daddies."

"Which friend?" I ask. "Anna, old roommate Anna?"

"Actually," Poppy says, "it's not a story from a friend. It's just a funny tweet I saw."

Poppy and I are wearing matching Danskos with socks. As we walk along the path at the edge of the Long Meadow, I take a picture of our feet standing on some old snow, open Instagram, put an orange heart emoji in the corner of the screen, and upload it to my stories. I don't tag Poppy because she doesn't like to be tagged in things.

Within minutes, I have a story reply from an account I don't recognize: getwellwithwendy. The only Wendy I know is our mother. I open the message and see that getwellwithwendy has sent me a thumbs-down emoji and a single line of text: horrible shoes... A very Wendy thing to say. I click on her profile. Sure enough, it's her. She has zero followers, but she's uploaded her first post: a blurry picture of a smoothie that she's captioned with #getwellwithwendy #kosher #smoothie #koshersmoothietime.

I'm about to show the message to Poppy and ask her if she knows what our mother is doing on Instagram and how long she's been eating kosher, but she starts talking before I can: "Have you heard that thing about how it would be as easy to bite off your finger as it is to bite into a carrot but there's something in our brains that won't let us do it?"

"Everyone's heard that," I tell her.

We sit on a bench. Poppy pulls out her phone. "Why didn't you tag me?"

"You hate when I tag you."

"Well," Poppy says, "still."

We hear a commotion from the field. One of the children playing soccer is on the ground, clutching his leg. When the coach pulls his hands away to get a closer look, there's blood.

"My bone," screams the child, "I see my bone!"

"Okay," Poppy says. "Let's go."

I stand up with her, but I stare out at the kid, trying to see what's happening. "Hang on," I say. "I just wanna see—"

"You're sick," Poppy says. "Come on."

I follow her out of the park, surprised; normally she's the one who wants to look at awful things. Once, when we were in high school, I got up in the middle of the night to use our shared bathroom, and Poppy was in there, on the toilet, with her school-issued laptop; *Oh my God, fuck, oh my God, oh my God,* said a voice coming from the computer speaker; I shut the door quickly and went back to bed, and she followed me, and climbed up on top of me, and dragged the covers off of me, and held her laptop turned around to face me, whisper-screaming: *It wasn't porn, it wasn't porn, it was 9/11 footage, it was jumpers, it was people filming people jump.*

Poppy wants to go to the Brooklyn Museum gift shop on the way back to the apartment, so we do. She holds up a forty-dollar T-shirt that says *CITY OF NEW YORK* in curly script and waves it at me. "Would Daddy like this?" she asks.

"Probably not," I say. "But you'd know better."

"I don't know. He's so old now, it's hard to say what he likes." Poppy folds the shirt poorly and reshelves it. "He replaced all the lights in the house with LED bulbs, and now every room looks like an operating room. It took three days of him carrying his ladder around, and every room he finished, he'd call me in and turn on the lights and go, 'So? How about that? Isn't that something? Isn't that *something*?' Now when I lie in bed with the overheads on, it feels like I'm about to go into surgery." Our father, a dermatologist, has an obsession with good lighting. Until a few years ago our relationship was pretty good, pretty normal. Then I started wanting things done. Now every few months my father takes my face in his hands, evaluates it, determines what part of it could be bigger, or smaller, or smoother, or better. *I have a new laser, it'll get those hairs on your neck. I have a new filler, it'll get your chickenpox scar. I have a new neuromodulator, it'll open up your littler eye.*

I laugh, then I pick the shirt back up and fold it a little nicer. I pull a piece of lint the color of Poppy's ugly scarf off the front.

"You're always undermining me," Poppy says. She touches the T-shirt one last time, just to touch it last, before we head out.

One of the Mormon mommy bloggers I follow on Instagram posts about having a "mom crush" on her "mini boyfriend," referring to her month-old baby. He's like a tiny husband I get to hold on my hip! She asks if any other moms feel this way, urges them to answer in the comments. The filter over the photo makes her newborn's just-opened eyes an icy, bright blue.

We need more blue eyed babies like yours!!!!! someone comments.

Amen!! the original mommy replies.

Omg, someone else writes, I always want to makeout with my baby boy!!!!! is that weird?, followed by three crying-with-laughter emojis.

SICK, another replies.

no this is totally normal, it's a hormonal thing, a different person writes. it's like how touching your nipples makes you feel homesick

I have a separate handle that I've started using just to follow these religious girls. A couple of years ago I used it to hate-stalk the accounts of brands I liked but couldn't afford, writers who were younger than me but whose careers were so far ahead of mine I'd never catch up, my craziest cousins and their craziest acquaintances, the worst people from high school. But then I started getting a lot of Mormon mommy bloggers on my Discover page, and I kept following them, collecting them like Beanie Babies: dani_lambofgod, servantwife1515, and so on, each compressing their lives into posts, posts, posts: uncountable shining garnets of the sickest, most deranged content imaginable.

Not all of the mommies I follow now are Mormon—some are evangelicals, fundamentalists, tradcaths, homesteaders. A few nights ago, when I was really high and looking at some mommies, I found a ballerina-turned-prepper who very much resembled my own mother, and I started crying in a way that felt otherworldly and out of my control. Looking at these women makes me feel full.

The last few years my mother, too, has started getting religious, but in a weird way; it's weirder, I think, when reform Jews suddenly find religion. She won't call herself a Jew for Jesus, but that's what she's become. My parents used to make fun of such people around the dinner table; now my mother attends services at a messianic congregation in Boynton Beach with a sign out front that reads *Congregation L'Chaim: Where Jew And Gentile*

Are At LAST One In CHRIST! She told me through tears not long ago, *When I was growing up, I always thought Jesus died for everyone but me. And it made me feel lower than a frog. But now I know he died for me, too.*

Sometimes my mother emails Poppy and me YouTube recordings of their services, which are led by a guy in a bad rug called Pastor Bruce. She always includes a note like *Amazing wisdom in here if you two would bother to pay attention.* One video, I remember, was called *THE BEST IS YET TO COME!* I've never known a Jew who thinks this way.

"Jesus," Poppy says when I tell her about my secret Instagram handle, Wendy's new account, the late-night L'Chaim browsing, how they connect, how concerned I am about our mother. "Leave all this behind. Don't think about it. How is this fun for you?"

I get ready to explain to Poppy that what I'm doing isn't about fun, but I stop myself because I don't know what it *is* about yet. I could tell her about the ex-ballerina, about what seeing her provoked. I could try to describe the feeling I get watching Pastor Bruce's lectures in the middle of the night, browsing the TEACHINGS section of L'Chaim's website (Teaching Number Four: *We affirm Jewish Culture and Jewish practices [that do not contradict the Direct Word of God!]*). I could tell her that I sometimes get the same feeling when an ad pops up for Endless Shrimp Mondays at Red Lobster while I'm trying to watch the Zapruder film on YouTube; when I see a linen clothing company post about how the "vibrational energy" of linen is 5,000 hertz, which is why wearing linen makes you magnetic to others.

Sometimes the things I see on the Internet—even and especially the anti-Semitic dog whistles, the worm-brained sociopolitical infographics, the mommy bloggers salivating to make out with their fauxhawked blond boychildren—feel like holes in the fabric of time only I am special enough to glimpse. If I'm not stoned already, they make me feel like I'm stoned. I can see the end of art and culture and sometimes even human life if I've been scrolling through the right pages for long enough. Sometimes I feel like my own ancestor. Sometimes I feel like a Tamagotchi. There's no way to fully describe these feelings to Poppy or to anyone. So instead, I show her a recent post by a woman who celebrated her husband's vasectomy reversal by posting a picture of him, asleep in a hospital bed and clothed in a paper gown, captioned Today is the day!! Can't wait 'til my amazing man wakes up and we can start trying to make babies! If you have a spare moment y'all please pray for us! followed by two closed-eyed-tongue-out emojis and then the one of the white man and white woman kissing with a heart between their faces.

"Okay," Poppy says, "wait," and she grabs my phone out of my hands. I watch her hungry fingers pinch to zoom, and I smile.

I take Poppy out for a welcome-to-Brooklyn dinner, hurrying her through the subway tunnels, shushing her when she starts talking on the train.

"People usually try to be quiet on public transportation here," I tell her. "Out of respect."

Poppy frowns at me and cuts her eyes toward a guy standing near us, watching *Gladiator* on his Samsung: full volume, no headphones.

"Respectful people," I say, "try to be quiet."

At the restaurant, there aren't any tables. "I just don't think we can seat you tonight," says the hostess. It's seven p.m.

"Not all night?" I ask, trying to Bambi my eyes.

"Like I said." The hostess smiles.

We walk a few blocks until we come to a place that Poppy thinks looks good, some kind of poke fusion restaurant with an annoying sidewalk sign: a hideous, badly chalked Pokémon tele-kinetically levitating a bowl of rice.

"What are you, five years old?" I ask, but Poppy's already in the door, holding up two fingers for the hostess.

At our table, a blond guy with a frightening tic of rocking back and forth on the tips of his toes takes our order.

"And what protein would you like on that?" he asks me. I don't want to eat any kind of fish or meat in this place; I don't like the look of the tabletops. Ever since I had some bad chowder for the first and only time when I was nine years old, I've had miserable anxiety about food; there are safe foods and non-safe foods, places where it's okay to eat and places where it's not. The restaurant I wanted to take Poppy to is a safe one; I've been eating there for years, having started with a limited sampling of meatless dishes and slowly, one by one, adding on plates I can confidently tell myself won't make me sick. When pudding's a day past its expiration date, when the inside of the lid on a jar of pickles has too much condensation, when the liquid in a jar of tomato sauce has separated, when a recipe calls for chicken thighs, when yellow flowers have opened on a head of broccolini, when it's a Tuesday night and someone wants to order calamari for the table: that's when I'm having a bad time.

"No protein, please," I say, offering him my menu.

"Oh, you have to select a protein."

"I don't want any protein."

"Unfortunately," he says, rocking toward me, "you have to have one. Otherwise it'd just be a plain rice bowl, you know?"

"What if I just want a plain rice bowl?"

"Unfortunately," he starts again.

"Look," I say, surprising myself with how feral and bitchy fear can make me sound, "I don't want a protein. Sorry."

"It's policy," he says, "for this dish to come with a protein. Like: I can't ring this dish into our system without one." He holds his pen above his pad, waiting.

"I just—I can't really, um—think of a protein I'd like to have." Is this guy hearing the word "protein" the way I'm hearing it, how pink and slick it feels right now, how revolting?

"Give her tofu on the side," Poppy says, grabbing my menu and passing them both up to our waiter.

"Tofu," he says, writing on his order pad, "on—the—side." He looks at me like: *Wasn't that simple?* I feel ashamed and drop my eyes.

After he walks away, I lean across the table and whisper to Poppy, "What the fuck was that? Why was that so weird? Did you hear the way he said the word 'protein'? Protein, protein, protein. I have, like—the ickies now, I don't want to eat here. Why wouldn't he just let me have no protein?"

Poppy unrolls her napkin and puts it in her lap. "Sometimes you have to pick a fuckin' protein." She stares at me. Her eyes are powerful, sharp; different than I remember them. "Stop making things harder for yourself. Things don't have to be so hard."

I want to buy a SodaStream, but Poppy doesn't want to support Israeli apartheid. So we're inert in the middle of Brooklyn's worst Target, just looking at one. Poppy has swiped some Babybels from the dairy section. She's eating them while we shop.

"I thought Pepsi bought SodaStream," I say, my need deepening by the second.

"The sanctions still apply," says Poppy, her mouth full of cheese.

"You're gonna pay for those, right?"

Poppy rolls her eyes and stashes the wrappers in her purse. "What's with you and paying for everything," she says.

I google *sodastream bds* and stare at a picture of Scarlett Johansson, dead-eyed, being unveiled as the company's first-ever global brand ambassador during a ceremony at the Gramercy Park Hotel. The picture is attached to an article in which Scarlett, under fire for hawking SodaStream in a Super Bowl ad, says that SodaStream is a bridge to peace between Israel and Palestine, supporting neighbors working alongside each other, receiving equal pay, equal benefits, and equal rights.

I show Poppy the article.

"Did you see *Under the Skin*?" she asks.

"No."

She grabs my arm and widens her eyes. "Oh my god," she says, "we're watching it later. As soon as we get home. Scarlett Johansson plays this alien—I'm not spoiling anything, but she's an alien, I mean, that's kind of the twist but there's a bunch of other stuff, it's not even a movie that's really *about* the twist—"

"I'm, like, thirty," I tell Poppy, even though I'm two years away from being thirty. "I don't care about spoilers." Of course, I'm furious that she's just spoiled the movie for me. I grab the SodaStream off the shelf.

"You can't break the boycott," Poppy says.

"I don't care where it's made, it doesn't matter to me. I don't wanna have to keep buying Perriers for the rest of my fucking life." On the back of the box, there's a little Israeli flag with text underneath that reads: *This product was produced by Arabs and Jews working side by side in peace and harmony*. "Look," I say, "there's this sticker."

Poppy inspects the sticker for a second. "How stupid are you?" she asks. "If you don't stand up against the behemoth of fascism—"

"That's not how you pronounce that word. It's 'behemoth.'" Instantly I feel like a bitch. It's possible—probable—that I've just incorrectly corrected Poppy's perfectly correct pronunciation of the word "behemoth." But she doesn't call me on it, so I blink and keep going. "I literally am not going to deny myself something I need right now because I don't think Israel should be bombing the shit out of everyone. Everyone bombs the shit out of everyone. Who owns Babybel? Is Babybel fascist?"

"I've googled this. They're fine. Also, you have this new thing I'm noticing," Poppy says, moving her hands at me like a mime in a box, "where you don't think anything means anything."

"Because nothing *does* mean anything."

"When did this start?"

"I don't know," I say.

"Have you talked to someone about this?"

"No."

Poppy makes a self-impressed face. "Well, I've found therapy to be really helpful in uncovering why I think certain things, and in building a belief system, and in, like: doing things like not supporting Israel."

"I don't support Israel."

"You're supporting Israel right fucking now."

"Keep your voice down," I say as a throng of school-age Hasidic girls walk past. "You can't talk about Israel in public here."

At the self-checkout, Poppy scans a tub of chocolate-covered pretzels but secrets a nail polish into her plastic bag. "It's like twelve dollars," she says when I give her a look.

Not very long ago, Poppy tried to kill herself. No one knows but me. For years before she'd been clawing through a brown depression; the summer after college, she sunk into herself. My parents hustled up to the Research Triangle, moved her out of her roachy studio, and shuttled her back home to Florida, and she stayed there with them in our childhood house for several years: she attended outpatient therapy groups where she had to make inspirational mood boards out of decade-old magazines without the crucial use of scissors, flared with the hives that'd plagued her since puberty, ideated daily about throwing herself down the stairs. I visited rarely those first bad months, hardly called. I was too icked by the new way Poppy cried: constantly, close-eyed, keening like an old tea kettle.

Once she was doing a little better, she got a temp job in the college advising office of a local private high school helping rich children slide into their places at good enough universities. She stayed in group longer than anyone she went in with, made friends, loved therapy, read about the brain. She talked about grad school. About returning to Durham, about local office. Then, on a nothing Friday in October the year before last, a day ahead of her birthday, she pulled hard on the wheel of her Jetta and crashed into a guardrail along the turnpike. All she did was break a wrist and total the car. She didn't tell anyone but me what she'd been trying to do.

Please don't do it again, I remember begging her over the phone.

Not for a while, at least, she said, *and probably not with another car.*

Shoplifting—being interested in any material thing at all— combined with her move to Brooklyn must be a sign that Poppy's shaken away the pull of suicide and turned to face her future; that she is even, that she is whole. At least that's what I tell myself.

Then again: who has ever finished a bottle of nail polish?

Poppy's standing in my doorway holding her laptop. "I think I found a place."

I sit up in bed and clear my own computer and some clothes away from the space beside me. Poppy kneels on the mattress and passes me the laptop. On the screen there's a StreetEasy listing for a boxy studio on an annoying stretch of Eighth Avenue in Chelsea. Red pipes hang from the ceiling. Unmistakable: it's the first apartment I lived in when I moved to the city.

"It's so cheap for the neighborhood," Poppy brags.

"Poppy," I say, "this is my old apartment."

"No," she says, taking the laptop back. "No, it's not."

"Across from the Foragers."

"I don't remember that apartment."

"You stayed with me for, like, a week during spring break. I had the daybed, we slept feet to feet like *Willy Wonka*."

"Oh my god," she says, letting her mouth hang open.

"See, you're pretending," I say. "You're pretending like you don't know that's my old apartment. There's no way you saw those pictures and didn't know." I grab the laptop back from her. "They raised the rent like eight hundred dollars. What are you talking about, cheap for the neighborhood? You can't afford this. Look for roommates on Craigslist, like a normal person." *Everyone lives in Chelsea when they first move to the city,* I remember saying to Poppy once years ago, *even if only metaphorically.* Did she think I was being serious?

"If I get a really good job I can."

"Did you, like, become a software developer in the night?"

"Well, maybe Mommy and Daddy would help me and pay half of it for a year and I *could* become a software developer and then I'd be able to afford it on my own."

"They're not gonna help you," I say, needing to believe it.

"They helped *you* when you moved here. Even when you were not showing signs of becoming a software developer, so if I *was,* then maybe."

"Yeah, but I was, like, twenty-one. You're too old to ask for help. And they didn't pay my rent, they were just my guarantors, and I had to beg for even that." I'm lying, so I make things colorful. "I remember they were so horrible about it, Daddy was like: *I'm not thrilled to have my ass on the line here.*"

"My psychiatrist said I'm emotionally underdeveloped by about four years." Poppy says this with an unnatural superiority. "He said I could even be displaying signs of undiagnosed ASD, that's how far back I am emotionally. So four years, that's— It doesn't matter, I think they'd help me out." When I don't respond, Poppy blinks at me. "ASD means autism."

"You *are* fucking autistic, Poppy," I say, "if you think you're gonna be able to get Mommy and Daddy to pay your rent." I feel bad right away, but not quite bad enough to apologize, or to stop. "What you actually need to do is find a real apartment, with roommates, that you can afford, and stop sleeping on my ex-boyfriend's old air mattress, and get a fucking job, and get a fucking life." I feel a motor in me, whirring, cutting up my guts.

If Poppy takes over my old apartment and starts here where I started, she'll slowly take over every part of everything I've ever done, and my experience of the last seven years will not have been what I thought it was, which was *my* life, but something else: a map of shouldn't-dos for Poppy, a map she has been watching me reach the edges of in real time; watching and noting my failures, watching and preparing to do it over and do it right.

"That was a low thing to say," Poppy says, "and I know you didn't really mean it, because I know you're not that low of a person. When you're ready to talk to me without actively trying to wound me *and* yourself, then we can have a conversation, and maybe it'll be just slightly less rife with cruelty and profanity and rabid ableism." She stands up and walks out, leaving the door open behind her.

"Don't talk to me like you're one of your five therapists," I shout after her. She doesn't take the bait.

SHE'S MOVING INTO MY OLD APARTMENT, I text our mother. I know I shouldn't, but it feels so good when she and I can be a team—even though it seems, more and more often these days, that we can be a team only when we're against Poppy.

A minute later, the answer comes: I told you when you were 12 to stop encouraging her to spend so much time with you if you didn't want her to. But you encouraged her nonetheless.

I can't actually think of an instance in which I ever encouraged Poppy to spend more time with me; if anything, I was always begging her to leave me alone. I never understood why she couldn't play by herself like I could, why she had to join the clubs

I joined, why she would always wait to see what I was wearing before putting together an outfit of her own.

She's just trying to understand herself, my mother writes.

you're right, I start typing, but before I can finish, another text comes in:

But she never will and you will be stuck with her forever.

Jon, the guy I've been seeing, comes over for dinner. i always like meeting people's siblings, he texted earlier. it's like: there but for the grace of god goes that person

Over pre-dinner snacks, he and Poppy talk about Sor Juana Inés de la Cruz, whom they both love, while I scroll on my phone. A girl I went to high school with is Instagramming about mindfulness: your energetic frequency determines what comes toward you. energy is everything. everything is energy. the people and opportunities that vibrationally mirror your unique level of energetic sovereignty are what will come into your life. do not stay bogged down by the same old low-vibe loops. attune your heart to your true energetic blueprint. when you are aligned with your own energy, everything else will arrive.

"What do you guys think my level of energetic sovereignty is," I ask them, unable to say anything meaningful about Sor Juana. They ignore me.

"I might be a nun, too, one day," Poppy tells Jon. "Nuns are, like, having a moment." Poppy wants to be anything her girlboss feminist idols are. A nun like Sor Juana, a showrunner like Tina Fey, a communist like Frida Kahlo.

"You're not going to be a nun," I say.

Poppy looks at me with ruthlessness. "What if being a nun is, like, in alignment with my level of energetic sovereignty," she says. So she was listening; she just didn't feel like my question was worth a response.

I go back into my phone. I don't like having Poppy and Jon in the same room. I don't know how to be; I feel naked and tense. Jon and Poppy get along, though, and I wonder if it's the two of them who should be dating. This makes me feel more naked and more tense. I've been on the apps for nearly a year, clawing my way toward some lick of tenderness, making out with terrible kissers in Washington Square Park, making out with terrible kissers on Pier 46, making out with terrible kissers in that weird triangle at Atlantic and Washington, and then a couple months ago along came Jon: a marginally better kisser, smart, French on his mom's side, rich even though he won't talk about it, uncircumcised but whatever, with an MFA in poetry and half a PhD in poetry and poetics, and with all his hair, even, at least for now. He pretends he knows things about wine and I let him. I pretend I know things about Russian literature and he lets me. It's all very tentative. And now here's Poppy, squatting atop every part of my life.

There's this moment halfway through the night when Poppy asks Jon who his candidate is, and he says, "We're for Bernie," his "we" meaning him and me, and Poppy looks at me with hatred because she knows I'm secretly for Warren. But the thing is I'm not actually for Warren. I just told Poppy that so she wouldn't tell me I'd been brainwashed into liking Bernie by Jon, which I haven't been, because I was for Bernie four years ago, too, but I never said so to Poppy, because four years ago I was still with my ex Gage, who was also for Bernie and was also a poet, and Poppy would've said that he had brainwashed me, too.

After some food, Jon and I show Poppy the first episode of *Rick and Morty,* which she hasn't wanted to watch because of Reddit, but which Jon and I have been enthusiastically watching together, and at the end she says she doesn't get it.

"It gets better in the second season," Jon says. "Like *Community*? You know how it took them a while to find, like, the heart—"

"The heart of the show," Poppy says.

"Yeah," Jon says.

"It takes every show a while to find its heart," I say, feeling stupid. "That's why they're shows."

Poppy ignores me. "And then they lost it again."

"And then they got it back, kind of."

"Kind of."

Jon and Poppy talk about Dan Harmon's story circles while I peel the skin around my thumbnails off in limp strips, opening myself some raw little holes.

Poppy is reading a book about a woman who's marrying the man of her dreams: a rich Brit who owns land and calls her "darling." The woman's central problem is that her boyfriend is outed as secret royalty, and she has to decide if she wants to be royalty along with him. I think Poppy's too smart to read these books, and I say so.

Poppy makes a disgusted face. "How dare you judge what I read in my personal time. What should I be reading, a fucking textbook? Freud? Sometimes I need comfort, sometimes comfort means turning off your brain. You of all people know that, mommy stalker."

"The mommies are different."

"Different how?"

I don't have an answer. "Um," I say. "I'm studying them, kind of."

"For what?"

"For this essay I'm writing," I say, "about America, and Jews, and assimilation, and militancy, and god, and conspiracism, and whatever." There's no essay I'm writing. There's never anything I'm writing—anything real, at least. For a while I was writing copy for the online shopping vertical of a middling magazine, "20 Cute Puffers Under $200." "33 Reasons to Check Out This Amazon Sale Right Now." "These Influencers Love HomeGoods and HERE'S WHY." Now I work remotely for a company called BookSmarts editing study guides to books like *Of Mice and Men* and *Sapiens*. I'm supposed to be the final word on whether rabbits are, in the context of *Of Mice and Men,* a symbol of the futility of escapist fantasies in the Depression-era West, but in reality my job is mostly just blindly approving content the writers have pulled out of their asses and then formatting it to go up on the site so that high-schoolers can bullshit their way to fours on their AP exams. A few years ago I was writing a novel, just like everyone else I knew. Now I'm afraid to finish it because I keep trying to think of it in terms of what the BookSmarts guide for it would say. But I can't. And if I can't figure out the major motifs of my own book, how could it possibly be a book of any merit?

I look out the window. On the street I see a dog and a woman walking it. The dog trots forward, nose to the ground, then hunches its body into a horrible stance and shits. The woman picks up the shit in a green bag, twists the bag shut, and keeps walking. Then she stops. She looks at the sleeve of her jacket. She stomps her foot. It seems like she got shit on her. She stares at her sleeve for a second, then keeps on walking. Snow flurries fall around her; in an hour it'll probably all melt.

"I want a dog so bad," Poppy says.

Jon texts me a picture of his dick. I save my work before taking a five-minute break to go into the bathroom and text him back one of my boobs, but when I lift up my shirt, my belly's got those pink wrinkles it gets when I sit with bad posture for too long, so instead I write back god i love your cock and hope that's enough. Of course, when I come out of the bathroom, I see that iMessage is open on my computer, and Jon's cock is on the screen. Poppy is staring at it, shaking her head.

"You straights," she says. She points with her bookmark at the penis. "You like that? You—no, I'm not being mean. You like looking at that?"

I hurry to the monitor and X out of the app. "Of course I don't like it."

"You can demand more," Poppy says. "It's 2019."

On Instagram I see a meme about being a Scorpio. I send it to Poppy, because that's what she is. I send her another about Pokémon and abortion, and another in which someone has captioned a picture of gargantuan prehistoric arthropods swimming around in the primordial sea I was born in the wrong generation♥, and another in which someone has redrawn Blue, the dog from *Blue's Clues,* as a large and hellish hound. "*I REQUIRE THOSE CLUES, STEVEN,*" nightmare-Blue is saying, hovering over a cowering Steve. I think the *Blue's Clues* meme is so funny that I send it to Jon, too. He writes back: ????

blues clues!!!!!!! I write.

He sees my reply but doesn't respond.

I try again: the kids show!!!!!!!

i never saw that, Jon writes.

FORTY, I write. "Forty" is what I say to Jon when he's acting forty, which he isn't but obviously wishes he were. He's thirty-two, only four years older than me, but he's always pretending like there's some huge generational gap between us.

come over, he writes.

My throat feels sore. The idea of spending more than an hour on the train to Harlem just to go sleep on Jon's lumpy IKEA mattress—lumpier, even, than my IKEA mattress—makes me sad.

feelin icky, I write. i think i have a cold :'(The conversation is getting too long to be happening on Instagram, but it feels too late to switch to texts. Jon doesn't respond to my thing about maybe having a cold. I take a picture of myself with my arm flung over my face, place an enlarged thermometer-in-the-mouth emoji in the corner of the photo, and post it to my stories. I make up a whole fantasy in which Jon brings me chicken soup from Barney Greengrass and we watch the wordless Disney cartoon about the old barn while spooning, and then we go to sleep without having any kind of sex at all. Hours pass. Jon doesn't acknowledge my story. I stare at the sprinkler pipe running across my ceiling and consider where I am, where I ought to be. In childhood, I thought I'd be an orthodontist.

"I'd be so good at BookSmarts," Poppy says. "I'm book-smart. You're not really that book-smart, you were always kind of bad at school and studying and having a work ethic, so it's crazy you have that job and I have no job." She's heinously drunk after a night out with some college friends she hasn't spoken to in three years. They're all in law school now. Earlier, Poppy attended the last of her job interviews; she texted me when it ended that the interviewer had concluded by saying, *And you have a lovely afternoon,* code for *See you never.* So now Poppy's blackout.

"I have lots of knowledge," she tells me. "I have to do something with it. I have to start making money. But I don't want to have to make money. I want to just have big piles of it for nothing. I have this dream for my life, but I'm so embarrassed to tell you. It's so bad, it's against—it's not anything I believe in, but. But I'm gonna tell you anyway. So I'm at the Met in the middle of a weekday. I drop a glove in that big room full of the marble sculptures, and a kind tall dark handsome stranger picks it up and

hands it back to me, and he compliments the glove, it's velvet—
it's a velvet glove—and I make a joke, and he asks if I'm free for
dinner, and I am, and then we go to a dim restaurant, and there's
olives, and candlelight, and a private party happening in the back
room, and every once in a while we hear these big loud laughs, and
we know that everyone is having a good time, and that makes us
feel safe, and the man keeps telling me these great sophisticated
political jokes, and at the end of the night he kisses me on my
stoop, and we go out again and again, and on one of our dates he
tells me he's the sole heir to this huge fortune, billions of dollars,
but like—he's a good person, still, and I am just"—now Poppy is
crying—"I'm just so happy, and so relieved, because he proposes,
and my future is set, and I know in my heart deep down I'll never
want for anything, ever, I can have anything I want, and my new
husband's gonna buy me a townhouse with all this old pottery in
it, just cabinets and cabinets of that smooth, white, fucking useless pottery, and a Hamptons house with beach access and insane
jewelry for my birthdays and our anniversaries, one year he'll buy
me, like, a forty-thousand-dollar watch, and I go with him to the
store to buy it and the people working there all treat us nicely and
give us bottled waters for free," and here Poppy, having reminded
herself of water, gets up to go to the fridge, "and this husband
just loves me so much, and he gets me pregnant, which you know
I'm so grossed out by but then we have twin girls, so—sorry to
be gender essentialist, sorry, we assign them female at birth, but
they both grow up to be girls—and I get to dress them in pretty
things, and then I send them to—to school at"—Poppy nearly

gags with joy—"*Barnard,*" she wails, "they'll go to Barnard when they're old enough, and when we drop them off on drop-off day I'll help them Lysol their mattresses, I'll start spending more and more time out on Long Island, which is what I call it so that I don't sound so fucking rich, which I of course am, because I've been so fortunate because of my husband, because I've never had to stress about paying sixteen dollars for—for MOVIE SNACKS," Poppy says, weeping, her chin atremble, "or, like, a hundred dollars for a filling in my tooth, because my husband has made things so easy for me, and he's such a good father to the girls, and like—Maya Rudolph speaks at their graduation, and she has flowers on her podium, and then after, they go to law school at Princeton, and they find their own rich husbands, and even though the husbands will never be good enough for them, they're these clean nice boys in Sperrys, and even though I know they'll never take care of my twins as perfectly as me, you can tell they're the kind of boys that—they'll never hit them or call them bitches or fuck other women without their consent, you know? And my daughters will go off with these boys and have daughters of their own, and those daughters will also always be taken care of, and will also go to the Ivy Leagues, because of the generational—the generational wealth, you know, and there'll never be any, like—any, like—oh, hold on," Poppy says, and she goes to the bathroom to throw up. She stays there, retching, for hours. As I fall asleep, I'm jealous that Poppy can articulate such a clear, raw vision of want, that she can fantasize so deeply. Every time I think of something I want I manage to talk myself out of it. I close my eyes and tell myself to think hard about my deepest wish for my future life. I tell myself it's okay to imagine; that I'm safe inside my own head; that I can get specific; that my desires are worth considering. Before I know it, it's morning, and I don't remember dreaming of anything.

When I get out of bed, Poppy is on the couch, in a blanket, reading. There's a single hive in the middle of her forehead. Poppy sees me notice it and waves her hand at me.

"Don't," she says. "It's just normal allergies, I'm not flaring. Look." She turns her book around so I can see the cover. It's about the psychology of trauma.

"Did you buy that because I made you feel stupid for reading *Surprise Mystic Royal Wedding Three?*"

"No," Poppy says, defensive in a way that confirms I'm right, "I'm reading it because I want to solve the secret of our childhoods."

I remind Poppy that our childhoods were not traumatic.

"My childhood was traumatic," she says.

"What, because you were, like—forced to wear tights to temple?"

Poppy points a finger at me. "That was our mother policing my gender expression, and you know it." She says it half as a joke, screwing up her face and voice and eyes in an impression of someone irate about their gender being policed, and then she laughs. She waits for me to laugh, too.

I make Nespressos and Poppy puts on Hulu. We watch five hours of *Sailor Moon* and then realize it's night.

"Shit," Poppy says.

"The whole day's over," I say, feeling a loss.

"But we, like—needed that. To just do nothing."

I feel like what I needed, actually, probably, was to go on a long walk and read something dense and boring and impressive, to drink some juice, to see a neighbor or pet a dog or make small talk with the barista at the coffee place on the next block. I get this vision of Poppy and me on this couch forever, watching *Sailor Moon* and never showering and never leaving, growing old, developing bedsores.

"You're only staying here three more weeks," I say to Poppy. "I just need you to remember that you're only staying here while you look for somewhere else."

"I know that."

"But, like—*truly* you can only stay for three weeks. And three weeks is, like, the absolute maximum."

Poppy frowns and gestures to the empty bedroom. "There's literally an empty bedroom."

I've told her repeatedly not to talk about the empty bedroom. "It's not a bedroom," I say, "it's my office."

"'Yeah, your 'office,'" Poppy says, putting the phrase in air quotes, which she knows annoy me more than any other gesture, then stands up. "You have this, like—narrative," she says, waving her hand in the air in a gesture that suggests the creation of narrative, "where I'm this leech, where I'm trying to stay here forever and, like—feed off you and not do anything with my life. But that's not the narrative."

"What's the narrative, then?" I ask. "What are you *doing* here?"

Poppy doesn't answer me. She tucks her laptop into the crook of her elbow and puts her glasses on her head and picks up her mug of cold coffee. She starts clomping toward the empty bedroom and sloshes some on the floor.

"Clean that up," I yell, nearly spitting.

"You clean it up," Poppy says, stomping along. I follow her to the door. As she shuts it, I can see that the faulty air mattress has deflated into a sheet. I push against the door. Poppy pushes back. We push and push this way for several seconds. I start to cry. I let go of the door, and Poppy falls forward on it with all her weight. "Fuck," she screams in pain.

"What," I say, pulling the door open, "what?"

Poppy has her foot propped on her knee. She cradles her big toe, which is covered in blood. With a rip, she pulls her toenail off and holds it aloft.

"You better not get your blood all over my office floor," I say.

As Poppy walks past me on her way to the bathroom, she throws the toenail at my head. I let it hit me.

In the dark, in my room, I look at my mommies. They're all doing pyramid schemes. One's selling hair stuff, one's selling nail stuff. One's selling classes on how to be a better wife. She has a highlight of stories featuring questions that other women have asked her about how to "prosper" their husbands.

Advice on prepping (apocalypse) when hubby doesn't think its necessary but wife does but wants to submit? one woman has asked.

Lady, this mommy has written back, we are in the same boat. Submit. Express your concern and offer him supporting verses. Pray for the Father's mercy and leading. Pray and obey. See my free podcast link in bio

The most upsetting scheme involves essential oils sold by WayLife, a huge company out of Utah. All over my feed, this company's brand partners—WayLadies, they call themselves—claim that the oils cure illness and offer closeness to the Lord. Madysyn's fever was 104 last night......2 drops of the Abundance blend on her chest and it dropped right down......He is God! Once my mother sent me a link to a thing of hand sanitizer sold on WayLife's website. I wrote her back, don't buy that!!!!!!!!! She sent me a screenshot of a receipt for a twelve-pack followed by the snort-face emoji. Don't you ever tell me what to do, read a text that came in an hour later. I am the parent, and you are the child.

I fall asleep to a video of a small girl, probably three or four, reciting the story of Daniel in the lions' den for her offscreen mother.

"The nions didn't scare Daniel," says the girl, "because he was bwave and God said be bwave and save him from the nions and King Dawius."

"Yes," says the voice of the mommy, "yes, Myla! Very good! Myla—now, Myla," she says, because Myla has started to play with a doll, "Myla, listen sweetie—can you tell me, what's the meaning of this story?"

"Obey God," Myla replies.

"Amen!" says the mommy. "Amen!"

The cold I've been imagining myself to be getting for the last two days never materializes, so I meet Jon in Harlem, where he lives, for lunch. I'm on StreetEasy daily, looking for places in his neighborhood, nervous that if I don't move close to him soon, this whole thing will be over before it starts. I realize how moronic it is, flirting with the idea of uprooting my life and leaving my rent-stabilized place to live forty-five minutes closer to a guy I've been fucking for nine weeks—and not even really fucking, technically, because after the first blow job I gave him, I got strep, which I always get when I give someone new a blow job, and which necessitated oral antibiotics, which dulled the efficacy of my birth control, but Jon didn't want to use condoms, so we couldn't have intercourse, and he was going down on me so much that I got a yeast infection, which then turned into bacterial vaginosis, which necessitated a vaginal antibiotic inserted with an applicator nightly for a week, which caused a rash, which I convinced myself, after seeing an Instagram infographic about how HIV can live undetectable in the human body for up to ten years, had to be late-stage AIDS, a line of thinking that gave me debilitating diarrhea, which is of course a symptom of late-stage AIDS, which got me so worked up that I made an early-morning trip to urgent care for an HIV test, which was negative, which relieved the diarrhea but not the rash, which required a trip to the gynecologist, where I saw not my regular gynecologist but a different one who took a swab and prescribed me another cream administered via another applicator that gave me another, more terrible rash, at which point I demanded to see my original gynecologist, who took one look at my situation and said, *Don't touch your vulva, don't put anything in your vagina, don't do anything to it, don't put anything on it, wear loose-fitting cotton briefs, and leave it alone.* So in reality the fucking has been happening only about five weeks, and for some reason, it feels like an apology I'm making to him every time.

Jon buys us bagels, chips, and drinks, plus a cookie to share. Our total is something like thirty bucks. I offer to Venmo him, and he says it's fine; he'll send me a request, or I can buy him something of equal value later on. His father works for Goldman. There are no seats in the deli, so we sit outside on a bench getting smacked around by the wind. Neither of us finishes our sandwich. Jon suggests the Natural History museum, and I say okay. On the way he takes a phone call from his mother, his tongue spooning out words in French. I love hearing Jon speak another language, but when I've told Poppy that he speaks it in front of me, she's warned me that it's a calculated and exclusionary act meant to make me feel small and unintelligent and uncultured because I speak only English.

At the museum we watch a short film about the ocean. As we settle in our seats, I feel excited, but the movie tells us nothing we didn't already know.

"The sea's a tease," I tell Jon on the way out, flirting. "Like—there's gotta be stuff in there we can't imagine. What's really down there, you know?"

"The ocean," Jon says, "is pretty fully mapped."

Back at his apartment Jon pushes aside his ex-girlfriend's weighted blanket—they've split up, but they didn't want to break their lease, so they're sharing the apartment until August but supposedly sleeping in it only on alternate nights in an arrangement I don't fully understand because Jon never sleeps at my place—and we have some uninspired sex on the half-made bed. Every time I look at his weird dick with all its skin, I wonder: If we get married, will I get used to it? After he comes, he puts on a Bo Burnham special, then gets bored and switches to *Minority Report*.

"Fucking cops," he says three times, once in French. The night's not about me. I sigh. Jon doesn't notice. I get up to go to the bathroom and take my phone with me. "Get me water?" Jon asks.

On the toilet, I see I have a text from my mother. It's a screenshot of a heinous pair of $650 Gucci espadrilles. These would look adorable on you, she's written. Much better than those hag shoes you and your sister wear.... the two of you just bring out the worst in each other

I sit for a few minutes, staring at it, unsure how to respond, trying to stop myself from hyperventilating because something in me feels she's right, until Jon knocks on the door. "Are you okay?" he asks.

"I'm fine," I say.

"Can I come in?"

"Sure."

He comes in and sits on the floor in front of me. "Is your vagina all right?"

"Oh, yeah. I'm just stressed. My mom's being weird and, you know, my sister's here."

"I liked her," Jon says. "She's funny."

"She tried to kill herself like a year ago," I say. "It was really bad."

"Oh my god," Jon says, but he doesn't look concerned, exactly. I don't know him well enough to know what kind of face he's making.

"She had some big injuries," I say, exaggerating. "It took her, like, three months to recover. No one even knows but me. So I've been carrying around this big terrible secret all by myself because the only person I can talk to about it is her but I don't want to talk about it with her, you know? And all I can think about when I look at her is, like, what's she gonna do next time? Is she gonna drink bleach? Is she gonna jump off the roof of my apartment building? Every day I think about her dying, I see it happening in all these gruesome awful ways and I see it so clearly, and I make myself see it over and over, it's like I'm trying to prepare myself but it's exhausting because when it really happens it'll never be like what I'm imagining. It's this enormous, like, psychic weight that's with me every second. So I'm sorry if I haven't seemed like myself." This thing happens sometimes when I'm talking to a sexual partner where I can't tell if anything I'm saying is real.

Jon's looking at the floor. "She seemed so vibrant the other night. Very full of life."

"It's all an act. She majored in theater," I fib—she minored— "so she's really good at hiding herself."

In the morning I help Jon bring some jizzy towels down to the laundromat and then we get coffee. Over a crossword he tells me he's not ready for a relationship right now, seeing as he's still living with his ex.

"Plus," he says, "it sounds like you've got a lot of stuff going on in your own life, with your sister, and," he says, spinning his wrist in circles rather than finishing his sentence.

I blink. "Nothing's going on with my sister. It's fine. Oh my god, she's totally not suicidal anymore. She told me. And I would, like, see it in her eyes if she was. I'm just emotional about it. I just thought I could share my emotions with you. And she's only here for three weeks. She's probably not going to find a job and she'll realize it was a stupid idea to come here and she's going to just move back home."

The timer on Jon's phone beeps, prompting him to turn the towels over. He stands up and says, "Well," kisses me on the cheek, and then takes his body and the crossword out the door. I spend another twenty minutes at the coffee shop, trying not to cry while putting together an extremely sad playlist for the train ride home.

Poppy's toe is bandaged, her foot elevated on one of my fuzzy couch pillows. She's underlining things in her book about trauma.

"Hey," she says, using a gentle *we've been fighting* voice.

In response I lie down on the floor. I texted her from the subway; she knows what's going on.

"Do you want to talk?"

"No," I say, my throat swollen, my voice a horn. I can't tell her that I told Jon her biggest secret, or that I did it partly to try to get him to want to take care of me, or that it didn't even work. If she hadn't come to stay, none of this would've happened. I would have fallen asleep to *Minority Report* while Jon softly tugged my pubic hair; we would've woken up, continued our lives. Maybe he would've taught me French so that I could've understood the things he said to his mother. Maybe one day *he* would've bought *me* a forty-thousand-dollar watch.

"He wasn't nice to you anyway. You can do a thousand times better. He fucked up your vagina, he didn't understand any of your memes—"

"Memes don't *matter,* Poppy," I shout. Now I'm crying. Of course memes matter.

"Do you want coffee?"

"Had it," I say.

"Do you want to take a shower?"

I nod. Poppy gets up and goes to my room and brings out a towel, which she hangs on the back of the bathroom door.

"Do you want to smoke? Do you want a gummy?"

"I have to work," I tell her. "I have this big deadline tomorrow, and I haven't even started, because I just kept putting it off, and then I was getting nervous on the way to Jon's about doing it, but I told myself I'd rather be happy and get, like, fucked, or whatever, not fucked, but just, like, held instead of doing my work, and now I'll never finish and it's not the first time this month

I've gone over and I'm such a slacker piece of shit they're going to fire me." I'm weeping.

"Do you want to feel better?" Poppy asks.

"No," I say, flinging an arm over my face, but Poppy opens my hand and puts something into it.

The pill is small, chalky-looking, tangerine. *4QHL,* says its smooth hull.

"Henry gave it to me the other night," Poppy says. "It's like Adderall but stronger? Him and all his 2L friends take it."

"I don't think I have ADHD," I say, passing it back to her.

"You probably don't, but you also probably wouldn't even know if you did. Women go undiagnosed like ninety percent of the time," Poppy says, "because their symptoms are different than men's. Like how women have different heart attack symptoms than men? Everything's different for women, but we're constantly measured against men's standards for things, and that's why the patriarchy is literally killing us."

"Okay," I say, "I need for my home to be the one place in the world where I don't have to hear about the patriarchy. Every time I hear someone talking about the patriarchy, I lose brain cells."

"Look, there's two pills. I'll take it with you. There's literally nothing to be afraid of. It's not just for ADHD. It's for having a nice time. It's for seeing things clearly." Poppy puts a pill on her tongue and swallows it. I don't think Poppy, who's already more heavily medicated than most people, should be experimenting with law-bro drugs, but it's already down her gullet. Across the street, a man walks back and forth along the sidewalk, moaning.

Poppy shuts the window and hands me my pill, firmly this time. The gesture reminds me of our mother. Like a good girl, I take what I'm given.

For a while, nothing happens. "Okay," I say, "now I want a weed gummy." Poppy and I take gummies and put on some TV and sit on our phones, scrolling.

"The floor's kinda dirty," Poppy says, her phone on her tummy. She points at the small tiled part of the living room that is the kitchen. She gets up. She folds my jute runner; beneath it, the floor is covered in hair and old food gunk. I stand up to help her. Now I have gloves on. Now I'm on the floor, scrubbing. My arm hurts but it doesn't matter. My cheek is cold. It's on the tile. It feels nice. I remember why I came down here. To make sure of no crumbs. To remove the crumbs. From my life.

"Princeton doesn't *have* a law school," Poppy says. "I just remembered. So my future children can never go to law school there." She has her head in the fridge. She pulls out a pepper swaddled in tinfoil. We unwrap it like a gift. It's shriveled, completely black. She holds it in her palm. We can't stop staring at this pepper. Now it's in the trash. It's glistening as if someone's licked it.

"Wontons," Poppy says, her voice different. Thirty minutes go by and then I'm pretty sure we're eating wontons. Poppy's gone to the store. She walks in the door with five boxes of cereal. She arranges them atop the fridge. "The cereal aisle," she says, "is the most beautiful place on Planet Earth." Poppy wants to write a sitcom about us, she tells me. She's been wanting to write it for years and now she finally knows how to do it. We squish together in front of her laptop. INT. DEPRESSING BROOKLYN APARTMENT, Poppy writes. Two SISTERS are CLEANING. An UGLY SCARF that signals NOTHING ABOUT EITHER OF THEM hangs on the coat rack with the coats. I start to ask Poppy how she knew what I secretly thought about the scarf but then realize maybe I wrote that line. We finish three pages. I understand very suddenly that I won't be married by the time I'm thirty. "I'm not going to be married by the time I'm thirty," I say. Poppy says we should watch the Keira Knightley *Pride and Prejudice* because it will make me feel better about not being married by thirty. "But the point of *Pride and Prejudice* is they're all married by thirty." Thirty, Poppy reminds me, was different then. I notice a bug on the wall. It's the worst bug I've ever seen, nightmare-colored with two hundred legs. It's making a sound. I get up to kill it, but I can't. "What are you doing?" Poppy asks me. I tell her. "There's no bug," she says. "This is so going in our sitcom."

"Stop calling it a sitcom," I say. "I don't wanna do a sitcom. I wanna do a miniseries like *Band of Brothers*. I wanna revive the form."

On Amazon, we order candles. "I hate Amazon," says Poppy, "but I'll never stop using it." We spend some time googling Bezos. We spend some time googling a visual representation of 160 billion dollars. We spend some time on the Spend Bill Gates' Money website. We spend some time crying. We spend some time looking at dresses on department store websites. We sort prices high to low for once. I'm on the toilet. Whatever we ate, it wasn't wontons.

I wake up with wet hair. I don't remember showering or falling asleep. My phone tells me it's the next day. My eyes feel like pudding, and when I open up my computer, I see that all of my BookSmarts work is done. I added it to the team Google Drive at 4:43 a.m. I read the files; the work is exceptional. I get an email notification that my order is on the way. In the email there's a picture of a three-hundred-dollar party dress. It's pink, with tulle.

I get up and go into Poppy's room. She is asleep in the very center of my deflated air mattress, tucked in tightly beneath smooth blankets. Outside, it's snowing. I kneel on the floor and shake one of Poppy's feet. I call her name.

"Poppy," I say. "What did you give us?"

Poppy smiles at me, her eyes still closed. "Mommy," she says, happy. "I dreamt we had the Spanish flu."

Shouts and jolts of jackhammering come from outside: recently, a piece of someone's balcony fell down into the courtyard, nearly nailing a smoker. Now sixty feet of scaffolding and netting are going up so that pointing can be done on all the balconies. Poppy and I haven't seen the sun in days.

Our building, which used to be a Jewish hospital, is very, very old and largely unrenovated; the basement, one of my neighbors told me, was once the morgue. I often wonder if the whole building's haunted, if they've stabilized the rent in case the place is cursed. My life's certainly gotten worse since I moved in.

Poppy leans over the back of the couch to look out the window, sticking her head outside and peering upward. "Wow," she says; "this is really gonna suck for you for the next few months." She's still, I guess, pretending like she's going to be living anywhere other than in this apartment with me, even though she's been here for more than a month. So far Poppy's housing hunt has brought her to the East Village, where a broker opened the door of a basement-level studio to reveal a naked model sleeping on a mattress in the middle of the living room; to Windsor Terrace and a sixth-floor walk-up where the shower was the whole bathroom; to Clinton Hill and a place with a large brown stain on the wall in the shape of a human body.

Poppy gets up to floss something out of a tooth. "Have you heard that thing," she shouts from the bathroom, "about how you could bite off your finger like it was a carrot but something in our brains stops us from being able to do it?"

"You told me that, like, weeks ago," I say.

"Oh," Poppy says, looking unsure of herself. "Maybe I did."

All the medications Poppy takes together make her sleepy and forgetful. They make her digits tingle, they make her sclera blue, they make her back scaly, they make her face puffy, they make her stomach revolt. Poppy was in seventh grade when the hives started coming. She could never predict when a flare would hit. Her eyelid would swell shut in English class; she'd go to the bathroom at the movie theater halfway through a film and find her wrist had grown a golf ball while she was sitting in the dark. She went for tests. Stress, hormones, the usual nothing answers. Someone suggested vasculitis. Someone suggested lupus. Poppy went on steroids. She got moon face. Her body softened. Our mother tested the house for black mold. Then she tested it again. Then she decided the tests were bogus, manufactured by crooks and idiots. Poppy started staying home from school, doing everything online. One of her classmates saw her at the grocery store, fatter than she'd been, and started a rumor that she was pregnant. Poppy, who'd just started tending to the spiky garden of a Facebook account, posted a status telling people she wasn't with child, actually using the phrase "with child," and shortly after that the hives grew worse, which made our parents say things like, *See, it's all in your head,* which made Poppy flare more horribly, because of course the hives were in her head at least a little, even if she refused to let herself think it; even if the seed of them was somewhere deeper, deep in her blood, deep enough that for years she swore at night she could feel her organs, too, bubbling with hives, swelling and contracting, making her wish she could turn herself inside out and rub her body on the carpet.

Last week I got a data-collection text from someone with the nurses' union. A question for you, POPPY: Have you had a personal experience with our broken health care system? According to some computer somewhere, we're each other. I tell Poppy about the text now, thinking it'll make her happy; she laughs, but I can tell it doesn't. I can tell by her dead eyes.

Night falls and we decide to FaceTime our mother. Neither of us has heard from her in almost a week. Apparently, when Poppy left Florida, our mother warned her that our living together would be disastrous and she didn't want to hear about anything, good or bad, that happened during our cohabitation. Poppy told me about this the other week after I finally showed her the ominous text I got about us bringing out the worst in each other.

Do you think we do? I asked Poppy.

She thought for a minute. *In some sense,* she said, but she never clarified which sense she meant.

Now Poppy and I squeeze close together on the couch so we can fit on camera. I try to hold Poppy's phone at an angle that will please both of us, and we bicker over whose face looks fattest. We're always self-conscious about our chins.

"Oh, my chin," our mother says as soon as the call picks up and she sees her own face. She clutches at her jaw. Poppy and I look at each other and laugh. "What's so funny?" our mother asks.

"Nothing," Poppy says. "We were just saying we're so insecure about *our* chins."

"You should be," our mother says. "One day you'll get my chin. Every woman in my family gets this chin."

"Your chin's fine," Poppy says.

"You're beautiful," I say. "Your chin is beautiful."

The call ends. Our mother, it seems, has hung up. I ring back.

"If you're going to make fun of me about my chin," she says upon answering, "I'm not doing this."

Poppy and I look at each other and laugh again. "No one's making fun of you about your chin," Poppy says. "You're the one who said something about your chin, and then we said something about our chins in solidarity."

"Poppy, I was looking on Instagram just now, and I was very distressed by your post."

"What post?" Poppy says, just as I'm thinking, What post? and reaching for my phone to open up her Instagram and see what rare missive she's sent out into the world. Ever since the Facebook thing, Poppy's hated social media.

"You know what post," says our mother.

There on Poppy's stories is a blurry picture of some yellow graffiti spray-painted across the bridge over the Atlantic train yard: COPS KILL ☺

"Why do you even have Instagram?" Poppy asks. "And why don't you follow us?"

"I follow your sister," she says. "I made it for a secret project. It's none of your business why I have Instagram or why I do anything I do. Stop changing the subject, thinking I'll forget. You can't play me. That sign in your post should have said COPS HELP PEOPLE."

"Graffiti, not a sign," Poppy says.

"Story, not post," I say.

Our mother ignores us. "Do you remember when we called the police because the neighbor's horses were running in the street? And the police came and put the horses back where they belonged? And then came to our door and introduced themselves and asked if we needed anything else? Cops *help*."

Poppy laughs. "No one likes cops, Mommy."

"I like cops. I like them very much."

"No one in New York likes cops," I say.

"You're being very combative, Jules," says my mother.

"*Me?*"

"Yes, you."

"It's out of my control, this is like the ninth day of my period."

"I don't know how you girls have become like this. Picking on everything I say. Spreading lies about the police. Talking to me about your periods. I didn't raise you this way. Do you have any idea how devastating it is for me? To hear you talk like this? About the people who *protect* us?" My mother's voice sounds so profoundly hurt that I briefly wonder if I'm on the wrong side of the whole cops thing after all.

"Let's drop it," I say.

"How about I drop you," our mother says. "Poppy, have you found a job? Or are you going to live off your sister for the rest of her life?"

Poppy and I look at each other, raising our eyebrows.

"Don't look at each other like that," our mother says.

"Like what?" we ask at the same time.

"Clearly," our mother says, "you're having your own conversation. Call me when you get whatever's going on out of your system." The call drops—she's hung up again. We try her one more time, but she rejects it on the second ring. We text our mother that we love her. She gives the text a thumbs-down.

"I don't understand why the three of us can't ever just have, like, a nice conversation," I say. "Not even a conversation, just a moment even. What's her deal with us? Why doesn't she like us?"

"Oh," Poppy says without looking up, "it's because she's a narcissist and we're her appendages. It says so in the trauma book. Have you noticed how whenever we say 'I love you' she never says it back?"

"Yes," I say, "but I thought I was crazy."

"Also, I'm not trying to live off you," Poppy says. "I have

another job interview tomorrow. I promise you I'm not trying to take advantage of you, but I'm sorry if it seems like I am."

I'm trapped. If I tell Poppy I think our mother's being cruel, it's like I'm excusing her failure to find footing, like I'm telling her it's okay to be a fuckup; if I say something like: *Well, you better hope you get it, because I'm kicking you out next week,* I'm feeding something bad inside me: The part of me that agrees with my mother. The part of me that wants to be alone for no good reason.

"I pity her," Poppy says, frowning in a way that makes her seem strong. "I really do."

"Pity her for what?"

"Um," Poppy says. She thinks for a minute. "I don't know. I guess I don't. I just thought it would make me sound like I had power or something."

"It did," I say, patting her. *Just stay,* I want to say, *just stay here and get some real furniture and pay me a couple hundred bucks a month and let everything work itself out. When you are aligned with your own energy, everything else will arrive.*

ONE MORE CHANCE TO FUND ABORTION AND GET SWAG, says an email in my inbox from an Alabama abortion fund I donated seventy-five dollars to last year. I'm all for abortion, but the email seems insensitive. I ask Poppy if thinking this makes me a bad leftist.

She puts on her deep-thought face. "It doesn't make you a bad leftist," she says eventually. "Your issue is with—what?"

"With swag," I say. "It seems casual. And abortion is serious."

Poppy points at me. "*That's* what makes you a bad leftist. Abortion shouldn't be serious. It's a normal medical procedure. It's like a corn removal or a tonsillectomy or whatever."

"Well, yeah, but. It can be a serious decision. I mean, it can be an emotional decision for some people."

"Have you had an abortion?" Poppy asks.

"No."

"Then you're not an authority on how serious or unserious abortion is."

"Have *you* had an abortion?" I ask her.

"No," she says.

"So how are you an authority?"

"I'm not an authority," she says, "and I *know* I'm not an authority, so I'm not labeling abortion as serious or unserious."

"I'm confused. You just said it shouldn't be serious."

"I'm saying it shouldn't be, but I'm not saying it isn't."

A thought hits me. "What if I'm pregnant?"

"You're on your period."

"It's day twelve. Or something. I've lost count. It might be implantation bleeding."

"What's implantation bleeding?"

"I read about it. It's bleeding from the egg attaching to your uterus. Or from the sperm attaching to the egg. Or the egg traveling wherever it's supposed to go to become something. I don't know."

"If you were pregnant right now, would you have an abortion?"

I don't answer right away. "Obviously, I'm not pregnant. I just want an excuse to text Jon about a medical problem."

"Get the fuck *over* him," Poppy says. "You dated for, like, three weeks."

"Nine," I say. "Nine weeks. And he's the first person I've dated since Gage."

"Jon, Gigi, whatever. Move on," Poppy says.

"Don't call him Gigi, only I called him Gigi."

"You're making me crave death." She's trying to be funny, but I don't laugh. I feel the top of my head prickle and my pupils embiggen. I don't like it when Poppy talks about death, even in jest. I hear myself take a weird breath. I try to think of something that'll change the subject. Poppy heads to her room, though, before I can come up with anything else to say that's clever or silly about abortion, or swag, or the two things in combination, or anything else that's ever happened in the long, long history of the world.

That night I go online and make an appointment to see my gynecologist later in the week. Then I stay up very late looking at mommies. One of them, an anti-vaxxer who sells WayLife oils at the coveted Diamond level and claims she cured her son's autism by feeding him camel's milk each day, posts an image to her stories of her gel-manicured hand gripping a small yellow envelope labeled *VARICELLA*.

A safe v@x option for all you mamas! These are Homeoprophy-laxis. While I do not use them as a way to "avoid" getting sick (I firmly believe weathering illness has incredible benefits) I use these as a way to allow the immune system to be exposed to diseases we cannot seem to get naturally anymore, says the caption, followed by a crying-face emoji. On the next slide, there's a video of her rubbing her hand along the handle of a shopping cart before bringing her palm to her mouth and licking it because all germs are good germs. On her next slide, her tongue hovers over the shopping cart handle; overlaid text invites her followers to join her "Warrior Base" group on Facebook. Membership costs twelve dollars a month, but it's a safe space to talk about alternative methods of healing, methods that might upset other people, methods that the government doesn't want hardworking warrior moms to ever find out about. And if you join the Warrior Base, of course, you get a 25 percent discount on a WayLife oils starter kit.

I go back to report the image of the varicella envelope for violating community guidelines, but I can't choose which category to report it under: *Violence or dangerous organizations, False information, Scam or fraud, Sale of illegal or regulated goods.* I give up and move on to another mommy; on her stories, she begs her followers to *WAKE UP.* She posts a slide featuring a screengrab of a tweet from a former Playboy Bunny who is purportedly blowing the whistle on secret tunnels that run beneath the Playboy Mansion, allowing an elite cabal of Hollywood stars and D.C. politicians to traffic children across the country to the sex dungeons of people like Tom Hanks and Hillary Clinton. She must not have finished adding slides, because when I tap through to see more, I find myself on the story of Elizabeth Smart, who is shilling eighty-five-dollar leggings. Things aren't so bad in my life, I think. At least I'm not one of these people or one of their followers. Then I realize that I am, of course, one of their followers—a devoted one, even, in my own fucked little way.

Poppy shows me all the dogs she loves on Petfinder. For some reason, there's a group of puppies from one shelter who are all named after fuel corporations: ExxonMobil, Shell, Hess, Chevron, Valero.

"Imagine having a widdle dog," Poppy says in a dreamy voice as she scrolls past images of dogs with bulging, bleeding eyes and skin mottled with mange. "No, like, really imagine it. Seriously." She pulls up the profile of a small black-and-white dog with a fluffy face, some kind of corgi-Jindo mix, it looks like. The dog's name, inexplicably, is listed as "Amy Klobuchar." Poppy explains that all the dogs from this shelter have been temporarily named after current Democratic primary candidates: there's also a Kamala Harris, a Mayor Pete, a Bernie Sanders.

"Why do they do this?" I ask.

"To draw people in and, like, charm them with cultural references. I guess it makes them want to adopt the dogs."

"How does being called 'ExxonMobil' make someone want to adopt you more?"

Amy Klobuchar's eyes are cute, I'll give her that. Her ears are notched, though, and she has a bald spot just below her nose that gives the ickily humanoid impression of a top lip; she holds her tongue in a strange posture in many pictures, like she's licking the air; she is missing her front right leg.

Even though I'm only a year or two old (I'm not sure how old I am!) I have been through a lot, says Amy Klobuchar's profile. I am still learning about the world—I don't like cars, I am scared of all other doggies, and I need some help socializing with hoomans, too! With the right home (no other pets OF ANY KIND or children, I'm a diva who likes my own space!) and some tender patience from my new paw-rents, I will be your best friend for life.

"That's code for 'I will eat your baby's face,'" I say to Poppy.

"No, it's not," Poppy says. "It's code for she's been through a lot and she needs good owners."

"I hate 'paw-rents.' I hate being a millennial, being targeted like this. I don't think I like her. I want a nice dog," I tell Poppy.

"Amy Klobuchar does seem nice."

"I want a nice dog and a nice-*looking* dog."

Poppy breathes through her nose. "Amy Klobuchar really needs a home."

"A three-legged dog is going to need so much help."

"They're animals," Poppy says. "They're not like us. They adapt. She can do anything a four-legged dog can do, I bet."

"I don't want that ugly fucking dog," I tell her. "You could never take care of one anyway, you can't even take care of yourself. Get a plant, get a fish."

This, I realize, is a step too far. Poppy takes her laptop into the room she calls her room and shuts the door. I pick up my phone and look up Amy Klobuchar the dog and stare at her all by myself. She's not so bad, as far as shelter dogs go. I could have been nicer. But I remember Poppy at all her lowests—back when she had to take a leave from high school, back when she was covered in dinner-plate hives, back when she came home from college and let tissues fill her bed, let food sit on her nightstand for days; I remember the high-pitched cry she'd make halfway through most sentences, the way she'd just lie down on the floor sometimes, unable to even make it downstairs to the kitchen. I tell myself I'm saving Poppy from something, keeping her from a failure that could break her.

I stare at Amy Klobuchar's busted face, her lip, her teeny Snoopy nose. I take a screenshot, knowing that from now on I'll look at it any time I want to feel like shit.

A text from my father lights up the top of my screen: a rare occasion. There are no words, just a grainy image of what looks like a credit card bill. I zoom in on the photo and see that it's an invitation from a crisis response group: an offer to complete an online survey about how the mass shooting that took place a year ago at the high school five minutes from the house where Poppy and I grew up and that killed seventeen people, making it the deadliest high school shooting in United States history, has affected local residents in the long term.

Here come the words: They're paying $25 for responses. Could Be worth it. I signed up! Luv u!

will do! I write back.

How r my shmegegges? That's what he calls me and Poppy: Yiddish for, roughly, "airheads."

we are good daddy!! thanks for checking in! I write back.

It is the joy of my life to know u 2 r 2gether, he says. I luv u Girls.

It's true: all his passwords, I know, are either *ILuvPop* or *ILuvJul*. Our relationship's fairly weird—once a year or so for the last several years, I've gone to his office to have him plump my lips and smooth my jawline and fix my gummy smile, which he does while asking me questions like: *Now remind me, did you ever watch* Breaking Bad? —but I send him back a heart.

GO TO TEMPLE, my father texts. FIND A GOOD RABBI. EVEN IF THINGS R SWELL NOW, U WILL NEED ADVICE ONE DAY.

I lost almost all my friends in the breakup with my ex-boyfriend Gage; it was my first real relationship, and I let our lives get too entwined without looking ahead to what I'd do if things ended. The only friends I managed to keep are two women from grad school, both named Leigh, who have been secretly in love with each other for five years. Every time I see them individually, they tell me about their love for the other; every time I see them together, they both direct the conversation entirely toward me, dive-bombing me with questions about how my writing's going and how my reading's going and what I'm buying online these days.

At a bar, the Leighs ask me what's new. When I tell them Poppy's here, that she's living with me, horror of horrors, they pat my hands. They assure me she'll find her people soon and move out to live with friends.

"Your beautiful office," Leigh says, contorting her eyebrows, making it worse. "She *took* it from you."

"She did," says Leigh, "she took it."

"How do you feel about it?"

"When can you kick her out?"

"But where will she go when you do?"

I try to ask the Leighs about their own lives, their own writing, their own apartments. But all they want to talk to me about is how unfortunate my situation is, how Poppy is leeching from me. I know they're being supportive, but leaving the bar, I decide not to see the Leighs for a while.

My gynecologist performs an ultrasound, which reveals a small uterine polyp.

"There's nothing you need to do right now, but we'll go ahead and get you scheduled for surgery," she says, poking around on her iPad. "I'd like you to do it within the next six weeks or so, if possible."

"I don't wanna have surgery," I say involuntarily. "I've never had surgery."

My gynecologist blinks at me. "It's a very minor surgery," she says.

"I, um—if I have to have anesthesia, I don't think I can have it, because my second cousin Paige, she went under anesthesia to get breast implants for her eighteenth-birthday present, and she died on the table." *All for a pair of boobs, the death of their daughter,* I remember my mother saying when Paige died.

"I'm sorry for your loss," my gynecologist says. "You'll be very lightly sedated, and we'll give you some pain medication to take when we're finished. It's a simple D and C procedure. You will not die on the table, because there isn't a table."

I stare at her. "An abortion." *FUND ABORTION AND GET SWAG.*

My gynecologist breathes heavily and swings shut the magnetic cover on her iPad. I always suspect I'm her least favorite patient. "It won't be an abortion, because you're not pregnant." She puts her hands in her lap. "Are there any other questions I can answer for you at this time? Otherwise, they'll get you scheduled at the front desk."

Outside the gynecologist's office, there's a fish tank sitting next to a streetlamp. The tank is filled a third of the way with water, and a fat orange fish swims around in it. *I AM FREE,* says a sign on the tank, *BUT I AM VERY OLD.*

I run back inside. "Excuse me," I say to the woman at the front desk, "can I get one of the pee cups?"

I use the plastic cup she gives me to scoop the fish out of its dirty tank; I walk it home slowly, my nose dripping, my face stinging. Inside, I set the fish on the kitchen table and fill a flower vase with sink water; this, I tell myself, will do for now. Who leaves a fish outside in the cold? I luxuriate in my own benevolence. I do some BookSmarts work and wait for Poppy to get home; I can't tell if the fish will charm or enrage her. It doesn't matter. An hour later, when I go to check on the fish, it's extremely dead. Its blood tinges the water; its eyeballs have popped out of its head and sunk to the bottom of the vase. I flush it down the toilet and throw the vase in the recycling. I tell myself the fish was probably mostly dead when I rescued it; I try not to think about how, after all the fuss I made over Amy Klobuchar, I'm the one with a dead pet's blood on my hands.

"Radishes in everything," Poppy says. "I never saw a radish until I moved here."

The language of "moved here" strikes me as odd. Poppy didn't so much move here as migrate here, drift here. She's still living out of her suitcases. "Moved here" suggests success, autonomy. I begin to wonder if, by these standards, I have even fully moved here.

Poppy stabs at her radish-laden salad, wolfing it. Our movie starts in ten minutes.

We hurry into the theater. The ticket-taker tells us our movie is downstairs, straight across the lobby. On the way to the door, I spot a bathroom and tell Poppy I'm going to pee. I hand her my jacket to save my seat with.

"Don't use that bathroom," she says. "That's the handicap bathroom."

"I'm just peeing."

"Use the bathroom that's for you, the one upstairs."

"But it's gonna start—"

Poppy passes my jacket back to me. "You are so insensitive," she says. "Use the normal bathroom." She goes into the theater.

I stomp upstairs, contemplating Poppy's use of the word "normal" while acting holy about my ableism. Poppy's a fraud, she doesn't know anything. I have a uterine polyp. I've been bleeding for weeks. It's probably so large that when they remove it, I'm going to hemorrhage; I'm going to die on the table like Cousin Paige. I sit on the toilet in the upstairs bathroom thinking about these things for so long that when I finally come downstairs, Poppy is standing in the lobby.

"You missed the first fifteen minutes," she says.

"I don't care."

"Come on, let's go. We'll see it when it's streaming."

I feel a sob coming. "Let's just go inside," I say. "We paid already."

"It's not worth it," Poppy says. "It was one of those movies where right away someone threw up as a way of, like, signaling that they were emotionally overwhelmed. I hate that, it always makes me afraid that if I ever have something emotional happen to me, I'll just start throwing up. Let's go."

"You're ruining the night."

"*You're* ruining the night," Poppy says, raising her voice. I shush her. "Don't shush me," she says, and walks out into the cold. I follow her home, where we settle uneasily on the couch and watch some bad TV. At one point, someone on the show gets bad news and throws up in the sink.

"See?" Poppy says. "See what I mean?" A small hive has risen on her cheek, bright and glistening as an Advil.

"You have something here," I say, touching the hive.

Poppy jerks away from me. "I know," she says. "Shut up. Don't say anything. Don't even look at it. It's my third one this week. If I stress out about them they'll only get worse." She stares at the screen for a few seconds. Then she looks at me. "It's like: do I try to stop *feeling*?"

"I don't think that's a good idea." Any time Poppy talks about shutting down a part of herself, it makes me nervous. "I don't think it's a good way to move through the world."

"Or," Poppy says, "it's the secret answer to moving through the world."

I don't say anything, pretending to really like what we're watching.

Outside an enormous apartment building across the street from the botanical gardens, we wait for a broker to show us a studio for Poppy. It's freezing and raining; that it's the first week of May means nothing. Poppy and I huddle in our coats. A man and a woman, a couple, stand nearby, whispering to each other.

Soon we spot the broker from the apartment's StreetEasy listing jogging down the street, tzitzit flapping. He's wearing a kippah and a Cubs jersey and he's vaping. When he gets to us, he's out of breath. He coughs and introduces himself as Benny and starts flipping through a key ring.

"Fourteen D?" Benny asks us. We nod. "Here to see Fourteen D?" he asks the couple.

"You're showing it to all of us? To them, too?" the woman asks.

"Uh, yeah," Benny says.

The woman looks at me and Poppy. "You can have it," she says to us. She spits on the ground, then turns and walks away. Her boyfriend follows her. "I'm tired of fucking fighting these guarantor-ass bitches who don't pay their own rent for these fucking rathole shitholes," she screams. Her boyfriend puts an arm around her. She shakes it off. He tries again. She shoves him. I feel terrible. Poppy's not going to live here. She can't afford it; she doesn't even have a job. She's just looking at places to look at places. The couple could have lived here, made something here. I watch them stop in their tracks halfway down the block and argue. Maybe they'll break up.

"Woof," Benny says. He smiles at us. "Well, less worries for you now, ladies?"

To make up for the movie we missed, Poppy and I attend a play: an updated version of a Greek tragedy. The script is very of the moment; every time the characters mention something from the real world—Uber, TikTok—the whole audience laughs a self-satisfied laugh. Poppy and I rest our heads on each other's shoulders every time we hate something, which is every other minute of the whole play.

"I think art is dead," Poppy says on the walk home. "I really think it's dead. We're all so—in our devices, like—there's no *funding* in *schools*—" I roll my eyes. For twenty minutes she whines about the state of the American theater, trying to put words to the reason why the play was so intensely bad. *We hate big ideas and big emotions. The Greeks felt but we don't feel. We have TV in our hands. Art is dead.* She's right, probably. But the thing is that when something's dead, you can't say anything about it that'll bring it back. Poppy's ideas about dead art, to me, are just as numbing as the ideas in the play. The shows I watch are dead. The middling novels I take apart bit by tiny bit for BookSmarts are dead. Dead art is everywhere. Dead art is my life. By the time we get inside, I'm exhausted. My ears hurt from the unseasonable cold, and when I put my hands on them in the elevator to warm them up, Poppy misinterprets the gesture and starts with the silent treatment. I try to explain, but all she says back is "I get it, no, seriously, I get it." Inside the apartment she goes straight to her room and closes the door. I do the same. A few minutes later I get a long text from her about how she thinks I'm a real artist and a good one and how she always wants to talk about art with me and really figure out her sense of hermeneutics, but I never listen to her, which is frustrating, because all her life all she's done is listen to my ideas about art and movies and television and internalize them and make them her own and emulate them, and now she's in her twenties and doesn't know what parts of her are real and what parts of her are just parts of me, and sometimes she feels like she has no core, no beliefs, no ideas, and that frightens her, and I should know all of this intuitively without having to be told, and about how she'll be out of my way by the end of the month. I could try to explain again about my ears being cold, but it seems like too much work. I press the thumbs-up reaction to Poppy's message and put on a documentary about Laci Peterson.

"I got it," Poppy says. "I got a job. Oh my god, thank god." She throws herself on the sheepskin rug at the foot of my bed with a relief that seems performative. "It's at another private school," she says, rolling over to face me, "in the guidance office this time. Doing, like, admin, but whatever. Do you wanna hear something insane?"

"Sure," I say.

"The whole school is about blocks."

"Blocks?"

"Yeah, like, building blocks. Every classroom in the whole lower school has wooden blocks in it, and there are giant foam blocks on the roof that they play with even in their downtime, at recess, and a lot of the curriculum is structured around these big monthlong in-class block-building projects. And you can tell even in the high school how there's all this weird stuff about building, and, you know. They're making a lot of dioramas and stuff? It's all— The school's whole ethos is like: building things together."

"That sounds cool," I say.

"Personally I'd venture that it's bourgeois and fairly *dangerous* to structure a kid's whole life around blocks and not much else for eighteen years, seventeen years, or whatever, but that's just me. I don't have a kid. I don't know how kids learn yet."

"That seems harsh, calling it dangerous."

"You *don't* think it's dangerous to structure a child's education around blocks?"

And now I have to spend my time thinking about this.

That afternoon my mother calls.

"Have you heard the news?" she asks.

"Yeah, it's cool, right?"

"*Cool?*" she asks. "Cool?"

"Yeah—it sounds like Poppy's gonna get to work with kids again, she likes kids—"

"Not about your sister," she says, "about the *Frangis*."

The Frangis are a family from our hometown whose kids I went to school with from elementary on. "No," I say.

"Jason Frangi," my mother says, "is in prison."

"Oh my god," I say.

"Or might go to prison. I don't think he's in prison yet, or maybe he hasn't had a trial. But still."

"What happened?"

"You won't believe me even if I tell you. God, it's so horrible I can't even say."

I doubt that very much. If there's one thing my mother loves, it's saying horrible things. "Child porn?" I ask. Many people from our hometown have been caught recently with child porn; my father's pulmonologist, one of my old history teachers, so on.

"Worse," she says. "He fucked their dog."

"He *what*?"

"He fucked the family dog. Fucked it right to death."

I think of Amy Klobuchar. *I am still learning about the world.* "Oh my god," I say. "A dog can die from that?"

"Of course a dog can die from that. A little dog like that, imagine the physics. And then he *dismembered* it. And *then* he buried the pieces all over the yard."

"No."

"And the *gardeners* found them. Imagine his poor parents."

"Imagine the poor gardeners. Imagine the poor dog."

"There's real evil in this world," my mother says. "Real evil everywhere. Right under our own noses." There's a long pause. "And *that's* why we need the police."

Free to talk? my boss messages via Slack. Right away my armpits pour.

Sure!! I write back.

He calls two seconds later, greets me, asks how I'm doing. I tell him I'm doing great. I don't tell him I'm Winnie-the-Poohing it while watching clips from the movie version of *Mame* on YouTube.

"So," he says, "we got some user feedback this morning that we wanted to talk to you about."

"Oh, sure," I say, my vulva sweating.

"So, uh, this guide you edited last month for *The War Unending*? That was you, right?"

I recall a nonsensical speculative novel about a civil war in Iceland. "Yeah," I say, "I remember."

"Okay, well, uh. We got some feedback from a user in Iceland who was upset because it looks like whoever wrote the guide, when they were filling out the historical context section, they, uh, treated the civil war from the book like it really happened."

I laugh. My boss's silence tells me this is the incorrect response.

"And, you know, listen, mistakes happen. But as an editor—senior editor—it's your job to, uh, fact-check rigorously? And I just don't know how we could've missed it." By "we" he means "you." Why do bosses do that?

"Oh my god," I say. I'm scrambling to open my old files, which are in a folder called *OLD FILES*. "Yeah, I don't know how— Hang on, because, obviously there was no civil war in Iceland."

"Yeah."

There is silence.

"I'm looking for the file—"

"No, no, you don't need to look for the file. I just— It feels pretty obvious to me that you skimmed this one, and that seems indicative of something larger? Tinkel has been sending a lot of emails."

Tinkel is a man from an unknown part of America who reads every BookSmarts guide as soon as it's published, hunting for typos and errors and inconsistencies. He is meticulous. He emails the general info@ email on the website several times a week to report his findings. He signs his emails Mr. Tinkel.

"Oh, Mr. Tinkel," I say, unsure of what else I can offer.

"Let's just, going forward, really try and—sort of *emulate* Tinkel. Let's get that laser focus back." Again with the "let's."

"I'm so sorry, Joe," I say. "I don't know how it got past me." I know exactly how it got past me: I don't pay attention. I can't explain to the people I work with how small a concern work is to me: between the mommies, and my polyps, and the street goldfish, and Poppy's apartment hunt, and the Frangis—how am I supposed to focus?

The call ends. I'm so embarrassed I go back to bed. When I wake up again, at five minutes to one, the sun is high and there's a house centipede on the ceiling, hopelessly out of reach. I watch it crawl around my room in a circle four times, convinced that if I keep an eye on it, it won't fall on my face. When I get tired of watching the centipede, I pull out my phone. On Instagram, a mommy is preaching about the importance of throwing out shoes, which she calls "feet prisons," and walking the wide earth barefoot, as God intended. She posts a carousel of pictures: her bare feet in grass, her bare feet in sand, her bare feet on the linoleum floor of her local Target. Of course I will step on things and get scrapes from time to time, she writes, but God heals all my wounds.

Poppy and I watch a confusing movie, a film about child soldiers in an unnamed but at-war South American country near the Amazon. It's not clear what year it is or what the genders of most of the child soldiers are, and the movie ends, abruptly, in the middle of a scene that seemed to be leading to another scene. Right away I google the name of the movie plus *ending* plus *Reddit*.

"What are you doing?" Poppy asks.

"I'm looking up what people said about the ending."

"It doesn't matter what people said about the ending," Poppy tells me. "What did *you* think about the ending?"

I roll my eyes and keep reading on my phone.

"So for everything that challenges you, you're gonna google the ending and let someone else tell you what to think?"

"I wanna get it," I say.

"There's nothing to get," Poppy says.

"Where were they? What year was it? I couldn't figure out anything the whole time, and it ends like that?"

"None of that matters," Poppy says. "That scene? Where the girl was under the waterfall?"

"Yeah?" I ask, excited, hopeful that Poppy has figured this thing out for the both of us.

"That's what it was about. The scarcity. So now you feel that same scarcity. And instead of sitting with it, you google? You google?"

My police blotter app makes its terrifying notification noise, letting me know that something bad has happened in the borough.

NYC ALERT: Jumper down off the Brooklyn Bridge. NYPD Harbor Unit has recovered the body.

I re-download the apps. In a hopeful move, I'd deleted them after Jon and I had sex for the first time. The interface already looks different, but I can't put my finger on precisely what's changed. Here are guys, legions of guys. An alarming number of them have made their profile picture an image of their wanderings through the Holocaust Memorial in Berlin. They look somberly at the ground or sunnily over their shoulders, their bodies made small by the concrete slabs around them. I screenshot about five of these. Now that I have a collection going I consider posting them to the socials. I imagine my tweet about them going viral, but then I imagine it getting seven likes and three retweets, so instead I show the screenshots to Poppy when she gets home.

"Do these guys know what that place is?" she asks.

"I can't tell if it's worse if they do or if they don't."

Poppy helps me swipe for a while. She tells me she thinks one of the guidance counselors in her office is anti-Semitic, but when I ask her why she thinks so, she doesn't have an answer.

"I just get a vibe," she tells me. "You know how sometimes you just get a vibe?"

Unfortunately I do know how sometimes you just get a vibe. Last week, when it was Passover, an annoying literary-world striver I know through the Leighs posted that she'd just been to her first seder, and that it was *actually really beautiful*.

"Put in your bio that you don't want to date anyone who makes less than three hundred thousand dollars a year," she says.

Cackling, I do it.

"By the way, what's 5G?" Poppy asks, pawing nervously at her phone.

"It's what we have but better, I think, but scientists are saying it might be unsafe? Or maybe just conspiracy theorists are saying it's unsafe. I don't know."

"Show me something safe," Poppy says. She gestures around.

When I wake up in the middle of the night, I have nine messages from men who, in response to my newly added income threshold, are calling me a greedy gold-digging kike cunt, threatening to take my life.

Poppy comes home from work puzzled. She reaches into her pocket and pulls out a pair of earrings: dingy, oxidized silver wire loops poking from the heads of a pair of those tiny plastic baby figurines they give out at baby showers.

"What the fuck are those," I ask.

"The first day at work, you know, I thought it was so weird—I went into one of the bathrooms near the guidance office and there were all these baby figurines on the floor. But I kind of— I didn't know what to do, I had to pee, I kind of just stepped over them. And when I came back out of the stall, this girl was, like, gathering them all up in her shirt. And then today, it turns out, she made all these pairs of earrings for people. And she gave me one at her guidance appointment this afternoon."

Poppy and I consider the earrings.

"What do they mean?" I ask.

"I guess it's some teen thing."

We open my laptop and ask it about "teen mini baby earrings"—one link on Etsy. At least four people have bought and reviewed them. The shop owner looks teenish in her picture, but the item description holds no clues.

"Maybe people just like them," Poppy says.

Feeling this to be impossible, we search *teen mini baby earrings tiktok*. Now we find a video called *HIDING MINI-BABIES AROUND SCHOOL*. It has four million views. Poppy screams with joy. We play the video. A teen in college, lonely on campus while "everyone's at Coachella," orders a lot of mini-babies and, together with his friends, hides them around school in strange places. While the teen and his friends place the babies delicately atop urinals, changing stations, stacks of napkins in the cafeteria, water fountains, Poppy and I forget all our troubles. A baby on an ATM. A baby next to a dispenser full of cardboard coffee sleeves. A baby in the mouth of a statue of the college's mascot, a panther. The teens enter the library and head to an upper floor to place babies. One of them says, "No one even comes up here."

"But when they do," another says, "they'll find a surprise!"

Soon Poppy's laughter quiets. "The kids at my school did it wrong," she says. "It's about sneaky babies in sneaky places, not a pile of babies in one place." She laughs some more, then gets serious. "Probably it's the block learning," she says. "They can't understand certain things once blocks aren't part of the picture."

One time Jon told me about playing the choking game while visiting family in France. He was seventeen, hanging with his cousins' friends. I imagine the living room. Nice floors, big windows. He choked a girl and she blacked out. And stayed that way. The scariest five seconds of his life until she coughed. This is what

I'm thinking about as I stare at the ceiling of my gynecologist's office, against which is plastered a photo of Tim Tebow, and wait for the sedative to kick in.

Once it does, a great calm descends over me. Nothing's the matter. It is okay that I'm here alone. Poppy couldn't drop me off, but she'll be here to pick me up. It's okay to get only half of what you want. Poppy's job is new and I can tell she doesn't want to use up her sick days. She wants to prove that she is good, attentive, committed. I wonder why I can never harness this energy in myself; why I always want to do the wrong thing even when I don't want to. What's the wrong thing, I wonder. There's no wrong thing. Life is what you make it. I lock eyes with Tebow.

"Life's what you make it," I say out loud to the nurse. She measures my blood pressure and tells me it's elevated. I feel like a marshmallow. "Marshmallow," I say.

A doctor who isn't my regular doctor comes into the room. This is an old, old man, with tall yellow teeth and slick white hair. He snaps on some gloves.

"You're not my doctor," I say.

"I'm the anesthesiologist," he says.

"No anesthesia," I say. "My cousin died by anesthesia."

"It's twilight anesthesia," he says.

"I love *Twilight*," I say.

"You ever had your wisdom teeth out?"

I nod.

"It's just like that."

"You're talking to me like I'm a baby," I say.

"Well," he says, "you're not a baby."

"And I never will be again," I say, and then I'm aware of very little.

·Next thing I know, I'm in a new room. I'm in a bed that's softer than my own. There are some other people in the room, in their own beds. Poppy's there. The old-man doctor's there. There's blood on my sock.

"I bled a lot?" I ask the doctor.

"You bled," the doctor says.

I have apple juice and I have my phone. But Poppy's not there anymore. "Poppy," I say.

"She just went to the bathroom, honey," says a nurse.

"When you become a nurse," I ask, "do they make you call everyone 'honey'?"

The nurse is not amused. I look at my phone. I think about Poppy on the air mattress and feel sad. "She doesn't even have a bed," I say to the room. No one answers me and I feel sadder. "She has to have a bed so she can stay." A woman in a bed nearby looks at me funny. I go into my phone and search for my favorite picture of Poppy when she was a baby, to show the woman how cute Poppy was, to show her why I feel so much. It's a picture of her sitting on the kitchen counter in pajamas, eyes closed and sleepy. She's holding a banana. The peels drape down around her teeny hands. On the counter beside her is her favorite baby doll, Baby, her arms pulled off from being loved too greatly. When I go to show the woman, though, she's gone, and so is her bed. "That's okay," I say. I switch to the Internet and google *soft hospital bed* and *get hospital soft bed in house for sister* and *best beds for little sister.* The Internet replies: Casper, Nectar Sleep, Article, Tuft & Needle, Crate & Barrel, Raymour & Flanigan. Trundle twin bed, upholstered twin frame, boho natural daybed, gray fabric sofa bed, beautiful kids' beds with storage for sweet dreams. I look at beautiful beds. I get an ad for a child's toy that's a mouse that comes in a box that looks like a bed. I get an ad for a charcuterie board. I get an ad for unique mugs. I get an ad for unique knives. Then Poppy has my phone.

"No more of this," she says. "You don't need to call anybody."

"Phones aren't for calling anymore, Poppy," I say. "Phones are for everything."

Poppy brings me home, where I sleep for four hours. I wake up in time for dinner. Poppy serves me a bowl of lentil soup on the couch so that I can lie on a heating pad and look at my phone.

An anti-vaxxer mommy I follow posts on her stories about how, in order to protect her son from standard vaccinations, which she spells "va((in@t!0n$," she feels she must take him into hiding—like Anne Frank. I swipe through a few more people's stories—a girl I got my MFA with has been blessed with a book deal; a girl I knew in elementary school has lost custody of her daughter and, to announce it, has recorded a video of herself crying over a cover of "Make You Feel My Love"; a guy I went on four dates with when I first moved here wants to know if any of his followers are down to discuss some theories about *Neon*

Genesis Evangelion. But I can't enjoy any of it—the Anne Frank mommy's smug face won't leave my head. I go to her profile and start writing her a message.

anne frank, I type, went into hiding from a regime that sought to systematically exterminate her people on the basis of their religion. I'm feeling smart. comparing your situation to hers is deeply anti-semitic. i'd urge you to think about what language like this signals to jewish followers of yours, I finish, knowing this woman has no Jewish followers.

Ten minutes later, she writes back a reply written like a poem:

I disagree.

We will have to go into hiding.

Va((ine$ are also a religion.

Tell me how it's different?

My son will be killed if he is not hidden?

My Jewish Followers get it.

Please unfollow my page.

Please do not message me again.

"What are you doing?" Poppy asks, appearing over my shoulder. "Oh, come on," she says. "Jesus Christ. Don't pick fights with these people. You're high."

"I'm doing it for my project," I tell her.

"Yeah, you have a project, just like Mommy's *wellness* project—"

"No, this is serious, this is real. I'm thinking it's maybe gonna be a kind of interactive website with all these little gifs." I surprise myself with how easily I can picture a website covered in sticker-like gifs of mommies.

"The water you swim in," Poppy says, sighing, "is the water you swim in."

"I know, but—I really feel like I'm—piecing together something about America?"

Poppy doesn't respond.

"I feel like I'm maybe even gonna be able to write a book, you know—it's probably even bigger than I'm thinking of it as being—something on the failure of the larger American experiment, America as a death cult, America as—"

"Stop calling it America," Poppy says, taking my empty soup bowl. "You're creeping me out." She goes into her room and shuts the door. I block the Anne Frank lady and keep scrolling. My mother has posted an image. It's a pyramid labeled *THE PYRAMID OF QUALITIES OF SUCCESSFUL INDIVIDUALS.* At the bottom of the pyramid is a long row of qualities: industriousness, friendship, loyalty, cooperation, enthusiasm. The triangle top of the pyramid is divided longitudinally into two smaller triangles; the qualities they hold are faith and patience. *SO TRUE!* says my mother's caption. #faith #patience #faithandpatience #getwellwithwendy #comingsoon. I comment what's coming soon, wendy???? and then toss my phone over to the other end of the couch. Something about my phone facedown on the sofa reminds me of a baby drowning.

The next day Poppy comes home from work with excited eyes. "I have a story." This morning, she says, a student's father came to her desk and asked to talk to the head counselor about his son.

Poppy told him that the head counselor was out for the week; the father, though, had an urgent concern. His son's latest block-centric project had earned a C—unheard of. Poppy suggested the parent talk to the teacher directly. The guidance office, Poppy reminded the parent, was probably not the best equipped to handle a classroom situation.

"Then," Poppy says, "the guy throws his *business card* at me, he, like, *flings* it and it hits me in the face and he's like—'Do you know who I am? Do you know who I am?' and then he goes—this is verbatim—he goes, 'I would like you to talk to me about my kid as if you were talking to Mark Zuckerberg about his kid.'"

We laugh so hard I feel it in my stomach. It feels so good to laugh. I'm so happy about laughing that I don't stop. Then I feel something threaten to drop out of my vagina.

"Oh," I say, and hurry up and waddle across the apartment.

"What," Poppy says, "what?" and she follows me to the bathroom and stands in the doorway. I undo the drawstring of my pants, pull everything down, look in my underwear—nothing. I squat over the toilet and pee, and I feel something slither. An enormous clump of tissue lands in the toilet: pink-brown with a kind of pale tail attached that reminds me of the cloudy white part of the inside of an egg. It makes a horrible noise as it drops into the water.

"Oh my god," I say, looking away from the bowl as fast as I can, "I'm gonna throw up."

"What, what is it?"

"This huge—this huge thing just came out."

"Is that normal? Did they tell you something would come out?"

"No, I don't know, I don't know."

"Let me google," Poppy says, readying her phone.

"No," I say, and I wipe. Small black grits cling to the paper. "It's okay. I think it's normal. They said something about the numbing stuff, I think." There's a sweet smell, like ointment, coming from inside me. I wipe again, then move my hand to the flusher.

"Wait, wait, before you flush," Poppy says, "can I see it?"

Before I can answer Poppy, the buzzer rings.

"Hello," I say, gesturing to my body on the toilet. "Go get it, please."

Poppy rushes to the buzzer. "Who is it?" she asks.

"Delivery," says the voice on the other end.

"Did you order something?" Poppy asks.

"Maybe? I order from Amazon, like, every day—" I take one more peek at the thing floating in the toilet, consider scooping it out to look at it more closely, then flush it.

"Hey," she says, disappointed, pressing the button that opens the lobby door. "I wanted to see."

I stand up and wipe one last time. "I'm gonna go down and see what came." But by the time I've washed my hands, there's a knock at the door. When we open it, there's a sweaty delivery guy standing beside two brown boxes as big as refrigerators.

"One of you's Poppy?" he says, holding out a digital machine for someone to sign.

"Where is this from?" Poppy asks, not taking the machine.

"Sleepy's," says the guy.

"Oh," I say. *Best bed for little sister.* "I ordered it." I look at Poppy. "It's a bed. For you. I think you should stay."

Poppy starts to argue with me.

"It's what you want," I say, "and I think it's a good idea. It'll be good. It'll be fun. You'll stay for the year. And when the lease is up, we'll see. But you should stay."

Poppy smiles at me. It's not her usual smile. "Okay," she says. "We can do this for a year." Her voice sounds thin. Poppy wanted what she wanted from me until I gave it to her.

I sign the man's small machine. Together, Poppy and I scoot the giant boxes into the apartment and open them with scissors. Tiny Styrofoam fluff flies at our faces and gets stuck in Poppy's hair. In one box there's a tightly rolled twin mattress. In the other box there's a frame for a slim pink four-poster. I tell Poppy what I googled to get us here. She hugs me.

"This is so sweet," she says, "but is there any way I can, like—can we send it back and you can just give me the money?"

When I check my email for the invoice, I see I've bought Poppy a hybrid gel grid model, top of the line, best bed for little sister, $1,649.99 before tax. And I've paid for rush delivery. And another thousand for the frame. All night I rant on the phone to Sleepy's: *My card was stolen, my bank account was hacked, I'm not responsible for these things, I can't accept them.*

But you signed, they keep telling me. *You signed for the boxes. It's here, right here. You did accept them. You did.*

"Remember your first boyfriend?" Poppy asks me one night.

"Isaac?" I ask. Isaac was gay, and he had huge teeth, and he fought with his father physically and often, and he regularly came to school bruised from these fights. We dated for three weeks; sometime in the second week, I lost my Motorola Razr. I was always pretty sure he stole it out of my backpack. But his parents were fairly rich, and my parents were fairly rich, so there was no motive for him to take my Razr. When we were breaking up, I asked him if he'd stolen it, and he rolled his eyes and replied, "Sure, Julie," which was what he called me, "I stole your Razr."

"Yeah," Poppy says. She holds up her phone. "He died."

We huddle our heads together over her phone. Sure enough, Isaac's Facebook page now says Remembering Isaac Stein where it used to say Isaac Stein.

"Oh my god," I say, reexperiencing viscerally the sensation of my big teeth knocking his big teeth in one of the school library's private study rooms.

"Are you sad?" Poppy asks.

"Not really," I say. "He stole my Razr."

"I wonder how he died," Poppy says, scrolling.

"Drugs," I say. "I think he did a lot of drugs."

"Just because he's gay doesn't mean he did a lot of drugs."

"Is it a stereotype that gay people do a lot of drugs?"

"No, but just, like—the way you said it made it sound like you think it is." Poppy switches to Google and searches *isaac stein south florida dead*. "Oh, hang on." She clicks a link to a PDF on a government website: an arrest affidavit claiming Isaac extorted and defrauded his father, stole over a hundred thousand dollars from him, and fled to Montenegro with a boyfriend, where he evidently at some point died.

"Send that to me," I say, and she does. We sit in silence reading it side by side. On the warrant for his arrest, his hair is listed as brown. When I knew him, he was blond.

"This is so intense," Poppy says.

"Yeah," I say, zooming in on Isaac's listed occupation: un-employed.

"How are you feeling?" she asks.

"I'm feeling like now I know he *for* sure stole my Razr."

The mommy whose husband recently underwent a vasectomy reversal is now pregnant with her third child—a miracle, a sign from her God—and Isaac Stein is dead, and I'm done bleeding, and I have what Poppy calls the jobbies. I want a new job, but mostly only in theory, and probably only because Poppy's job is still new. When I open my laptop to start work, a little black square falls out of it: the e key is broken. A perfect excuse to neglect BookSmarts for the day.

hi! I Slack my boss. I am about to type *the e key on my laptop just broke* before realizing I can't. quick call? I type instead, and then I deliver the news verbally.

"I'm gonna go out and get it fixed right now," I promise. "I'll have everything in tomorrow." Today was my deadline. My boss assures me he'll shuffle things around, it'll all be fine.

"But," he says before hanging up, "if you could maybe work on some stuff today that doesn't require you to type out any e's and get that uploaded to the drive, it'd be great."

Feeling deeply indignant that I could be expected to get any work done without an e key, I go to a publishing house's shitty website and hunt. I decide to apply to a role I'm both under- and overqualified for in the marketing department of a haughty imprint. I could do marketing.

Which of these statements is true? the application asks, offering a drop-down menu.

Aesthetics enhance our surroundings

Rules should be followed

Ideas should be studied

Charity improves society

Rules should be broken

Money makes more money

Individuality expresses uniqueness

I stare at the list for a while, then choose Money makes more money.

What gets you out of bed in the morning? the application asks me next.

Seeing beautiful aesthetics

Maintaining order through rules

Encountering exciting ideas

Helping my neighbors

Breaking the mold

Making money

Expressing my individuality

Now I'm furious. I take a picture of the screen with my phone and send it to Poppy.

what IS THIS lmao, I say.

Within seconds she's typing back. tag yourself, she writes; i'm "encountering exciting ideas."

i can't tag myself, I write. that's why im texting you

She doesn't type back.

tag meeee!!!!!! I write.

you're a pleaser, she says. put "maintaining order"

I select Maintaining order through rules, effortfully edit a lukewarm old cover letter saved to my desktop as *bonappetit_editorial_letter_2*—every time I encounter a word that needs an e, I have to copy-and-paste one from somewhere else in the document—and submit the application. Then I move to the couch, where I lie down and look out the window and think about what it means that I'm a pleaser, and about how Poppy can just articulate something about me so clearly when I've never even glimpsed that something in myself, and moreover about how I can start working very hard to stop people-pleasing entirely in the months and years to come. Starting now, I think, and starting with everyone, I'm going to try very hard to shed my pleaser skin; I'm going to devote myself to myself. Already, though, I know it won't work.

I put off the trip to the Apple Store until the evening. While I sit at the Genius Bar waiting for a Genius to help me, Poppy inspects some new iPhones on a nearby table. After a few minutes, she hurries back over to me.

"I'm about to blow your mind," she says. Her eyes are wide and her face is sweaty.

"Okay," I say, using my skeptical voice.

My tone deadens Poppy's eyes. "Fine," she says, turning back toward the table of phones. I can spot a big hive on the back of her neck.

I grab her arm. "Okay, tell me."

She jerks her shoulder up. "No, it's fine."

"Tell me."

Poppy turns back around. Her eyes are enormous again. "Are you ready?" she asks.

I sigh.

"Okay, so. You remember your dreams pretty well."

It's true. "I do . . ." My skeptical voice creeps back in. I try to restrain it. "Yeah, I have really vivid dreams, usually."

"But you never dream about your phone, do you?" Bush-baby eyes.

I think about this for a minute. I never do dream about my phone. I'm never holding it or looking at it or searching for it, whereas in real life, I spend probably ten hours a day holding it or looking at it or searching for it behind the couch, in the bed-clothes. "Oh my god," I say.

"Right?" Poppy screams. "It's insane! We never dream about our phones! Ergo . . ." Poppy makes an *ergo* gesture with both hands.

"I don't know?"

"Er*go*," Poppy says, "the government."

"Absolutely not." I turn to my laptop and open Google. "Let's look." Drams about iphons, I type, before remembering.

"Hmm," Poppy says. "You can't really do much on a computer," she observes rightly, "without the e key."

Poppy and I have started doing most of our grocery shopping as a unit. She doesn't feel that both paying for groceries and schlepping them is fair; someone should pay and someone should schlep.

Today the grocery store is playing frenetic jazz over the loud-speakers. Immediately our shopping takes on a sense of urgency.

"Do you want a pear?" Poppy asks me, and the question seems

loaded. I shrug. "Will you or will you not eat a pear in the next three to four days?" she tries again.

"I can't know that about myself," I say.

Poppy sets the pear back atop the pile from whence it came, sending several pears toppling to the ground. She makes a face like *yikes* and hurries away. I pick up the pears. I start to put them back in the bin, but then I think how vulnerable it is to shop for produce; you could get a dirty old pear someone dropped on the floor. The pears probably touch worse in the shipping process— probably things so horrible I can't even imagine them. Once a friend of my father's told me that when he worked at a pickle factory in his youth, relish was made from cucumbers deemed too disgusting to brine whole; workers tossed the most revolting specimens right back onto the conveyor belt after inspection, sending them down the line and off the edge into a large vat where they were mashed up and mixed together so that their hideousness could still be made profitable.

Certain that I'm never buying a pear again, I bring my armful of them over to a man unloading produce onto the shelves.

"These fell," I tell him, holding the pears out in front of me. "I don't know what to do with them." He accepts the pears, then tosses them into a large black trash bin stuffed with stems and leaves and onion skins and corn silks. "I didn't drop them," I say, "they just fell."

I'm looking everywhere for fresh basil, but I can't find it. I walk up to a woman in dark pants and a collared shirt. "Excuse me," I say, "where could I find fresh basil?"

The woman turns around. "I don't work here," she says. "I'm just Black."

In the dairy section, things are even worse. There, we spy a pretty famous actor evaluating tiny glass jars of yogurt. Poppy lives for celeb sightings. She grips my arm tight. "Oh my god," she says.

The pretty famous man moves toward us, a basket on his arm. He's going for the smoked salmon. I busy myself at a shelf full of nut butters and fruit spreads. I pick up three things in a row that are past their expiration. To distract Poppy, I show the dates to her. "We should really tell someone who works here," I say.

She laughs unnaturally. The pretty famous man squeezes past us. He smells nice.

Poppy pays and I schlep. She tells me about a small boy who slips into the guidance office each day at lunchtime and asks to eat with Poppy. Lower-school students, however, are not allowed to eat lunch outside of the lunchroom. Every day Poppy walks this boy back to the cafeteria and he cries and tries to hold her hand the whole way. He carries a washcloth around like a safety blanket and rubs it on his cheek. *I can't do it,* he tells Poppy on his daily march back to his classmates. *Please don't make me.*

"There must be something going on at home," Poppy says as we cross against the light. "It's a weird situation. Even my boss thinks so. And I want to tell this kid every day, 'It's okay, it'll all be okay, school will be okay,' but obviously I can't know that things will be okay for him, so I can't *say* that to him. And I don't know why it's *me* he's latched on to?" A hot wind comes, kicking up dust and tiny bits of street crap, and I struggle to breathe. "Do you think it's because I have that mom instinct, I seem like a mother figure to him? Like I'd be a good mom?"

"No," I say. "I don't think you'd be a good mom."

Poppy stops walking and looks at the ground. "That's so fucking mean."

"I don't think I'd be a good mom, either."

"That doesn't mean I wouldn't be."

"Obviously it does," I say, lifting the paper grocery bag onto my hip so I can hold it in my arms. "Since we're, like, the same in a lot of ways."

"I'll meet you at home, I think," Poppy says. "I need time to process here. I'd be a great mom. That kid comes to me every fucking day for comfort." She peels away from me, shimmying between the cars parked on the street to cross to the other side.

"And you don't give it to him," I say.

She looks back at me. Her eyes are wet. We walk home different ways.

In the morning I wake to a Facebook message from one of my college poetry teachers.

And what are you up to, he's written, in the big city?

For thirty minutes, as I rise and hydrate and eat a KIND bar and pick at my sebaceous filaments and dry-brush and shower and lotion myself and begin my day, I ponder the "and." What's that "and" doing?

"And what are you up to," I mutter to myself as I slick my hair into a bun.

"And what are you up to," I whisper as I tamp ground espresso beans into the bottom of the Moka pot.

I scroll through my useless Facebook feed while I drink my coffee, trying to ignore the gnatty feeling my teacher's waiting message creates in the base of my skull. A page called Five-Minute Crafts, which I do not follow but which always pops up regardless, shows me a video full of Easy Escape Techniques. In the time-lapsed video, a bored-looking blonde escapes being zip-tied to a chair, handcuffed in a field, bound at the ankles with nautical rope. She wriggles free with ease over and over. A man playing her kidnapper pops on screen each time to huff and puff.

And what are you up to? I hear in my head.

Hi Robert! I start writing back, determined to make it sound like I'm up to lots. Things are good! Writing a sort of experimental book-length hybrid essay about the assimilation of Jews into American life and the loneliness of the internet and a whole bunch of other things—not finished yet but making good progress! I work for an online academic publisher and live with my sister, whom I love a lot—she's also in the education sphere. Look at me using "whom." I add "-al" to "education," then google *education sphere vs educational sphere,* then get stressed and delete it all and switch apps.

One of my mommies, rooted_saffron_mama, has started posting about Jews and the New World Order. Beneath a picture of a cartoon lamb with a single tear falling from its light eye, its head bleeding and ringed in a crown of thorns, she writes:

ALL OVER THE WORLD FAKE J00Z ARE TRYING TO ESTABLISH A FALSELY J00ISH, COMMUNIST, BOLSHEVIK, ONE WORLD TOTALITARIAN GOVERNMENT AND TAKE AWAY ALL RIGHTS BY COVERTLY INSTALLING 5G TOWERS AND DENYING MEDICAL CARE TO THE ELDERLY (THE ONES THE GLOBALIST J00Z CALL "USELESS EATERS") WAKE UP PEOPLE!!!!!!!!!!!!!

you hateful fucking antisemite, I write to her.

WHAT ABOUT WHAT I SAID IS ANTI SEMITIC, she writes back. TORAH AND TALMUD ARE DIFFERENT. J00DAISM TODAY IS FALSE J00DAISM LED BY F@KE J00Z. CLEARLY YOU CAN'T FUCKING READ SO DON'T COME FOR ME.

A girl I went to high school with is a lesbian celebrity's newest girlfriend. They're photographed together everywhere. Getting green juices, walking dogs. In high school this girl was known for never wearing Soffe shorts underneath her uniform skirt; you could always see her thong when you were walking up the stairs behind her. I think in high school she was actually really mean about lesbians. Suddenly I feel I need a pair of Soffe shorts. When I was eleven I had some black ones that said *ANGEL* on the butt. By the time I get to the Soffe website I'm bored. It's the ease of my childhood I want back, not these shorts.

I tweet, there was a day you put on soffe shorts for the last time and you didn't even know it. Five people like the tweet. It's 9:48 in the morning. It occurs to me that I haven't left the house in days.

At the park I sit and breathe while the grass dampens my pants. An old bald woman slumps on a bench. She's wearing a long skirt that reveals her bare calves, both of which are swollen and bright red, cellulitic, infected, weeping—she has a plastic Target bag tied around one of them. Beneath the nearest tree, a man in one of those short beanies sips a cold brew. He has a large neck tattoo that says *NECK TATTOO*. His girlfriend has hair that looks to have recently been dyed the color hairdressers are calling "rosé." Some mothers sit in a circle with their babies. I wonder why I ever come outside. I wonder why I'm in Brooklyn when my work is remote and I have no friends, nothing tethering me here. I try not to stare at the old bald woman, but I can't help myself. It's just too sad. I stare at her and get sadder and sadder. I told myself I wouldn't look at my phone while I was in the park, but I feel the only thing that will stop me from plummeting into sadness is to look at my phone. No one has texted me or sent me any memes. Moments after I unlock it, though, Poppy calls. I answer.

"I had a feeling you were about to call. I always get a feeling when someone's about to call or text. I swear I'm psychic."

"I think it's just that you're always on your phone," Poppy says, "and you only talk to two people, and the enormous amount of time you spend on your phone combined with the smallness of the number of the people you talk to means that of course it seems like you always get a feeling."

"That's so mean," I say, staring at the old bald woman and trying not to spiral out because she reminds me of my loneliness, and my mortality, and my fear of dying alone; not just of dying alone, but of dying alone in Brooklyn.

The old bald woman heaves with sobs. She's crying; it's the noiseless, open-mouthed crying of a person in unbearable, layered pain.

"Can you believe that shit?" Poppy asks. I realize she's been talking for several seconds. "Do you think I did the right thing? What would you have done?"

"I'm sorry," I say, "I wasn't listening at all."

"I knew it," Poppy says. Then things are quiet.

"So?" I ask. "What happened?"

"It doesn't matter. You don't give a fuck."

"I do," I say, hoping it sounds true.

"You don't. You never listen to the stories I tell you about my kids. You can keep up with a thousand things on Instagram, but you can't, like, bother to listen to actual stories about actual fucking human beings in my life."

"Those kids are not your kids," I say. "They're your job. Don't get obsessed with them."

"Did you ever think maybe I'm quote-unquote obsessed with them because I have no one else? Because I have a mothering instinct born of neglect? That I'm just fucking good at my job as a caretaker of the vulnerable? That it could be my calling in life?"

The bald woman is leaning over, trying to reach a bloody tissue she's dropped on the ground. "There's no such thing as a calling," I say. "I'm having an emotional crisis. I can't really process what you're saying to me right now."

"Is it a crisis you've made up in your head because you have no real crisis in your life?" Poppy asks.

Aping our mother, I hang up on her without a reply. My phone's not done with me yet; there's a new text from one of the Leighs.

how are you doing, it says; then there's the emoji with the big pleading anime eyes. Why, I wonder, is she talking to me like I'm a cancer patient?

great!!!!!!!!!!!!!!! I write back. how are you!!!!!!!!

im ok! i just have not heard from you and i wanted to make sure things were ok w your living situation

I write back with the tears-streaming emoji followed by thank you!!!! you are so kind to ask!! everything is ok. poppy seems ok

good!!!!!!! writes Leigh.

I start typing: yeah it's just like......idk!!! it's nice to have her around and we laugh a lot, i guess i just feel like i don't really fully know her, or the person she wants to be? or whatever idk. its comfy!!! to live with family!!!! but also jkladjflkajsdf. and it feels like oh my god am i going to be grey gardens one day and my whole life has passed and it's just me and her.

Why does every message I send make me sound completely devoid of personality, perspective, intelligence? Why have I decided *jkladjflkajsdf* is an acceptable replacement for language, for reckoning? I backspace and backspace, knowing Leigh doesn't want to hear it all anyway. Instead I write, lets get together soon!!!!! and Leigh writes, absolutement!!!!!! for drinks and treats!!!!!! and I say, yes please!!!! knowing we won't make a plan, we won't see each other for months, we won't reveal ourselves to each other; I will look back on this one day as a moment in which I inched myself one step closer to total loneliness: to exactly what I was afraid of the whole time.

I text Poppy one afternoon to ask what she wants to eat for dinner. She doesn't respond. I call her; she doesn't answer. I wait until dark, then pour cold red sauce over linguine and turn on the pilot of *Lost*, which I've seen about eight times. I love rewatching. I love when things unfold how I remember them unfolding. Toward the end of the episode, Poppy walks in.

"Ooh," she says, looking at the hot people on the screen. "Did you know Evangeline Lilly's an anti-vaxxer now?"

"Everyone's an anti-vaxxer now," I say. I google *evangeline lilly antivax* while Poppy helps herself to some sticky noodles left in the pot, eating with her hands. I read aloud the first headline that comes up: "*Evangeline Lilly claims plant-based diet cured depression.*"

Poppy licks her fingers. "I actually have been thinking about going fully plant-based," she says, flipping her sensible work ponytail around as punctuation.

I make a face. "Why didn't you answer my texts?"

She makes a face back. "What texts?"

"About dinner."

"Oh," she says. "I was out."

Poppy having things of her own to do feels wrong. "Could

you, like—tell me? When you're gonna go out and not participate in dinner?"

"We don't have to participate in dinner together every night," Poppy says. "Not even couples do that."

"I know," I say, "but some nights you're like: *What's for dinner,* and other nights, you're like: not able to answer my texts."

"Well, like I said, I'm going plant-based soon, so I'm probably going to be making my own meals now, so you don't have to factor me into your dinner plans."

Alone in my room, I apply for ten jobs. One of them is a position writing horoscopes for Starlab, a moneyed new astrology app. The same way BookSmarts rips off SparkNotes without meaningfully differentiating itself from SparkNotes, Starlab seems to have been invented to rip off Co-Star without adding anything to the premise—why is it, I think, while getting stoned out of my mind off Poppy's shitty vape pen, that in this life, in our simulation, in whatever terrifying meaningless thing it is we're all doing every day, we can only create infinite and infinitely worse versions of the things we already have instead of good new things we need?

This role might be a *stellar* fit for you, says the job description, if you:

- Consider yourself to be the greatest aphorist of your generation.
- Bleed onto the page.
- Are a collector of of objects, words, people, experiences.

- Have some cursory knowledge of the fundamentals of Freudian.psychoanalysis (BA or BS in psychology preferred).
- Are always reaching toward your highest self.
- Have no ego.
- Caught the typo already.

I did catch the typo. I have an ego for sure and my bachelor's is in literature, but everything else sounds right. I start the application, typing faster than I've ever typed before.

The job prompts me to Describe the personality of the Virgo or Scorpio reading this. There is a blank text box below. Luckily, Poppy is a Scorpio. I let the text box have it.

Scorpio, I write, you've got fire. But that doesn't mean you can burn anyone who tries to get close.

I hate it.

Scorpio, I try once more, your hard crustacean casing keeps you safe—but it also means you're fucking clueless.

In the morning, when I wake up, I have an email from someone named Emily. She was excited by my application. More than excited—she's never seen a horoscope so good from someone whose résumé doesn't reflect any experience writing horoscopes. As a Scorpio herself, she says, she felt profoundly dragged by my description of Scorpios. She'd love to chat more. When can I come by? And, by the way, what's my sign?

It's almost time, it seems, for my high school reunion. A girl named Molly who was vice president of our graduating class invites me and two hundred others to join a Facebook group. '09 SO FINE 10-YEAR REUNION, it's called. A boy who pushed me against a locker and threatened to kill me in seventh grade has made the first post: he has a connection at a hotel near Universal Studios and is going to rent us a block of rooms with pool access.

hell yeah brother B), comments a boy who has become a cop. Obviously he tried to do the smiling-sunglasses emoji, but it didn't work. I click on his profile. He posts a lot about his boys in blue and about how officers these days need to *keep their heads on a swivel*. The part of my brain that loves hateful things is aglow.

My phone lights up. It's Gage. Every few months he texts me to ask if I need edibles; I haven't heard from him since right before Valentine's. One of the reasons it took so long for us to break up was because he has a medical marijuana card and I don't.

Just get your own marijuana card, Poppy would say when I'd call her to ideate about ending things.

But I don't want it on my record, I'd say. *For Gage it doesn't matter, he has no ambitions.*

The text he's sent now is just a leaf emoji and a question mark. I thumbs-up it.

come thru whenever, he writes.

An hour later I'm at his apartment, in his bed. After twenty seconds of kissing, Gage reaches into his nightstand for his penis sleeve, a nearly Vantablack device with terrifying whorled vortices swirled around its outside; like a real vagina, it suggests the void. He lubes up and inserts his dick into the sleeve. I'm rubbing myself through my underwear, but I never finish when we do this side-by-side thing; for me it's more about anthropology, about watching Gage to see if he's changed, to see if I can make him feel familiar again. We were together for four years—it's mystifying, not even a year after our breakup, to find that four years wasn't really anything. It always felt like we were just around the corner from getting married, but neither of us could ever seem to work up the motivation. Before Gage, I'd thought that relationships ended only when something huge and irredeemable happened: something that totally wrecked you both, something neither of you could move past. But at some point I realized relationships could just end. You could just feel done. For months I scrambled for an excuse to peel away from him. Finally I nailed one: he hated my mother.

I can't be with someone who hates my mother, I remember telling him, squeezing myself toward a cry, the morning I dumped him.

But you're *always telling me how much* you *hate your mother,* he said back.

I told him that my hating my mother and his hating my mother weren't the same thing, and that they were ultimately irreconcilable, and he bought it.

With Gage, I felt comfortable; I had someone who adored me, who cared what I thought, but who didn't know me quite well enough to tell me how I could grow as a person, to point out the places where I wasn't meeting my potential. When I'd complain to him that I felt like a piece of shit for not exercising or not working very hard or not writing or not trying to make new friends or not engaging intellectually with the culture, he'd tell me I was doing fine, I was beautiful and talented, I was sexy, I was smart, I was his whole world, I was enough. It was very nice.

Gage makes a noise of defeat. He stops jerking himself off and looks at the wall.

"What?" I ask.

"You're not really here," he says.

"I was thinking about our relationship," I say, being honest; Gage never thought I was very honest about my thoughts.

"I just feel bad now," Gage says. "I feel like I'm completely unattractive to you."

"You're not," I say.

"Can I be inside you?"

I look at the sleeve. "Well, not now that you used the thing."

"It's clean," Gage says. "I clean it every time."

"It's not clean enough for me."

"I wash it, like, *perfectly* with *gentle soap*—"

"You know how when I get BV, I can't get rid of it for, like, a month, I'm not taking that risk—"

"Okay, I'm not pressuring, I'm not pressuring, I would never pressure you," Gage says, unsheathing himself. He waddles toward the door, naked from the waist down.

"Put pants on," I say.

"Paul's not home."

"Can I pee?" I ask.

"Yeah."

"Buddy system?" I ask, holding out my hand. When we lived together and we had to get out of bed in the middle of the night to use the bathroom at the same time, we'd always say "Buddy system" and hold hands there and back.

Gage doesn't say anything, so I get up and put my hand in his hand, and we walk together to the bathroom. I use the toilet while he washes his penis sleeve in the sink.

"This is pretty fucked up," he says, using his hand to wipe out the inside. "I don't like doing this."

"Cleaning the thing?"

"No," he says. "Masturbating together, doing the buddy system. It hurts."

"I don't feel hurt or anything," I say, wiping. "Do you really feel *hurt*?"

"Yeah, I feel fucking hurt." Gage puts his penis sleeve on the edge of the tub and leaves the bathroom, closing me in. As I wash my hands, I notice a paper note taped up on the corner of the mirror: *every day,* it says, *you are getting better and better*.

Gage isn't in the living room when I come out; my edibles are sitting on the bench by the door. "I'll Venmo you," I shout. Gage doesn't answer. I was hoping he'd be able to orgasm, and he'd get the sweet newborn-baby look he gets when he comes, and he'd hold my head and let me talk about Poppy moving in, about Mr. Tinkel, about the bald lady in the park, about the goldfish, about how even texting feels hard lately; but it seems like he's reached some kind of cliff. "I didn't come over to be mean," I yell. "It looks really great in here." Gage has a cool wooden chair by the window. "I like this chair, where'd you get it?" He won't answer me. "Okay," I say. "See you?"

Gage opens his door. "Get your own fucking medical marijuana card," he says. He's crying. "It's not gonna stop you from getting a job."

"What's your job now? Do you have a job?" I know that he doesn't. "That's fucking right," I say. I pick up the edibles. They're all the wrong flavor. "These are wrong," I say. Gage cries harder. "Okay," I say, putting them in my bag anyway. "I'm going." I go.

At my Starlab interview I meet with Emily, whose job title is "Technical Astrologer." She looks the way I've been trying to look for years. She has the right wispy clothes and the right wispy hair. I'm in a long blue caftan-y dress that makes me look like a cone. I'm pretty sure I'm older than Emily, and I feel embarrassed.

"So, tell me about getting your MFA," Emily says in a tone of voice that tells me a secret part of her is considering an MFA. We're sitting at a long desk occupied by five people wired into giant iMacs. They all look pretty great, too. One girl with perfect lip filler has her shoes off and her legs tucked up on her chair beneath a blanket. She's on Spotify. I want this non-job so badly I can feel my throat closing up.

"Um," I say. There's not much to tell about my MFA. Mostly I remember going to dark bars and magazine parties after class to try to meet nasty editors and glimpse obscure literary celebrities. I was a sifting-dust-mote kind of writer then, always working on stories about middle-aged women named Maryanne looking out their kitchen windows and thinking about their wayward adult children while "good brown bread" or whatever baked in the oven. Then the bread would be done and they'd wrap it in a soft checked dishcloth and the story would be over. These women's houses were poorly heated, since I'd observed that the greatest characters across classic and contemporary fiction alike were always cold. There were never men in any of these stories, and in my workshops, all the men would be like: *Where are the men?* I tried working on a novel about a family of economically depressed women living in the Florida Panhandle, but I'd never been economically depressed and I'd never visited the Panhandle, and I stopped writing it after I went to a lecture where a novelist one generation above me entreated the audience to write only what was true. *Get a life,* he told us, *learn a trade. Go into the army if you want to write about the army. Go run a farm if you want to write about life on a farm.*

I don't mention any of this to Emily. "This is what I'll tell you about it. Once," I say, smiling coyly, "I showed one of my favorite teachers an essay I had written, and I was so proud of it, I thought it was really good and idiosyncratic, it was about climate change, and it was really sort of broken up and experimental and cool, and in our office hours meeting, she was holding a copy of the essay and she put it down in front of me and said, 'It's good, but so what?'" This didn't happen to me, but I heard that it happened to a girl in one of my seminars.

Emily clutches her chest. "Oh my God," she says.

"And so now," I say, doing the most naturalistic acting I can, "that's what I really try to think about when I'm writing. It's good, but so what? What am I trying to say?" I narrow my eyes. "What does it have to really offer a person, you know?"

Emily is nodding. "Yeah," she says. "Yeah, oh my God." She keeps nodding. "Wow."

Now I know for sure I am older than Emily.

Poppy has gone plant-based, just as she threatened. She eats large bowls of weird cauliflower pasta mixed with uncooked peppers of different colors, fake egg whites, lots of soups. She starts losing weight, so I start trying to lose weight, too. I notice that she smells. I thought, based on everything I've ever seen on the Internet, that going plant-based was supposed to cleanse a person's system, make them light and glowy and pure. When we watch TV together on the couch at night, I try to sit far away from her. All I can think is: She smells she smells she smells. Finally, one evening, I tell her.

"I guess I'll go fucking shower, then," she says, leaving me alone with the television. When Poppy is done, she comes to stand in front of me in her towel. "Do I fucking smell now?" she asks.

"Oh my god."

"Smell me," she says, and she presses her armpit into my face.

"It wasn't even your armpit that smelled, it was just this smell coming from your body."

"You are such a fucking cunt," she says, "it's my medicated lotion." She goes to her room and slams the door.

"I'm sorry," I tell the door. "I didn't know it was a special lotion thing, I thought it was a body thing."

Poppy doesn't answer me. I go back to my room and poke through the high school reunion group: lots of new members have joined. A girl who was captain of the dance team now runs a clean-living compound in Hawaii. A guy whose last name was Butts has changed it to Batts. One girl, who is definitely white, seems to be passing herself off as a Black activist at the university where she's a PhD candidate. The one guy who always talked about moving to Seoul has moved to Seoul. A girl who was on theater tech crew is posting about how Hasbro has started to release dolls with buttons on their genitals in order to groom young children for the pedophilic cannibalistic elite right under their parents' noses *#childlivesmatter*.

An email arrives from Starlab. I have the job. Of course they'd tell me I got the position over email, after work hours, in a note that begins *Hi, you—*

I read through the offer letter. I'm getting a pay bump and a work computer. I wish I could tell Poppy. So I decide to go in and tell Poppy.

Her door is unlocked. When I walk in, she's naked, her hair dripping. "*Excuse* me," she says, but she doesn't bother to cover up.

"I got the job," I tell her.

She rolls her eyes.

"What?" I ask. "Why would you roll your eyes? I get to, like, write dumb aphorisms for lots of money now."

"I just don't think you're going to be happy in a real workplace.

You've been working from home for, like, four years. Now you're gonna be commuting, eating salads. I don't think you'll like it. You like just being in the apartment, working in bed, wearing jammies." She picks up her towel and wraps herself in it.

"I'm gonna love it. What the fuck is wrong with you, my *jammies*?" What I want to ask is *Where'd you go*, but that doesn't make a whole lot of sense.

Poppy shrugs. "I'm happy you're happy, then," she says. "Or: that you're going to be happy. Soon. Maybe."

And I'm the cunt.

"Are you seeing someone?" I ask.

Poppy blinks her huge eyes. "I don't know what you mean by that."

"Seeing someone, dating someone. Don't be obtuse."

Poppy makes a face. "Obtuse? Hello. I'm not dating, per se."

"But you're seeing someone. Stop making fun of me."

She flaps her hands around in circles. "What does seeing someone even mean?"

"I don't know! What *does* seeing someone mean!"

"I think your idea of seeing someone and my idea of seeing someone are different. Like, dating isn't really part of my worldview. Love isn't really part of my worldview. So I don't know if I'm seeing someone by your standards."

"I swear to god," I say. "What the fuck does that mean, part of your worldview, you're always reading happy-marriage princess books."

"That's just entertainment, it's like—I'm not that person in real life, I feel like *you're* the one who really anticipates finding love, and you seek love, and you put yourself out there for love."

Not since you moved in, I think but don't say. I'm dying to tell Poppy about still semi-regularly fucking Gage, or at least still semi-regularly making him cry by not fucking him. Telling her now, though, would just confirm the idea she has of me: someone desperate, someone flimsy. "Can you ever just answer me about anything? You're queer, it's not like we live on different planets."

Poppy makes a sound of rage. "We certainly don't live by the same metrics."

"We're, like, literally the same person."

Poppy stares at me. "You keep saying that. Do you really think that?"

I'm confused now. I thought she thought that, too. "I mean, you're plant-based, but. We're really the same in a lot of ways."

"Oh my god. I can have my own life. I can have my own secrets. I can be somewhere you don't know about for two fucking hours. I don't have to talk about everything with you, you don't get to interrogate me like you're Mommy." Then she starts crying. Her face crumples chin-first, as it always does when a big cry is coming. I let her weep. I reach a hand out to pat her. She snot-rockets into her towel. "It's like—it's not even that I want to *be* here, messing with your life, living in view of you—it's like—a couple weeks before I decided to come, I had this conversation with Mommy, and it was just—basically she was like: *Are you a lesbian?* And I was like: *No, I'm queer,* and she was like: *That's a slur*, and I was like: *Not anymore, we've reclaimed it*, and she said, *Who's we*, and I said, *The queer community*, and she goes: *You mean THE LESBIAN COMMUNITY??????*" Poppy ruffles her hair, a move she does when she's frustrated. "And, you know, then she starts with, like, *Is the government encouraging you to do this, I think the deep state is trying to use the liberal media to get Jewish women to stop reproducing by convincing them they're men or they're lesbians, so they won't bear children, so there will be less Jewish children,* and then she goes on to this whole big tangent about 'nefarious motives,' how they're targeting people who are already 'deviant,' how they want fewer Jews in the world, they've always wanted a world without Jews, I'm asking her, *Who's they,* she's not answering me, so, it wasn't, you know. An extremely productive conversation or anything. And I offered to send her some links, or whatever, to articles about queerness, but you know how she won't click links."

Our mother fears spyware.

"And then she said, verbatim, *Well, I'd rather you date a shvartze than a woman.*"

"Jesus Christ," I say. "She never used to fucking talk like that."

"Yeah, well, now she does. So now you see. My being here isn't about me being really excited to be here. I'm, like, a refugee. Not a refugee, but, you know. I don't know," Poppy says, starting to cry. "Sorry," she says, "it's my period." She cries some more.

"I wanna hug you," I say after a minute, "but you're naked."

Poppy pulls her towel up. I sit on the air mattress and hug her. The fancy twin mattress from Sleepy's is still leaned, infuriatingly, against the wall; the pieces to build the pink princess frame, Poppy has squirreled away in the closet.

"What did I smell like?" she asks. "Before, when I smelled."

"Sort of beery, but not exactly beer, just that sour smell."

"I'm sorry."

"*I'm* sorry."

Poppy's shoulders heave.

"We should set up the real bed soon," I say. She puts her head on my shoulder and nods it. Things feel fixed.

That night, though, I can't sleep; every time I close my eyes, I see the face of the bald woman from the park, even more clearly than I could see it when I was feet away from her. Her leaking wounds, her death mask. I think about what Poppy said about love being part of my worldview. I think about using the buddy system with Gage. I wish I could remember why I felt I needed to be free of him. I pick up my phone and text him: I send a wyd, but in quotation marks, so that he knows I'm being charming.

i will not carry the weight of our past into my future, he writes back immediately. this will be the last time i speak to you intentionally. i wish you all happinesses.

lmao, I write back. have you been getting into ram dass or something?

Gage doesn't respond. I click my screen off. I'm all alone in the dark now, with the bald woman's face behind my eyes.

A girl I went to high school with, a real Obama fan named Briana, messages me on Facebook.

Hi mama!!!!!!! she says. Are you going to the reunion!!

I click on Briana's profile. She lives in DC and works at some kind of white-guilt-y education initiative that uses the power of theater to change inner-city kids' lives. We were in drama together all through high school and both got into NYU; my parents said it wasn't worth the price tag and pushed me toward state school, but Briana's parents thought it was, and so she went, and she did a lot of Shakespeare plays there, and she was always posting pictures of herself costumed in Elizabethan dress, and I grew squelchingly envious, and I deleted her number from my phone, and we fell out of touch. It thrills me to see that she has not made it as an actress, that she's working in nonprofits—the fate of the unremarkable—and that she's the annoying kind of married where she has her wedding date, bookended with hearts, in her little bio box.

not sure! I write back. depends on holidays. you?

Briana responds immediately. Yes!!!!

We'll be there!!!!

My husband and I :)

Or, to be grammatically correct, my husband and ME! Lol

Lifelong grammar Nazi!

Lol sorry grammar NERD!

What's new with you???

I tell her: not much! working, still in bk. how about you?

Amazing <3, she writes. At first it's unclear if she means that me working and still living in Brooklyn is amazing or if she means that she's doing amazing. But then.

We're actually going to have a baby!!!!

"Jesus Christ," I say. wow! I write. yay!

But it's been hard :'(Briana writes back.

oh no! I can't stop now.

I got pregnant for the first time about a year ago.....But the

baby's cranial cavity was malformed and my ob said that

it wouldn't have a brain and would likely die very shortly

after brith :'(

**Birth

So they had to give the baby this injection to stop his hard

so he didn't feel anything and then they induced labor

and I delivered and got to hold him which was so lovely.

**His HEART omg so many typing fails today!

oh my god, I write. Briana has known love, love enough to marry for. She has known the death of a thing that once lived inside her. She has birthed a half-dead thing and held it in her arms and buried it, probably, knowing Briana. And now she's opening herself to it again.

This is my first son, she writes, and suddenly before me is a picture of a pensive Briana in a hospital bed holding a small purple fetal thing to her chest. It's enough to make me believe in trigger warnings.

I can't imagine how I could write back to something like this, so I don't; instead I open a new tab and spend some time googling stop baby's heart in womb injection real. A few minutes later, my computer dings: more messages from Briana.

Are you there?

Did it not go through?

She sends the image again. She must be able to see I'm still online.

Are you mad?

Is it because I said grammar N*zi?

My mother calls.

"I'm very concerned," she says.

"Say more."

"You and your sister are up to something. I never hear from either of you. You have to be up to something together, shutting me out."

I think again of the teacher who wanted to know what I was up to; why does this keep happening to me? "We're not up to anything," I say. "What could we be up to?"

"I know she's turning you against me."

"I'm not against you! I love you!"

"What's she saying about me?"

"Nothing," I say. "She said you wouldn't accept 'queer' as a label and you called her a lesbian." As soon as the words are out of my mouth, I regret it. I know my mom will call Poppy next and tell Poppy what I've said, and then Poppy will scream at me, and then I'll suffer for days under her ire. No matter what I do, I'm always angering one of them, pushing one of them away to feel closer to the other for a bright minute.

"I never called her a lesbian. But that's what she is, and she can't admit it. I don't understand what's so bad about being a lesbian these days, no one can just be a lesbian anymore. Have you noticed that?"

I don't say anything.

"What, are you ignoring me? Have you *noticed* that?"

"I don't know," I say. "I still know some lesbians."

"I wish I could understand why she hates me so much. When she was born, even, she tried to kill me on her way out. I still have no feeling where I had my C-section, do you know that? No feeling for twentysomething years. Can you imagine that? What I went through for you two?"

I point out that I arrived by vaginal birth.

"Don't make this about you," my mother says. "Not everything's about you."

"I know," I say, but she's correct in that this is a basic fact of which I must regularly be reminded.

"Oh, did you see that photo of poor Hannah? With her *nose* pierced?"

"Hannah Wise? Of course I saw it. Hello."

"It's terrible."

"It's like: the placement's wrong—"

"—*All* wrong. Thank you. She has a fat nose. Pretty face, okay, but a fat nose, and they didn't get it in the crease right. I told Roberta, she should let it close up and then *redo* it if she's going to do it, but my God, if ever there was someone who shouldn't have one. What are your plans for Thanksgiving?" she asks.

"Mommy," I say, "it's summer."

"If you don't want to come home, don't come home."

"I want to come home for Thanksgiving," I say. I'm trying to tread carefully, to not undo the bonding we've just done over Hannah Wise's horrible nose. "I'm planning on coming home. But I just haven't gotten there in my year yet."

"It's not like you have much else going on," she says. "I know how much time you spend on that computer. Click click click, buy buy buy, Facebook Facebook Facebook."

"I'm not really on Facebook that much anymore, I only check it when I get messages from people who *are* still on it."

"It's an addiction. Just like anything else, it's an addiction."

"I don't have an addictive personality."

"Neither did my brother, allegedly," she says, "and he drank himself to death, but what do I know. I can't talk to you when you're like this. You sound exactly like your sister. If you don't want to come home, don't come home. I happen to be a very busy woman, I'm busy with temple and I'm busy with my new *business,* and I'd like to know *your* plans so that I can make *my* plans. If you're not going to tell me your plans, then I don't see what it is we're talking about."

"Are you doing Ring Around the Toesies again?" When I was in middle school, my mother went around selling upscale toe rings—pavé diamonds set in platinum and gold—to other housewives. She'd put her business cards in my backpack and ask me to pass them out, and when I didn't, she started counting how many she sent me with and how many I came home with each week. I loved her too much to throw them in the trash, but not enough to embarrass myself by passing them around. So I let her count them and scream at me while I cried. It felt like I was giving her something, even though I couldn't give her the thing she really wanted.

"It's much more substantial than Ring Around the Toesies," she says. "But I don't have time to talk about it right now."

"I love you," I say.

"Same," she says, and then she hangs up.

At Starlab there's a girl who goes by a name she chose for herself: Malone. She wears her black hair in Heidi braids every day and is always circulating emails about a new ritual she's leading out of her apartment deep in Red Hook. Stuff like *Let me be your spirit's*

*doula as we make our way through this brutal but cleansing mercury
retrograde with a potluck in my home.* Or *Join me in welcoming the
equinox with a screening of* KOYAANISQATSI *in my garden—please
bring a dish (if it suits your lifestyle to do so).*

VENUSIAN WORSHIP HOUR, she emails today, describing a
ritual she's prepared so that we can all get more deeply in touch
with our goddess-selves.

at this backyard candlelit slow burn on the astral plane, we'll
dress in pinks and coppers and invite venus into our bodies. anoint
your hair with perfume, adorn yourself in gold, drape yourself in
velvet. venus loves luxury.

I don't reply to Malone's email, but because she sits across
from me, I lean over the row of potted plants between us to tell
her I'm not going to be able to make it.

"I knew you wouldn't come," she says, smiling.

"Uh," I start.

"No no no, shh, shh," she says, waggling her tattooed fingers
at me. "I don't expect you to. You have a very independent aura, a
very intentional presence. You know how much of you there is to
go around, and you guard your energy carefully. It's exquisite, it's
a meaningful skill. I'll be fucking real with you: I envy it. When
you do come to one of my rituals, I'll know in here"—she taps her
heart—"that it was the one that was meant for you."

I tap my heart back.

"Also," she says, "I need you to proof this slide deck for me."
Malone puts a pair of pink headphones on and turns back to her
screen, her face emptying of anything.

Poppy was right about Starlab. I hate working in an office. I hate walking out into the sun every day and hoping I have enough on my MetroCard and realizing I don't have enough on my MetroCard and putting nine dollars on my MetroCard and missing the train and waiting for the train and getting on the train and seeing, every day, somehow, the worst thing I've ever seen, someone clipping their nails, someone bleeding, a woman announcing to the train car that she has AIDS before walking through, no one giving her any money at all, a rat that makes everyone pick their feet up and squeal, especially the high-schoolers, who push each other toward the rat, knocking into unlucky people holding poles, on the platform in the city a man peeing against a pylon and smiling, wet condoms on the street, people spitting, whatever, it's unremarkable; and then in the office, everyone with their questions, everyone introducing themselves, so many how-tos, an interactive online sexual harassment training slideshow to struggle through, a new insurance plan to choose, a primary care dentist to select, the crushing certainty that I'll end up paying fifteen thousand dollars for a hospital stay if I pick the plan that's cheapest and then have a medical emergency, an hour choosing a desk plant that costs me $69.99, having a bathroom code, inputting the bathroom code, fighting with the handle, being rescued by a coworker, talking while we pee, talking while we dry our hands, all the while thinking I came in here to cry, the catered lunches that are never hot when they're supposed to be hot or cold when they're supposed to be cold but room-temperature and soggy, making me so afraid to eat that I don't eat anything, and the coworkers who observe that I'm not eating anything, who exchange looks about me not eating anything, interpreting me as cool and anorexic rather than miserable and stoppered up with anxiety; then there's the actual work, the pithy *Pisces, this week look out for small atmospheric shifts,* the *Cancer, today imagine yourself light and whole,* the *Capricorn, tomorrow, avoid water,* all the while knowing in a dwindling few hours I have to walk back to the train, ride the train, walk back to the apartment, make a meal, etc., etc., and I start thinking about how I used to work in my own home on my nice couch with my own computer in my lap, the window open, a candle burning, something going on the stove; and I remember that I thought the whole time: Oh my god, I hate this so much, I so need to get out of the fucking house.

HAVE YOU EVER NOTICED, one of my mommies posts, HOW YOU SPELL INSTAGRAM?

IN STAG RAM

IN??? THE STAG???? IN THE RAM??? ANTLERS????

BAPHOMET, she posts, with a picture of Baphomet, a demon with horns. THEIR SYMBOLISM WILL BE THEIR DOWNFALL.

I switch back to my main account and snuggle down deeper into the couch, stretching my legs.

"Don't touch me with your feet," Poppy says, kicking me harder than necessary. She just loudly lost a game of online chess, and now she's looking at real estate. Both chess and real estate inspire violence in her.

The first post in my feed is from my mother: an American flag rippling in the wind. Ominous. I'm about to ask Poppy if she agrees it's ominous that our mother is posting images of the American flag, but she speaks up first.

"Bernie Madoff's house in Montauk is for sale," Poppy says. She turns her laptop around to face me. A middlingly nice nautical-themed home, right on the beach, for $19 million. Poppy clicks through the pictures. A roof pool, a sunroom, a whitewashed staircase descending the front of a friendly dune.

"What is it with you and the Hamptons?" I ask her. "It's not that great there. Everything's overpriced and overcrowded and the restaurants suck." I say this having never been to the Hamptons.

Poppy turns her laptop back around and stares at it. "I don't know," she says, then looks up at me. "It's just this beacon of, like: having made it."

"Made it by what standards?"

"By literally global standards, by everyone's standards. The Hamptons is having made it. What is with you and *not* being interested in the Hamptons?"

I don't even have to think. "I'm never gonna make it."

I want some good news, so I apply for a small writing grant offered by a tiny indie literary organization. I went to grad school with one of the guys who's on the board now, so I'm hoping my name will stand out. The grant is only $750. The money should probably be spent on something writing-related—a plane ticket to a quiet place, a good chair—but I can only envision buying this one really ugly dress from Rachel Comey.

In my application letter, for the part where I talk about what I'm working on, I craft a taut paragraph about being interested in how femininity is coded and recoded on image-centric platforms like Instagram, how capitalism and consumption fuel our desire to get on the Internet and stay there, and the ways in which the banal and the dangerous intersect as our investment in the mundanities of the lives of people we see but do not know deepens and deepens.

Two weeks later I get a response in the middle of my workday: I have not been chosen for the grant. In the rejection letter, there's a part that says:

In particular, the editors who reviewed your submission loved this bit from your cover letter:

"I'm interested in how femininity is coded and recoded on image-centric platforms like Instagram, by how capitalism and consumption fuel our desire to get on the Internet and stay there, and by how the banal and the dangerous intersect as our investment in the mundanities of the lives of people we see but do not know deepens and deepens."

This. Yes. One hundred percent to all of this.

"Yikes," says Jac, the girl whose computer is next to mine, the one who's always shoeless. "Rejection literally sucks."

I blink at her. "Are you reading my email?"

Jac blinks back. "Well, it's right there," she says, "and I'm right here, so."

I felt unfulfilled with BookSmarts because my work was anonymous and small and invisible. The site didn't get a lot of traffic, and the traffic it did get came in the form of frustrated high-schoolers who would write our info@ email to say things like booksmarts pls give me free membership :'(i have exam tomorrow or SOOOOOOOO stupid to put important quotations behind a paywall smh......... i need them to study... rot in hell motherfuckers.

I hoped at the astrology job, I'd at least feel the daily excitement of having my words "out in the world," whatever that means, that I'd start seeing people post screenshots of my predictions to their stories and timelines with the caption *omG IT ME* and know I'd done something, I'd reached someone, I wasn't pouring myself into a void. But still I'm waiting for any measure of satisfaction at all. Everything about this new job already feels stale, unimpressive.

When I told my parents about the switch to writing horoscopes, they both went *Huh*. They must think I'm writing fortune-cookie filler, but I don't know how to explain *Senior writer at the East Coast outpost of buzzy millennial astrology social networking application start-up based in Palo Alto* to people who thought I'd make a good CPA.

Worst of all, Poppy doesn't even seem that proud of me. When I show her things I've written, she'll often respond by saying things like *I think you think that because* you're *a water sign all water signs are just like you* or *That's wrong, a Libra would never.*

My most constant happiness these days comes from the few minutes each day when I can sneak away from my desk, make a shitty K-Cup coffee, and briefly sit alone on our WeWork knock-off's terrace while I drink it. From up there, if I crane my neck a certain way, I can see down Eighth Avenue almost to the first apartment I lived in when I moved to the city, back when my parents still put rent in my bank account on the twenty-second of every month and every siren that went by in the night still made me prop myself up on an elbow to listen, still made me think, Oh my god, where's the fire, I hope no one's hurting, I hope no one's dead.

Poppy and our mother had a huge fight on the phone, and now our mother has blocked Poppy's number. For hours Poppy has been lobbing emails and Facebook messages at her, and our mother has been texting me, ordering me to tell Poppy to stop.

Tell her to LOSE MY NUMBER, she writes; You girls are DESTROYING ME

I show Poppy the text. "Now you have her mad at me, and I didn't even do anything."

"You have to stop talking to her," Poppy says. "You can't control yourself. You told her that I told you that she called me a lesbian? When that's so completely not the point of anything I told you? Fucking tattletale mommy's girl. Get your shit under control." Poppy's phone dings. She looks down. An email from our mother. Poppy's off the phone plan; her emergency family Amex has been canceled. She sets her phone back down. "Whatever. I don't need a phone."

"We'll go to the Verizon store or whatever tomorrow and get you on a new phone plan."

"No," Poppy says, "I literally don't need this." She takes her phone over to the toilet and drops it in. "Literally: why would I need one? People lived without phones for thousands of years."

I join her at the toilet. "We're not living thousands of years ago, though," I say. "We're living now."

Poppy sighs. "Well," she says, gesturing at what used to be her phone, "I guess I'll get a new one."

That night, we sit on the couch and look at my phone together. One of my mommies is selling a giant water filtration system through an Amazon affiliate link.

I never knew what real water TASTED like until I tried my #Berkey, says one slide of her stories. The next slide is a Boomerang of her doing a shimmy, a big glass of water in her hand. #BerkeyPartner #BerkeyGirl, she's written over the Boomerang. The next slide is an up-close selfie of her looking sad. There's lots of text over this one. The #Berkey is so much more than a kitchen staple. Do you know what's in your tap water? The government does. Fluoride is a toxic substance that has been proven to cause disease, brain fog, and multiple health issues. I believe we are being controlled by fluoride in ways I can't discuss on here just yet. But for now I'll just say that fluoride interferes with the functioning of the thyroid and it is said to shut the door to your gateway to God, meaning it hammers down your pineal gland which is the gateway gland of your connection to the source. My kids have never had ANY fluoride or ANY cavities. The awakening is just beginning #freefromfluoride #totalitarianism #deepstate #governmentmindcontrol #connected #protectthesource #thematrixisreal

I go downstairs to pick up a package from the locked room in the lobby where all our parcels are delivered. When I step off the elevator, a mother is playing with her baby by the double doors. I walk to the right, go up the trio of stairs that leads to the package room, open the door, and fish around the crowded shelves for the candle I ordered from Amazon. When I leave, the mother and her baby are coming up the stairs, baby in the lead. She is, I can tell, just barely walking. Holding the wall, she clears the first step with ease, then the second one with a wobble.

The baby puts one foot onto the third step and releases the wall. As she lifts her other foot up, she begins falling forward. The baby is going to smack her face on the ancient gray tile and scream as her blood spills everywhere; she'll bite through her tender lip and need to be rushed to the emergency room. She will scar. Management will wipe away the blood, but I'll always remember, whenever I come down to look for packages from now on, the time the baby fell on her face in front of me and nearly died.

The baby makes the step. I tuck my package under my arm and clap for her. She looks at me, an emotion I can't discern in her big eyes.

When I call the elevator, the mother and her baby ride up with me.

"What floor?" I ask.

"Six, but can she push it? She's such a bitch if she can't push it, sorry," the mom says, guiding her baby's finger to the uppermost button. "What floor are you?"

"Four," I say.

The mother helps the baby push four. "There we go. Okay." She resettles her baby on her hip. "I'm just having this thing with her lately where it's hard for me to get her out of the house, so we just play in the lobby or I take her up on the roof. Don't tell Tomasz, he's already pissed at me for getting locked out like three times last month."

"She's super cute," I say.

"Galm," says the baby.

"To die." The mom slurps her baby's cheek. "I swear to God, I was so excited to meet her, I showed up to the hospital to have her nervous-laughing like I was going on a date or something. I laughed like that the whole time. Like, nine hours. I laughed her right out of me." The mother bounces her baby, making it laugh. "Right out, huh?" she says. Then she turns back to me. "God, sorry, I'm being gross. I hate when people talk about their babies like they're fucking them or something."

"Me, too," I say. I can tell this mommy is not like other mommies. My eyes wiggle. I try to think of something funny to say, but I can't, and then it's my floor. "Well," I say, stepping out.

"I'm Nina," she says. She pronounces her name "Nine-ah." "And this is June."

"Great to meet you," I say, "I'm—" but the doors shut and draw them up before they can meet me.

Inside the apartment, I tell Poppy about my vision of the baby injured and bleeding, helpless, wrecked.

Poppy's setting up her new phone. She frowns down at the screen. "Intrusive thoughts," she says. "Mine are about babies, too, sometimes, only in mine, I have a baby and I accidentally leave it in a hot car, and it cooks, and then I can't stop picturing the cooked baby over and over, and I get myself to this point where I can, like, smell the flesh, it's torture. Do you ever have the one where, you know, when you walk past Drano at the store, you're like, What if I drank a whole thing of Drano, and then you picture your insides burning, your tongue falling out?"

"I do have that," I say.

"Oh, and I have the one where—where—you'll be at a play or a movie, or on an interview or whatever, and you're like, What if I just shouted the most awful thing I could think of, like, something really violent or racist or disgusting, you know?"

I grab Poppy's arm. "I have that, too. Oh my god. Or like any time I'm using the kitchen knives it's like—"

"It's like what if I just fucking stabbed myself in the stomach."

"Where does that come from?" I ask.

"Death drive," Poppy says, dropping some bread into the toaster.

At Starlab, we have a team meeting about pivoting our brand's voice. No more sweet, encouraging horoscopes: it's time for us to get cheeky. More than cheeky. In fact, it's okay, the head of copywriting says, if the horoscopes get mean.

"Our users want to be dragged," he says. "Through the mud. They want to be hit by a bus. They want to be punched in the face."

Instead of offering a shoulder to cry on, we need to be that bitch of a friend who doesn't take any shit. We need to tell our users the truth about themselves whether they want to hear it or not.

Someone passes around a plate of questionably fresh danishes.

"Do you know where these are from?" I whisper to the girl on my left as she tries to hand them to me.

"They're danishes," she whispers.

"I know." I gulp. I love danishes, but these ones don't look right. "I'm just wondering if they've been, like, sitting out somewhere, if they're old—or if they just got here, or."

The girl on my left leans forward and scoots the danishes past me, straight to the girl on my right.

"Let's do an experiment here and think of any sign's worst trait. Who has one?" says the head.

One of my coworkers raises her hand. "Once I dated a Gemini for a few weeks," she says, "and after we broke up, he stalked me for two years."

He snaps his fingers. "Obsessive. Manchild. Needy. Terrifying. I love it. So instead of a horoscope like: *Gemini, sometimes you feel so alone that you,* I don't know, *that you seek yourself perpetually in others,* we need to be like: *Gemini, get ahold of yourself, you pathetic—you—pathetic obsessive needy manchild.* Right?" The head looks around the room, smiling. His eyes fall on me. "Jules," he says, gesturing at me, "no danish?"

When I come home from work, Poppy's flaring badly. She's on the couch, naked from the waist up, ice packs on her chest and stomach. She's been crying.

"Why me," she says. "Why all this for me? Why is it my head," she says, pointing at her head, "and my body," she says, pointing at her body, "and my—" she says, moving her hands very quickly and messily in circles all around her. "How can one person—how can one person—"

"Oh no," I say, dropping my shit and joining her on the couch. "When did it start?"

Poppy sniffs. "Lunchtime." I can see a flush of red peeking out from behind one of the ice packs. "I was sitting there, and all of a sudden I realized I was scratching, and then when I went to the bathroom—" She tears up. She rolls her eyes. "It's whatever. I just thought I was getting—I was on the least medication I've been on in like four years. And a couple months ago, when I had some new hives, they went away really quickly, so I was starting to think, like: Oh, if I get them now, they just go away. But now they're back and they're everywhere." Her chin crumples.

"Did you call your doctor?"

Poppy nods. She's not really looking at me—she's looking at an episode of *Sailor Moon* playing on the television.

"And?"

"And I don't know," she says, sitting up. "I'm going back up to sixty." That means six prednisone tablets a day, on top of the dapsone and the four antihistamines.

"You should call out of work tomorrow," I say.

Poppy rolls her eyes again.

"Seriously, you should. Just take a day. Who cares."

"Take a day and what? Sit around and think about it and feel miserable?" She lifts one of her ice packs and looks at her skin. "Fuck," she says, replacing it and crying a new gush of tears. "It's so bad." Poppy's knuckles, too, are swollen and red with hives. "My heart is beating so fast. Do you think I'm dying? I feel like I'm trying so hard, and the universe keeps being, like: *Why would you ever try anything?*"

"It's okay," I tell her. "It's just the steroids. You know they make you heart-attacky. And there's no such thing as, like, the universe," I say, waggling my hands and rolling my eyes when I say *the universe*. "You're fine. We're just gonna get super high and order a lot of food and you'll go to sleep and feel better in the morning."

"There is such a thing as the universe," Poppy says, "and I definitely won't."

She's right. In the morning, the hives are worse. Her hands and forearms are covered in tiny red mottles. It almost looks like she's wearing fancy Swiss-dot evening gloves. I tell her this.

She begins to cry. "It's the steroids making me cry so much, too," she says, wiping tears away with flat palms, but I know it's not. I know she's terrified.

She calls out sick from work and I do, too. I make a white-bean soup for lunch and remember how nice it is to be in the apartment on a weekday. Poppy cries on and off. We watch two more seasons of *Sailor Moon*. Poppy's doctor calls from Florida. Their conversation is long. Then Poppy is on the phone with the pharmacy.

"She yelled at me," Poppy says, meaning her doctor, "for not having an EpiPen. So now I have to go spend like a thousand dollars on an EpiPen." She puts her face in her hands. When she pulls them away, she is crying some more. "Will you come with me, please?"

It's hot out, but Poppy puts on long sleeves.

"It's New York," I tell her, watching her dress. "No one cares."

"No one cares if you're, like: singing along with your head-phones or dancing down the street in a cute way," she says. "People care if it looks like you have fucking leprosy." She pulls up her sleeves to once again show me her arms, which do indeed look like the arms of a leper.

"At least they're not on your vulva."

Poppy puts on a baseball cap, hiding her greasy hair, and looks at herself in the mirror by the door. "There is one on my vulva."

"Oh, shit. Well, at least they're not on your face."

She straightens the brim of her cap. "At least they're not on my face."

10 REASONS TO VOTE TRUMP NEXT FALL, posts one of my mommies. She's wearing a *KEEP AMERICA GREAT* hat and smiling maniacally. Her aqua eyes, made brighter by a filter, are huge and bulging. Her teeth are I-just-had-my-teeth-bleached white. On ten separate story slides, she lists the ten reasons she thinks people should vote Trump. TRUMP KEEPS HIS PROMISES, says one. When He says He will get it done, He means it, unlike the majority of politicians.

I reply to this slide: why are you capitalizing He in reference to trump as you would in reference to god? seems pretty blasphemous to me.....

I click on the line of text in the upper-left corner of her story that will let me try out the filter she used to get her eyes so blue and her teeth so white. I pose for the filter and take a picture of myself made anew in its glow. It doesn't look very good on me at all.

Then I notice Emily is in the background. "Crazy filter," she says.

"I'm researching," I say, bullshitting, "for the newsletter. Um, I thought we could do, like, a filter for each sign."

"Love it, chica," she says. "I'll talk to Helen."

I have actual work to do, but I can't stop scrolling. I get an ad for "in-the-moment" birth control, a vaginal gel called Phexxi. *STAY PHEXXI, STAY HORMONE PHREE!* it says. A list of side effects at the bottom of the ad includes bladder infection, kidney infection, vaginal burning, vaginal itching, vaginal yeast infection, vaginal discomfort, bacterial vaginosis, and vaginal discharge. Some male partners, too, the ad says, reported general discomfort.

I screenshot the ad and text it to Poppy, who's probably actually busy, since it's the first day all the kids are back for the new school year. WHO WOULD USE THIS LMAO??????? I write.

i can't tell if they're using ph as in vaginal ph?? which it seems this product ANNIHILATES ENTIRELY????? she writes back.

Then we get in a texting groove, sending jokes back and forth about Phexxi and vaginas and increasingly unlikely ideas for new methods of birth control. Sometimes all it takes for me to feel happy is to realize that Poppy, on the other side of the bridge, is feeling happy herself.

On Instagram I look at some accounts dedicated to the celebration of traditional femininity. One of them takes issue with how Kamala Harris's primary run is being celebrated.

HERE'S THE PROBLEM. Women have long believed the lie that somehow equality and progress are things to be celebrated. Women have always desired positions of power, even in the home. WHY? Because since the fall of creation, women have desired to RULE over men. CHRISTIAN WOMEN, our endgame is not equality. Our endgame is recognizing our DEPRAVED nature, REPENTING, and believing CHRIST was crucified and ROSE AGAIN.

I text Poppy some of the tradfem stuff—nothing gets her going like gender essentialism—but she doesn't respond. I bug her and bug her.

hello??????????

Nothing.

are you alive???????????

Nothing. The last time she was flaring like this, she tried to kill herself.

did you kill yourself????????

No answer.

are you mad at me for asking that????????

or did you KILL YOURSELF??????

When I open the door to the apartment, it's dark inside even though it's a sunny day—the mesh, still hanging over the face of the building, blocks out everything. I turn on the overhead. Poppy's door is open. She's in her work clothes, facedown on her deflated air mattress. Her phone alarm is going off, the one that tells her when to take her meds. She doesn't seem to hear it. I put my things down and go into her room. I know she's dead. She's lying just like a dead person would.

"Poppy?" I say. She doesn't answer me. "Poppy," I say, louder, meaner this time. She isn't moving. I can feel my pupils dilate. I can't tell if she's breathing. "Poppy," I say, and I crouch down and shake her. My vision tunnels. I'm picturing myself calling 911, telling our parents, eulogizing Poppy at her funeral, flowers everywhere, sitting in a dark bar somewhere in Crown Heights on a date five years from now saying *No, I don't have siblings*, not wanting to get into it, letting the memory of Poppy ripple through me as I swirl a stick of cocktail olives through a shallow martini glass. I shake her arm and say her name. I shouldn't have negged her so much or told her she smelled. I put my fingers on her throat but can't feel a pulse right away. "Poppy," I scream.

Poppy makes an eldritch gasp and pushes herself upright, swatting at my hand on her neck, her eyes still closed. "Who," she says, "who?"

"It's me, it's me. Jesus," I say. I start coughing. My chest feels empty, dry. It seems like maybe I missed a few breaths.

Poppy rubs her face. "Why would you wake me up?" she asks. "Why are you doing this to me?"

"Your alarm is going off," I tell her, still coughing. "Plus, I wanna get dinner." I don't tell her that I thought she was dead.

"I'm on the floor," she says, looking around.

"I told you, you need the real bed."

"I haven't been on this many antihistamines in years. And together, you know, with all the antidepressants and shit, it's like I go to space once I fall asleep, like I'm kind of awake, also, but I'm not? I can't dream, my eyes feel all glued—just now I was trying and trying because I kept hearing the alarm, but I couldn't."

"You didn't answer any of my texts."

"I've been sleeping—for—I don't even know." Poppy feels around for her droning phone. She picks it up and silences the alarm. "Four hours," she says. "I left work after lunch. They had an active-shooter drill on the literal first day the kids were back, oh my god. On top of everything." She rolls her eyes. "So boring. And so traumatizing." She stands up. "I have to go to the bathroom."

I follow her out of the bedroom. "The drills aren't even, like, sort of exciting?"

"What do you mean?"

While reading Anne Frank's diary for the first time in middle school, I started periodically hiding in my closet and pretending to be her. "Didn't you ever play Anne Frank?" I ask her.

"Didn't I what?"

"You know, pretend you were Anne Frank, hide in the closet in the dark for a minute, see what it was like, try and scare yourself? I played Anne Frank all the time. Have we never talked about this?"

Poppy's face is wood. She pulls down her pants and sits on the toilet. "Will you shut the door? I have to do something in here."

"You can poop in front of me."

"No," Poppy says, "I can't."

I pull the door shut. Then I shout through it: "Why won't you set up the real bed?"

"I'll do it later," Poppy says. "I like the air mattress."

"I can't get the money back," I say. "I've tried and tried. You need to sleep on a real bed. You're sleeping on the floor."

"I like it on the floor."

I fling open the door. "No, you don't," I say. "No one has ever liked it on the floor."

Poppy reaches for the doorknob. "Get out," she says.

"Set up the bed," I say, slamming the door again.

"You need some boundaries for yourself," Poppy calls after me.

In my room, I wonder if she's right.

A boymom of six posts a picture of all her children sitting on the front porch holding one of those customizable letter boards. WE ARE NOT FAILED ATTEMPTS AT TRYING FOR A GIRL, the sign says. Their mother looks down at them like she believes she is the Madonna. Her sweatshirt bears the phrase *RAISING BOYS*. On her stories she's doing a Q&A: her followers send in assumptions they have about her, and she confirms or refutes them.

Once you have a girl, you will stop having kids, someone writes in.

"False," the mommy chirps on video. "Unless that just happens to be the last baby that we're able to have. And then, in that case, it would look like it's true, but it's not. Also, look at these pictures of my little guys," she says, tilting her phone camera toward a living room wall lined with professional portraits of her little guys.

Poppy watches over my shoulder. "Imagine—holy shit, imagine the psychic trauma of being, like, eight years old and your mom is having you hold a sign up to two hundred thousand strangers that's like: *I AM NOT WHAT MY MOTHER WANTED AND IT'S VERY OBVIOUS THAT I'M NOT WHAT SHE WANTED.*"

"It's biblical," I say. "Six boys, it's Tribes of Israel vibes."

"That's what these people are all going for, obviously," Poppy says. "They're building an army for Jesus or whatever." She walks away.

I look again at the picture of the boys holding the sign. Some of them are smiling, but others are making mopey faces. A comment below the image sticks out to me. It's because the comment was written by my mother.

God bless you and your sweet boys, says getwellwithwendy. I take a screenshot for evidence, but I decide not to show it to Poppy. Just yet. I like my mother's comment, to see if she'll notice.

why would you do this to your children???? I message the mommy with six boys. you're ruining their lives!!!!!! one day they will find these images and be hurt by them!!!!!!!!!

She doesn't write back.

I devour her feed for another ten minutes; she has a lot of posts about how Donald Trump will soon expose the satanic pedophilic elites and sentence them to die by hanging in front of the Washington Monument.

I swipe over to my real Instagram, where a girl I went to high school with is posing on a yacht with a small dog she's dyed to look like a panda bear.

My father sends an email, wrenching my focus from the gorgeous, miserable-looking panda dog: FWD: FWD: FWD: SHABBOS BLESSINGS

Glittery, blinky, Angelfire-looking gifs ceiling a long chunk of cobalt-blue email text written in a scripty font that's hard to read.

A POWERFUL TEFILAH (PRAYER) FOR SHABBOS.
READ THIS CAREFULLY. EVERY FRIDAY NIGHT
WHEN WE SIT DOWN WITH OUR FAMILIES FOR
SHABBOS DINNER, TWO ANGELS PEER THROUGH

OUR WINDOWS. ONE ANGEL IS THE ANGEL OF
PEACE AND THE OTHER IS THE ANGEL OF CHAOS.
IF THERE IS PEACE IN OUR HOME THE ANGEL OF
PEACE SMILES AND SAYS "LET THIS FAMILY HAVE
ANOTHER WEEK OF PEACE." IF THERE IS CHAOS
IN OUR HOME THE ANGEL OF CHAOS SMILES AND
SAYS "LET THIS FAMILY HAVE ANOTHER WEEK OF
CHAOS." SEND THIS TO 18 PEOPLE FOR A WEEK
OF PEACE!

Poppy gets an invitation to a college friend's birthday dinner at a
small-plates restaurant in Cobble Hill. She hasn't been out much
in a few weeks—her face has bloated like a kabocha thanks to the
extra prednisone, and she feels embarrassed and ugly.

"I hate small-plates group dinners," she says. "You always end
up paying eighty bucks for five bites of, like, ceviche. But it's so
gauche and unremarkable to be the one complaining about the
portions or the prices or the splitting of the check or any of it.
There's no way to win, they get you both ways." She asks if I'll
go with her.

"I don't have eighty bucks to spend on ceviche," I tell her.

"I'll pay for us both," she says. Something in her seems ac-
tivated, like in spite of it all she really wants to show up for this
dinner, and so we do. I'm excited to see some of Poppy's college
friends—I liked them when I visited her in Durham a couple
times during her senior year, when she was living in a giant house

off-campus with six or seven roommates. The building was officially owned by the Duke chapel board, a group of Methodists who gave cheap housing to religious or religion-curious students. Poppy got a spot in the house after she wrote a long beseeching essay about how the core of Judaism was learning, and about how what she wanted to learn about at this particular juncture in her life was Methodists. The house worsened Poppy's hives: she lived in the basement, which teemed with black mold. You could smell it. I remember sleeping on her floor one weekend, dreaming that I was eating green bread. The year Poppy graduated, the place was condemned.

At the restaurant, Poppy and I sidle into a rigid leather booth with three people: Will, down for the weekend from Harvard Divinity; Nic, a second-year MFA poet at Brown; and Rajan, the birthday boy, visiting from med school in Chapel Hill. Will is engaged to a woman who wants to be a housewife, Nic doesn't put labels on their gender or their sexuality, and Raj is studying too hard to be involved right now. All of them are Poppy's age, only a few years younger than I am, but talking to them somehow feels like talking to children; all the things they're going through are things I went through three years ago. Someone's ex is calling them daily from a blocked number in the middle of the night; someone else has just learned that by the end of the year, they'll be off their parents' health insurance. I drink a glass of sangria and dispense advice. *Don't pick up the calls, even to tell them to fuck off. Start stretching in the morning or your hips will start locking up. If you're still on your parents' credit cards*

*right now, use them to buy everything you need before they cancel
them or kick you off.*

Poppy stares big-eyed at the menu for most of the meal.
The restaurant is hot and sticky and the booth is hot and sticky
and I can tell that Poppy is nervous that the temperature will
worsen her flare. She communicates with the waiter in Spanish
about what plates are coming to the table and when. She lets
her friends pick over the dishes first, then divvies up what's left
between her plate and mine, her mouth set in a weak line. She
doesn't drink anything; "I'm Cali sober," she tells everyone, but
I know alcohol makes her flare. Raj passes around molly capsules
for later; Nic talks about the plans they have to take mushrooms
at Storm King when the weather starts to get fall-ish in a few
weeks. I move a fork and knife around over some tough octopus
that's been dumped on my plate. It doesn't feel safe to eat octopus right now.

"Oh my god," Poppy says loudly, laughing at how I'm holding
my utensils. "This is a nice place, Jules. The food's not poison."

"I know," I say, feeling sweaty.

"Jules has this insane thing," Poppy says to Raj, "about *food*."

"Oh, like—bulimia?" Raj asks.

"No, like—she thinks practically everything at every meal she
ever eats is gonna give her food poisoning."

"I don't," I say. My voice sounds high and desperate. "I don't,
I'm just not that hungry."

Poppy makes a square with her elbows on the table and leans
toward me. "She throws out half the food we buy because she

says it looks bad. And she never eats in restaurants because she thinks they're all filthy."

"This place is Zagat-rated," Nic says, pronouncing "Zagat" wrong.

"Take a bite of the octopus, Jules," Poppy says. "Take one bite."

I look at the octopus. I look at Poppy. Then I get up to go to the bathroom and look at my phone on the toilet for fifteen minutes; I'm fed a Twitter thread about Caroline Calloway, a TikTok about how women can relieve constipation by sticking their thumbs into their vaginas and pressing backward against their rectums. When I return to the table, someone has cleared away all the plates to make room for the next round of tapas—all except my octopus.

"We kept it for you," Poppy says, "just in case. We weren't sure. The waiter was saying what a shame it is to waste octopus." She smiles at me. Now she's having a good time.

Another Duke guy named Fletcher shows up in a tie, coked out. "I'm so coked out," he says. Fletcher is working on his MBA at Columbia. He orders fried chickpeas and monkfish crudo and tells the waiter he wants to be on his own check, since he didn't participate in the first chunk of the meal.

Poppy's friends talk about their studies. Raj tells a story about a doctor who had a patient wake up in the middle of surgery. Nic says the modes of poetic expression available to us are insufficient and classist. Fletcher asks Will if Will is at war with what it means to be a Christian in the United States right now and Will says he isn't. Poppy mentions wanting to rescue a dog. Fletcher tells her she's an idiot if she doesn't go through a breeder and have the breeder train the dog for six weeks minimum before sending it home. He pulls out his phone to google a Bernedoodle ranch in Virginia. Raj says he's thinking about getting a dog, too. Will says he's not a dog person or a cat person but a bird person. No one reacts. Fletcher and Poppy coo over hybrids.

"You should totally get a dog," I say, spooning a tiny bite of blackened Brussels sprouts onto my plate because vegetables, in my mind, are always safe to eat, "when you live on your own."

"You love dogs," Poppy says. "You'd love it if we had a dog."

"Those aren't the same thing," I say. "I think it's really cruel to keep a dog in a small apartment."

"So you're saying all dog owners in New York are by definition cruel people?" Nic asks.

"Pretty bold statement," Will says, forking some oily broccolini into his mouth. "Ontologically speaking."

"No," I say, "no, that's not what I'm saying." I always thought I wanted smart friends, but after being around Poppy's smart friends, I'm reminded of why I don't have any. "I'm just saying, like: dogs deserve space to run around, they deserve to poop on the grass."

"So animals have basic inalienable rights," Nic says, "like humans?" I don't respond. Nic keeps talking. "That's a deeply radical stance. And I'm not saying it's wrong, just radical. To my mind, animal lives *are* essentially human lives, because humans are animals themselves."

Why, I wonder, is everyone who's ever gone to Brown like this?

"Obviously," I say, "I don't think that an animal life is the same as a human life."

"It's not obvious to people who don't know you," Poppy says. "Or to people who have different opinions from you. They're just trying to learn about what you think."

"I don't know what I think, like, existentially about dogs having rights. But I think in an apartment as small as mine," I say, really leaning into the "mine," "it would be unfair to the dog. And if you're rescuing a dog to give it a better life, you have to be able to actually give it a good life."

Poppy's mouth becomes furious. It reminds me of our mother's mouth when our mother is furious.

"At the end of the day," Nic asks, "what *is* a good life?"

"Anyway," Poppy says, "I'm thinking about *moving* and getting a dog. I found this one I love on Petfinder and I went to visit her at the shelter." She looks right at me, then she pulls out her phone and scrolls through it as she talks. "It's this no-kill place. She's been there for months. No one wants her because she has three legs. They told me she sits with her nose sticking through the wire *all day*, like she's desperate for someone to pet her snout." She holds up her phone, showing us all a picture of Amy Klobuchar. It isn't from Petfinder; it's a photo Poppy took. Amy Klobuchar is indeed sitting up against the wire edge of her enclosure, poking her nose through to the world outside. Poppy presses her thumb down on the photo, playing the live version; Amy Klobuchar opens her mouth into a smile and sticks her tongue out. Her tail wags. I can't believe Poppy went to see her without telling me. I stare at Poppy. She stares back.

"Stop," Raj says, "she's too cute."

"That's fucking tragic," Nic says, grabbing for Poppy's phone and zooming in. "I want her so fucking bad. You have to get her."

"I would," Poppy says. "But I wouldn't be able to give her a good life, you know, because I don't live in the Hamptons and make six fucking figures."

"You should apply to work at Xavier," Fletcher says. "I'll get you in the door."

"Or Henry could talk to someone at Dalton."

"His girlfriend went to Saint Ann's."

"If you really want to keep working in schools, that is."

"What do you do all day?"

"What's on your arm?" Raj asks quietly, touching Poppy's sleeve. It's ridden up, exposing a lingering welt on the top of her wrist. Poppy puts her hand on the bench, beneath her thigh, and reiterates that she's on medication. No one else asks her a direct question for the rest of the night.

The cake comes, a minuscule flan. Raj struggles with his candle. Everyone Instagrams him. At the end of the meal Poppy offers to put the whole bill on her card and have everyone Venmo her for simplicity.

"Steep," Will says when she tells him what he owes. "Are you sure it's that much?"

"Tax and tip," Poppy says.

Fletcher starts talking about how taxation is theft. Everyone groans. "Fletcher's a libertarian," Nic explains to me, picking their nail polish, as if I hadn't gathered.

Then the moseying from the table, the standing outside the

restaurant kicking the sidewalk, the cigarettes, the determination of next moves, the pretending to consider taking the subway, the calling of cars, the see-you-soons. I don't know why Poppy would bother to see these people again, soon or ever. In the backseat of our Uber, I ask what value they hold for her. She stares into her phone and refuses to answer me, so I look at mine. After several minutes, a text from Poppy arrives, right as she clicks her phone off and puts it into her pocket.

you know i don't like talking about serious stuff in front of uber drivers, says the text, but it's pretty shitty for you to say that you don't see the value in my friends—literally some of MY ONLY FRIENDS lmao????? obviously they're not the ideal perfect utopian feminist allies i want in a friendship but they're what i have and its mean for you to imply that just because they're not your friends they're not good enough. i have my own friends and i want my own life and i was serious about moving. im starting to feel like im not a real person, like i can't make my own decisions. like fuck yeah i want a dog and i want to sleep at weird times and i want to not live with someone who's always looking at me like im fucking crazy and gross. like i hate myself enough without your input lol

My stomach feels like it's expanding. Poppy hates herself and I've made her hate herself more. All the nasty things I've thought about her and said to her not just in the last few months but in our entire lives come back. The first time I ever called her a cunt: in high school, in a Sephora, right in front of the cashier, at full volume, all because Poppy wouldn't let me use a gift card she'd been hoarding for three years to buy a bottle of Moschino I Love

Love perfume. The time I ratted to our parents about Poppy using one of their credit cards to purchase $250 worth of *Grey's Anatomy* episodes on iTunes, then sat quietly on my bed listening with delight while our mother dragged Poppy—by her hair, I'd learn later—into the computer room and parked her in front of the desktop, screaming at her to *get the money back* so loudly I could hear it on the other side of the house. All those times I wouldn't laugh at a joke Poppy told, just to make her feel lonely. The times when we were small and I'd hold her down and tickle her and tell her that I'd love her only as many seconds as she'd let me tickle her, that she could bank minutes of my love by letting me torture her. The time I gave her the silent treatment so long and got her so angry that she punched our bathroom counter and broke a finger. The time I told her she needed a nose job but that even a nose job wouldn't save her from how Jewy she looked. The time I took her to the movies with my friends but didn't let her sit with us and instead set her up a couple rows back with a tub of popcorn buttered enough to be rough on her tummy.

Maybe, if I keep her with me, I can make these things up to her. She has it hard enough. If she moves out, she'll be alone, unguarded, stuck with some roommate who doesn't know her or care about her. Someone who won't watch her for signs that things are getting bad, someone who won't know how to tell the difference between what she's like when she needs new meds and what she's like when she's just on her period.

i am so sorry, I write, desperate to spin things. you're totally right. its not right for me to be judging or policing your life and your friends. its not fair to you and it's not fair to *our* friendship. I delete "friendship" and type out "relationship." Then I delete "relationship" and "our" and type "us." Then I delete "us" and type "you or to me." Then I delete "you or to me" and type "me or to you." Then I switch back to "you or to me." all i want, I continue, is for us to make this place a home for both of us. i love you and i want to make this work. i understand if you still need to move but i really hope we can have a conversation about all this and figure it out. i love you. i'm sorry.

Poppy takes out her phone. She reads my text. For three solid minutes I watch as she seems to type back to me. But when the text comes in, it is brief:

that's a whole lot of "i" statements

I notice a paper towel on the floor near the fridge. I don't remember dropping it there, so I don't pick it up. Poppy doesn't pick it up, either. It stays there all week, gathering our hair. Finally I mention it.

"You dropped that, like, two weeks ago," I say to Poppy, nodding at the paper towel. "I left it there to see how long it would take you to pick it up."

"I didn't drop it," Poppy says. "*You* dropped it, and *I* left it there."

"Just pick it up."

"You pick it up," says Poppy, "if it's such a big deal."

"You're saying you don't care if it stays there forever?"

"Yeah, it could stay there forever and it wouldn't bother me."

"So why were you waiting to see if I would get it?"

"Why were *you* waiting?"

"I can't do this," I say, and stoop to pick the paper towel up. "This is, like, the stupidest Beckett play ever, us living here like this. It's just never going to stop being stupid and petty."

"Because you're making it stupid and petty," Poppy says. "I'm having a great time except for when you're doing stuff like this. And *you're* having a great time when you're not laying traps for me and making it all harder."

I crumple the paper towel in my fist. "I'm not laying traps."

"You're trying to sabotage our experiences of this, you're trying to make our experiences of this weird and uneven—"

"Experiences of what?" I ask. "What the fuck are we experiencing?"

"The experience of living together," says Poppy, looking at the spot where the paper towel was, "of—of having this year together. None of it seems precious to you, it's like you don't want me to feel that we're sharing anything. I keep trying to do things and say things and create things that'll bring us together, but nothing works, it's like—it's like—"

"I don't know what you're talking about," I say. "You sound like you're on crystal meth right now."

"You do know," Poppy says. "You do and you're pretending you don't. You don't want us to share happiness and I don't get why. Why can't you admit that this is fun, that you have fun with me?"

"This isn't fun," I say. "This is fucking torture."

"Because you're sick in the head, Jules," she says, "because you hate everything, because you're ill and depressed and you have an eating disorder—"

"I don't have an *eating disorder*—"

"You have patterns of disordered eating that are incredibly concerning to me, and I've thought about talking to Mommy about it, but I don't want to blow up your shit."

My throat seizes. "I don't have an eating disorder, are you fucking insane? I'm on the high end of my BMI, even. I don't care how I look, I never weigh myself, I love to eat, I just only want to eat the things I want to eat when I want to eat them."

"Eating disorders are spectrum disorders," Poppy says. "You can have an eating disorder without stepping on a scale every day."

"Stop talking about how everything's a spectrum," I say, and I throw the paper towel at Poppy's head. It falls just a few inches from where it's been sitting for days, weeks, whatever. Poppy reaches out and grabs my wrist. I try to twist away. She doesn't let me. She grabs my hair. I laugh in her face as she grabs it and pulls.

"Holy shit, are you pulling my hair right now? Let go of me," I say, "let go," but she has my glory in her hands, and she scrunches her fingers right up close to my scalp.

"You never take me seriously, you never apologize for anything, you laugh at me every day—"

"I did apologize!"

"But not in a real way," Poppy says.

"You can't tell people their apologies aren't *real*."

"I can if they aren't, which yours *wasn't*."

We sound like small children. And eventually, like small children, we go to our rooms and slam our doors and don't speak for another several days.

I need to know your Thanksgiving plans NOW, my mother texts me. I don't respond. She starts calling me. The calls become FaceTimes. Finally I call her back and tell her that Poppy and I are in a tiff right now and that we're having trouble figuring out our day-to-day, let alone Thanksgiving. Then I cry to her about how sad I am about the tiff until she tells me to stop crying.

"Neither of you listen to me," she says. "I told you this would happen if you lived together. You can't stand each other. You want to just rip each other apart. Jesus, do you see we're *braking*?" She's on Bluetooth in her car; my father is driving. "I don't understand the two of you. I can't have this conversation right now."

I hear my father's voice. "Hi, sweetie," he says. "You're on speaker."

"I know," I say.

"We're driving over to your cousin's for dinner," my father says.

"That's nice," I say.

"No," my mother says, "it's not, because your father's driving like a maniac, he just rolled down his window to yell at some little *Russian* girl— Yeah, Steve, laugh, she could've had a gun in the car, people are shooting each other down here every day—"

"Did you read that email I sent you?" my father asks me, ignoring her. "About the angels?"

"I did," I say. "I liked it."

"Better get your house outta chaos before next Friday," he says. "Did you send it to however many people?"

"Steve, call her yourself if you want to talk to her. You're screaming in my ear. Watch that guy up— Do you see we're braking? God, you're the worst driver," she says.

"Will you give me a break?" he asks. "I mean, seriously, thirty-eight years, have I wrecked us *ever*—"

"Press end," says my mother. "No, don't *look* at the screen, look at the road, just *press*—"

They hang up on me before I can ask my mother anything about her Instagram. Her In Stag Ram. I send her a text: btw just in case poppy says anything to you about me having an eating disorder, i want you to know that i don't and she's lying like always.

My mother reacts to the text with a thumbs-down.

???? does that mean you think i have an eating disorder too????

My mother types for a moment, then stops; types and stops, types and stops.

I barrage Poppy with texts every hour of the day.

take out the fucking trash.

you left dishes in the sink. not acceptable.

i need something off the bookshelves in my office. please let me know if you're going to let me in to get it.

At work I write some mean horoscopes and submit them to my editor. Scorpio, I say, try and extend some gentleness to those in your orbit today. You're more rooted than most, so try to break through your tough shell and help those who are less tethered to the good, solid earth you tread to feel more at home in the world. Crack that carapace. Communicate. Once I'm done, I look at engagement rings in an incognito window dragged into the very corner of my screen and feel the trappings of my body sloop away as I stare at clusters of bright stones worth tens of thousands of dollars. By the time I realize I hurt from sitting in the same position for so long, it's dark and most everyone is gone. I have emails. I don't read them. I tell myself I'll focus really well tomorrow; I'll get all my tasks done, and I'll feel in charge of my life as a worker. I'll feel valuable to my workplace. Maybe I'll start making smoothies with anti-inflammatory powders in them that'll boost my concentration and my collagen. Maybe I'll start taking folic acid every day. Maybe I'll start a HIIT regimen. Maybe I'll go to HIIT classes on my lunch breaks. Maybe I'll only look at my phone for an hour in the morning and an hour at night. Maybe not even that. Maybe I'll get a Nokia like this one half-famous writer I admire and I'll never look at a candy-bright smartphone screen ever again. Maybe I'll start keeping fresh flowers in the house. Maybe I'll move to the woods. Maybe I'll finally find a life of plenty. Maybe tonight I'll tell Poppy all these plans and order her to move out by the end of the month so I can start my new existence.

As I stick my key into the apartment door, I hear barking coming from the other side. When I walk in, I am met by the deft, wet nose of Amy Klobuchar.

"So," Poppy says, "I can explain." Amy Klobuchar whines and whaps me with her scraggly tail. "Down, Rotini," says Poppy.

"Rotini?"

Poppy looks at me. "I wasn't going to keep Amy Klobuchar as her name, obviously."

I drop my tote. Amy Rotini Klobuchar licks it and barks at it. "What the fuck is happening?" I ask. "You don't even like rotini."

"I like rotini," Poppy says. "I'll eat a thing of rotini sometimes." The dog barks some more. "The one rule about her is we can't touch her ears, because apparently something traumatic happened to her involving her ears when she was a puppy, the shelter said, and she goes berserk when people get near them. So no petting the ears."

Amy Klobuchar looks at me and raises her bald lip a bit, showing me her tiny teeth and snorting.

"This is a fucking joke, right? You're like: watching this dog for someone else who adopted it?"

"I'm going to pay you an extra two hundred dollars a month," Poppy says. "I got a new job with more flexibility so I can be outside with her, you know, so I can take her to the park or the dog run and train her during the day—"

"You got a different job?"

Poppy blinks. "I got a job writing at BookSmarts," she says. "They were hiring your replacement, and they were moving it to part-time initially, but then they wanted me to come on as a full-time content writer instead of an editor because they liked my sample so much."

"This is fucked up," I say. "You're moving out. Like, today. This is so egregious."

"You don't want me to move out," she says. "I know because you told Mommy."

"You and Mommy are talking?"

Amy Klobuchar barks.

"Quiets," Poppy says. She turns to me. "That's the command she knows for being quiet. You have to add an s to the ends of dog commands, so it's, like, 'sits,' 'quiets,' whatever, so that whenever they hear the word 'sit' or 'quiet' in real conversations, they don't get confused and think you're saying the command and develop this, like, immunity to it. Look what else she can do. This is amazing. Are you watching?"

"I'm watching."

"Rotini, *pew-pews*," Poppy says, and she points a fake finger gun at the dog's nose. The dog doesn't do anything. "Amy Klobuchar," Poppy says, "*pew-pews!*" The dog lies down and sticks her tongue out. She's so happy. She's barking and barking to show us how happy she is.

"Good pew-pews!" Poppy says. "You love pew-pews! The shelter said she loves it, it's her favorite trick."

"How did a dog that was so abused and traumatized that her ears are off-limits manage to learn pew-pews," I ask.

Poppy shrugs. "I guess it wasn't all bad. I don't know, she's really smart."

"Dogs," I say as cruelly as I can, "have apple brains. Not even apple. Grape-size. Grape brains." I put down my keys on the butcher block by the door; I notice there's a Ziploc bag full of teeth sitting there. "What the fuck are those?" I ask.

"They're her baby teeth," Poppy says. "The woman at the shelter who took care of her gave them to me. This woman was so attached to her she wanted her for herself, but."

"But what?"

"I don't know, she couldn't take her."

"That means she didn't want her. Who would want this dog?" I sound like my mother.

"I want her," Poppy says. "I need her. She's going to be my psychiatric support dog. I'm going to train her and take her places. As an American with a disability, I can take her anywhere. She's—"

"What disability?" I say. "You're not fucking disabled."

"Depression is a major fucking disability. It's, like, on the disability list when you apply for jobs."

"Did you say you have a disability when you applied for BookSmarts?" My mother again, her voice through my teeth.

"This is going to be good for you, too. Because you're a wreck with no friends, like me, and you need a soft, cute thing to look at to keep yourself from, like, looking too deeply into your own emptiness."

"I hate you," I say, "and I hate this dog." And then I'm crying because I don't hate Poppy, and I don't hate the dog, but I do fear my own emptiness. It's why I can't stop looking at the mommies. It's why I can't eat certain octopuses in certain situations. It's why I don't write anymore. Poppy hugs me. The dog jumps up on us with her single front paw, trying to get in on the hug. I picture Poppy flaring badly, the dog sweetly licking each hive.

Crying, my face in Poppy's shoulder, I tell her about the things I am definitely not going to do for the dog. "I'm not walking her late, or in the rain or snow, or when it's above seventy-eight degrees out. And I'm not giving her wet food. I'll give her dry food, but I'm not touching a can of wet food. I'm not picking up her poop, and if they try to fine me for not doing it, I'm going to tell them it's your dog, and I'm going to carry around a photocopied picture of your driver's license, and I'm going to make sure they fine you and not me. I'm not expressing her anal glands. If she gets ticks or fleas or bugs she's out, I don't give a fuck, I'll put her in a trash bag down the trash chute, but I'm not getting bugs in my apartment that I've managed to keep bugs out of all this time. And if she throws up I'm not cleaning it. And if she eats a sock and needs a seven-thousand-dollar surgery to remove the sock I'm not paying for it or even chipping in."

The whole time I'm talking, the dog barks and barks, like she can understand me; like she's saying, *Shut up, you love me already, you're lying, you'd do anything for me, you know it, I'm family, soon you will stoop to pick up my shit and tell yourself it's just candy, it's just a small cake in the shape of a poop, and when we come inside, you will wipe my paws and you will give me a treat, and your life will be richer, and I will be the reason.*

Today, posts one of my mommies, I would like to share what I have come to think about the mother of all conspiracies!!! Now I do believe conspiracies can be a trap!! They can distract us from our faith!!! But this one is a highly Biblical matter directly related to Scripture!!!! I began researching the true shape of the earth three months ago and I began seeing how clearly the shape of the earth is described all throughout Scripture!!!! It's EVERYWHERE!!!! Our earth is NOT a moving globe like the secular world says!!!!! We are central and special to our Father God!! We are not some speck hurtling through some galaxy!!!! The Father and His Son Yeshua and all the Angels are literally right above the Firmament!!! Not in some remote otherworldly "space" trillions of "light years" away!!! Yes the Firmament over our heads is real!!! Yes the windows and doors of heaven are real!!!! And yes sadly Sheol the playground of demons below our feet is real!!!!

"Fuck," Poppy says, "fuck, Amy Klobuchar," talking to the dog, the dog who has just peed on the floor; the dog who has apparently been scratching at the front door for the last three minutes while I've been in a fugue state looking at flat-earth posts, sifting through the comments for my mother's username, hoping I find it, hoping I don't.

"I'll get it," I say, springing for one of the many rolls of paper towels and one of the many bottles of diluted white vinegar we now keep stationed around the apartment for quicker cleanups of Amy's many accidents.

"No, please, by all fucking means, you just sit there," Poppy says, putting her hand in my face, channeling our mother. "You just *sit* there, and I'll take care of her."

"I mean, she's your dog," I say.

Poppy leashes Amy and slams the door. I wipe up the mess. After washing my hands, I peek out the window, where I can see that, down on the street, Amy is looking up at Poppy expectantly, panting, wagging her tail, like: *Why are we out here, dummy? I just did my business! Up there!* A large truck goes down the street and Amy Klobuchar lunges for it, howling; she doesn't care about sedans, only really big vehicles that could end her life in a millionth of a second. They say dogs are like their owners, or owners are like their dogs—Poppy and Amy both want to get crushed to death.

I go back into my phone. The flat-earth mommy has reposted many colorful infographics that render earth as a flat disc floating in a large bubble. The top of the bubble is labeled *THE SKY* and the space above the bubble is labeled, in pretty, arcing letters,

WATERS ABOVE THE FIRMAMENT. Beneath the chunk of flat earth floating in the middle of the bubble are pillars labeled *THE FOUNDATIONS OF THE EARTH,* as in, *Where were you when I laid the foundations of the earth?*

Rotini didn't stick. Amy Klobuchar is Amy Klobuchar, now and forever, and her presence has indeed changed the rhythms of our lives. Now, instead of sleeping through our alarms, we're up at seven, ready for a stroll. Instead of watching TV after dinner, we watch the dog rip up a toy or clean a bone or chase and bite her own tail. *Look at her,* we say twenty-five times a day. *Look at her paws. Look at her weird head. Look at those eyes. Look at that tail wag. Look at that long tongue. Look at the way she tilts her head at new noises,* which is every noise, because Amy Klobuchar was kept locked up from birth on in a basement where she never saw sunlight and where she grew full of mange until she was many months old and someone, concerned and good, called protective services on her behalf. Now all she has is us. And we fight about her nonstop.

There's no way our fighting is creating a good or nourishing environment for the dog, but it's healthy, at least, for Poppy and me to have something practical to scream at each other about. *You didn't feed her, you didn't take her out, how could you leave this goopy caca in her eyes, use a Kleenex, clean her up, wipe her paws, Venmo me for her shots, Venmo me for her food, Venmo me for the dogwalker, I'm not Venmoing you shit, she's your dog, she's our dog, could you please let her up on the couch, could you please not let her up on the couch when she's this dirty, could you book her for a bath, can't you just wash her in the tub, could you not talk to her in that baby voice, could you not yell at her, walk her slowly, watch her leg, don't treat her differently because of the leg, she's your responsibility, she's our responsibility, she's an animal, don't be mad at her, she's such an animal, of course I'm mad at her.*

So that she can fulfill her destiny as a service dog, we get Amy Klobuchar a trainer named Finn, a nonbinary person with a teal-tipped shag mullet and many appealing tattoos. We meet Finn at the park two or three evenings a week so we can try to teach Amy to be mild in the presence of other animals, to obey us when we say things like "go to your place" and "stay right there." No matter how much we work with her, though, she shakes and yelps when other dogs come near; she rejects new commands; all she seems able to grasp is "pew-pews." Finn is always in shorts, even now that the weather's turning, and their shorts fit tight and long on their ropy legs.

Poppy and I both have crushes on Finn, and so does Amy Klobuchar. Whenever the dog sees Finn, she opens her mouth in a nervous yawn. When Finn is near, Amy Klobuchar keeps her tail high and moves at a ponyesque trot, clipping along smooth and close to the ground as she fetches the wet tennis balls Finn throws for her again and again until she tires out, sits down, drags her butt along the ground of the basketball court for a few seconds, then lies on her belly with her legs flung out behind her, awaiting our pats. Amy is the one thing we love mutually and truly. These moments are perfect, but then they're gone and my tummy hurts. Something in me's griping: it's not enough. On the way home from the park one evening, I ask Poppy if things feel like they're enough for her.

"Um," she says, panting slightly as she heaves Amy Klobuchar into her arms to carry her over a grimy puddle, "sure."

"Things feel better," I say.

"Yeah," Poppy agrees.

"What's wrong?" I ask.

"I don't know," Poppy says. She sets Amy back down. She looks at me. Something's going on behind her eyes. "I'm fine." She won't let me in. I wish I could claw her face off, get to her soul, understand who she is, feel safe in thinking I know her. We grew up together; we were hardly ever apart; we have the same rhythm to our voices and set the table the same way; even our phone numbers are different by just a digit. Still, there are parts of herself she keeps from me. If I were still writing, I'd write a shitty short story about us and what we're going through and how there are no words for it, and in it there'd be a sentence like: *Having a sister is looking in a cheap mirror: what's there is you, but unfamiliar and ugly for it.*

Starlab's getting canceled.

"But who isn't these days?" says our COO during a large informal meeting we hold to discuss said cancellation. We're packed into a conference room, sitting, standing; some suits from our parent company stand at the front of the room and urge us not to give in to "the mobs."

THIS APP IS TOXIC, an astrology macroinfluencer named Money (spelled like the currency but pronounced like the moon) tweeted last Wednesday; PLS DELETE <3. i have GOOD intel that they TROLL ppl in the middle of positive transits & make negative predictions to FUCK w them. dont let them toy w yer emotions. yer worth more~*

The tweet went viral, and a lot of users did delete the app. People sent long vitriolic emails urging us to take responsibility for our actions, but the company is seeded with so many sweet, sweet Silicon Valley clams that we don't really need to take responsibility for anything. No one trained me to write horoscopes or even told me anything about the patterns of stars in the sky. Every day I google something like *mars-mars aspects breakup* or *saturn trine mercury emotions mother daughter* or *dual venus square sun meaning* and copy what real astrologers have already divined.

"I made a commitment when I started this company," says our face-pierced female founder, joining the suits at the front of the room, "and that commitment was to telling people the truth about themselves."

A lot of people move their heads and make noises. "Yes," says one guy.

"And I don't want us to be shaken by this. Okay? We look at how hard and bad life can be, and we tell the truth about it, and we give people ways through it, and we are not going to apologize for that."

I feel like we should probably apologize.

Back at my desk, I have some messages, including some requests for rewrites on my latest horoscopes. When I open up the document, I'm met with red—Emily has destroyed all my shit. Deletions, insertions, comments that just read ??????

It goes without saying that we're now once again pivoting our editorial strategy toward a more positive discourse, says a big red note at the end, so please read through my comments and changes and let me know if you have any relevant questions. ☺

I consider writing back, *What happened to telling the TRUTH????* but think better of it. I sip some water, go to the bathroom, wash my face, return, make the changes, and send them back.

Thirty minutes later: Hmm, still not quite what we're looking for. Can I ask you to take a small edit test for me lady? Attached to the message is an edit test. Three pages of horoscopes, some confoundingly bad, that I'm being asked to reshape. Three times over the next two hours, Emily checks in on my progress via email. I tell her I'm really working to get it right.

It's not a big deal, she writes. We just want to see where your head's at and get more familiar with your thought process!

This, I know, is code for *You're doing badly; what you're turning in is crazytown.*

"Lots of revisions, huh," says Jac meanly.

"Stop looking at my screen all the time," I whisper.

"You looked at my texts," she whispers back.

"Everything okay?" asks the COO, who's been walking around the office in circles for the last hour, eating cashews and mingling.

"Yes," Jac and I both say.

The COO sits on the edge of my desk and says: "I hear your work has a mean streak."

"Um," I say. I've never seen this man before today; how does he know I'm mean?

"She's pretty brutal," Jac says. "We don't run her shit during eclipses."

This is news to me, but I don't know enough about eclipses to understand what it means.

After the COO has seen enough and moved away, I scroll Twitter and screenshot a helpful infographic someone has made in a soothing shade of sage: HOW TO POLITELY SAY "SORRY, I'M NOT DOING THAT FOR FREE." I wonder if it will come in handy in my near future, when my horoscopes prove so terrible that I'm let go and forced into freelancing. I keep scrolling. The BookSmarts account retweets an article into my feed: they've been bought by an ed-tech giant for $100 million. All their employees are getting wellness stipends and brand-new computers and free airfare to and from San Francisco for quarterly team-building retreats. I stare at the article, my whole body vibrating.

By the end of the day, the edit test is still unfinished; I'm stumped on a prediction about what will happen to sweet, stubborn Tauruses when Mercury—the planet of expression and analytical thought—and Jupiter—the planet of religion, law, and wealth—find themselves in conjunction near the filling of the moon.

In bed, I can't sleep. I download and delete a couple of dating apps. I check my mother's Instagram. She has three new posts. One is a meme that reads, SOMETIMES I QUESTION MY PARENTING.... AND SOMETIMES I QUESTION MY CHILD'S CHILDING. Her caption: eye-roll emoji, laughing-crying emoji, martini-glass emoji. I wonder which one of us, me or Poppy, she's trying to bat-signal with a post like this. The second new post is a picture of her dead mother. The caption reads, My Mother. Several people have commented hearts or crying emojis. WHEN DID SHE PASS, one of them wrote. Nine years ago.... I miss her every day. You do not know how lucky you are to have your parent until you do not have them. The last new post is just another smoothie. No caption, no likes.

I google a writer I hate. Next I google *endoscopic brow lift*. Next I google some direct-to-consumer shelving. Next I google *staph from food*. Next I google *pet cemetery*.

EVERY PETS LIFE
TELLS A STORY

says one place's website; I scroll through their images of pet graves for what feels like an hour. Next I google my grandfather's name, Sid Gold, and read his obituary from 2001. Next I google my grandfather's real name, Saul Goldbaum, the name he was born with, the name he had before he changed it to sound slightly less Jewish and slightly more shiny in the '30s; predictably, nothing comes up. Next I google the names of my grandfather's parents, Rebecca and Tuvia Goldbaum, plus *Long Island* plus *Jewish cemetery*—my father said something once about them being buried out there—and I poke around on databases of the tombstones in Jewish cemeteries on Long Island. Then it's 3:34 in the morning. I climb out of bed to get some Benadryl from the bathroom; Poppy is on the couch, lit by her laptop screen.

"Oh," she says, "hey. Did you know Hugh Grant has, like, five children with two women?"

"No," I say. I go to the bathroom, slide open our terrible rusty medicine cabinet, and pull out a pack of Benadryl. I walk back into the living room, popping two pink pills from their blisters. I look at the microwave. 3:36. It's a Friday. I pop out a third Benadryl.

"Well, he does. What are you doing up?" she asks.

"Googling our great-grandparents' graves," I say.

"Did you find them? We should go visit them. Clean the headstones or whatever. Bring flowers, ask for guidance."

"They're somewhere on Long Island," I say, "but I'm getting impatient with all the looking."

"You have so much patience for all the wrong things," Poppy says.

I ignore her. "What are *you* doing up?"

"Remember Knut the polar bear?"

"I don't think so?"

"Knut," she says, looking at me. "The polar bear."

"I don't remember."

"You remember."

Poppy always does this; she assumes that because some idea

or memory or piece of knowledge is hers, it's mine, too. "I'm telling you I don't."

Poppy makes a throaty, frustrated sound and starts typing something. "Knut," she says, turning around her laptop to show me a video of a small polar bear blumbering around his enclosure; a child's voice sings over it in German. "He was born at the Berlin Zoo in, like—2007?—and his mother abandoned him at birth in their pen and all these animal rights activists protested and sued the zoo, saying, like, it would've been kinder if they'd let Knut die rather than try to have humans raise him. Anyway, he had a seizure in front of all these visitors and fell into the water in his pen and drowned. And I was just thinking about him tonight because I was looking at Amy sleeping and she reminded me of him and I thought, There has to be a video. And there was. So I, like—watched the Knut death video." Poppy blinks. "And while it was playing, I felt like: there is a before and after of me watching this video, you know? There's the me who hadn't chosen to watch the video, and now there's the me who did. And I'm not the old me anymore." Poppy pauses. She has that expectant look on her face that tells me she's waiting for me to say something.

"I feel like you're trying to trap me into saying something."

"Trap you? Trap you how?"

"Trap me in a way where I, like—where I admit I believe that the videos we watch on the Internet can change who we are or something."

"Do you not believe that?"

"I obviously don't. I think I'd be great at those jobs where you have to, like, scrub all the beheading videos off Facebook. I think I could watch anything."

"You could watch a beheading and feel nothing."

"At this point," I say, "probably."

"That's disgusting. Come on, Amy," Poppy says, "let's go to bed."

"I could. It's not real when it's an Internet video. It's refraction on refraction on refraction. It's like looking in a toy kaleidoscope. So I'm saying you don't have to worry that you watched the polar bear death video, because it doesn't mean anything about you. You're the same person. The Internet isn't real, it isn't experience. It's moving dots."

Poppy sighs. "Then why are you always fucking talking about it?" She makes some kissing noises at the dog, trying to rouse her. Amy stays deep asleep, curled in a perfect circle on the sheepskin in front of the TV. "You could watch a video of her being beheaded and feel nothing?"

I look at the circle that is my dog and lie.

On the morning train, I spot the Leighs sitting together on a lonely stretch of blue bench, their legs entwined, their heads on each other's shoulders, their eyes closed. The first thought I have is: All they needed was for me to get out of their hair. I hate switching cars once the train is moving, but I don't want to be there when they open their eyes. I've seen the way Poppy looks at Finn, how hard she's working at BookSmarts, how nicely she's training Amy, how well she's sticking to her plant-based diet. She hasn't been holding me back from anything, I realize with a weird and scary clarity. I'm the one keeping her a prisoner of my own torpor.

In the big bathroom stall at work, I sit on the toilet and scroll, willing myself to shit; it's been days. One of my mommies posts an image of the evolution of the Starbucks logo over the years, from a black-and-white bare-breasted two-tailed mermaid to the sort of bland green princess she is now.

Who knew this about Starbucks??? she writes. Bill Gates (SHILL GATES) is tied to Starbucks. The logo is actually Lilith. She is typically described as the Devil's own Wife and a CHILD EATER. Lilith is a SEXUALLY WANTON DEMON that comes in the nights and STEALS NEWBORN BABIES. I've only ever had a Starbucks once. I'm glad I don't support them!!!! #RAPTURE #BEASTSYSTEM # SALVATION #FALLENANGELS #NEWWORLDORDER #JESUSISCOMING #JESUS #LASTDAYS #YAHWEH #FAITH #BIBLEPROPHECY #BIBLE #SATAN #ENDTIMES #ILLUMINATI #YAHSHUAH #MARTIALLAW #TRUTH #MARKOFTHEBEAST #FREEMASONS #GOD #JESUSCHRIST #HOLYSPIRIT #REPENT #DEMONS #DEVILS #ANTICHRIST #YASHUAH

love all the ways she's spelling yashuah, Poppy texts when I send it to her, but you really need to delete this account.

but i love them, I write back.

Poppy types for a minute. Then she stops.

like, I write, who has only ever had starbucks ONCE.

Poppy doesn't respond.

right?????

In comes a call from Poppy. "Okay, I don't know how you ever did this job full-time," she says. "I feel like my brain is a potato. The themes are this, the symbols are that."

Before I was an editor at BookSmarts, I, too, was a content writer, and I composed more than a hundred study guides. Poppy is on her fourth: *Watership Down*. "All these fucking rabbits," she says, "and their emotions and their motivations and all the allegories, my god. This rabbit hole symbolizes democracy. This other rabbit hole symbolizes totalitarianism. Five hundred pages, I could weep. Bunnies fucking bunnies, bunnies murdering bunnies, bunnies making fucking rafts and sailing on the rivers. How do I, like—wring meaning out of this? I'm struggling. I need Adderall or something."

"You don't have ADHD, Poppy. You already have enough things wrong with you." My belly shivers; I fear that was too mean. I motor past the moment so Poppy can't respond. "Just literally type words as they come into your head." I'm whispering into the little microphone on my dangly headphones. "You have to push through that ADHD feeling to a certain threshold, and then it's muscle memory and autopilot."

"Have you read *Watership Down*?"

"We saw the movie. It was really fucked up, remember?"

"No," Poppy says, "I'm probably blocking it out."

"Probably."

"So having seen the movie, and having been able to remember it, what would you say is the biggest motif?"

"Um," I say, "rabbits?"

"No, come on, a motif has to be, like—an idea."

I'm quiet, thinking. "Ingroups and outgroups?"

"That's a theme. You're getting me nowhere. Fuck, I have to walk the dog, she's licking the door, I don't know what that means. Okay. Text me motifs. Not themes."

"Trickery," I say, "trickery's a motif!" but she's already hung up. It doesn't matter. Trickery, I realize right away, is a theme, too. I set my phone down on top of the toilet paper dispenser, pee and wipe. There's a shock of blood on the paper. It's too early for my period, which always starts brown anyway. Uterine prolapse. Cervical cancer. Pelvic inflammatory disease. My whole body fills with heat. My lip sweats. I wipe again: nothing. I wipe again: a little pink. I wipe again: a little more pink. I wipe again: nothing. I pick up my phone and google *blood and pink fluid when wiping vagina*. Thousands of answers arrive in my palm. If I read one, I'll have to read five. If I read five, I'll have to read ten. Instead I click the screen off and close my eyes. I imagine my uterus, covered in sores. I imagine my cervix necrotizing, turning green with rot inside me. I imagine my bladder slipping out from between my legs while I sleep. I imagine myself in a hospital, dying, stinking, bleeding; then I flush and stand and go back to my desk. I try to tell myself over and over that sometimes, in life, there'll just be a little blood.

After work I ride a couple stops to the main branch of the public library, where a young and pretty and famous European writer I wish I could trade lives with is giving a craft talk. I didn't invite Poppy and I know she'll be hurt, but I haven't had a moment of free time alone since we got the dog. Being at the craft lecture won't really count as being alone, but I tell myself it'll feel that way.

In the basement of the library, about sixty people sit in chairs. Many of them have great coats and great haircuts. Every hot guy is already sitting next to a girl, cooing at her. I pick a seat toward the back, at the end of a row, and take out my phone. I go to my secret Instagram. One mommy has posted a picture of her five-year-old holding a fat stack of money to advertise the fact that she's doing a giveaway—winners can pick either fifteen hundred dollars cash or a Louis Vuitton Neverfull. All they have to do is like and follow and tag three friends and share to stories and subscribe to the mommy's newsletter about the best Bible verses for raising godly children.

"Hi," says a voice next to me. My first thought is that Poppy has found me. But when I turn to face the voice, I'm looking at a stranger sitting a few seats down from me. She's about my age, red in the face, with thick curly bangs and a huge gummy smile. "I'm Katie," she says. "With a K."

"Hi," I say. Katie has a stack of the author's books on the seat beside her. "Have we met?"

"Oh, no," says Katie, still smiling, "I was just saying hi."

I smile. "Hi."

"Have you read a lot of her work?" Katie asks me.

"Um," I say, "yeah."

"Me, too," Katie says. "I'm a completionist. Like, I've read everything she's written, even the random online stuff. She's so cool."

"She is."

"I'm always telling people: 'I want to be her when I grow up,'" Katie says, somehow spreading her lips farther back from her teeth than they already are. I hate that I've had the same thought. "Her or Ottessa Moshfegh." I've had this thought, too.

The lights dim.

Katie leans in and whispers at me, "So, are you a writer?"

"Oh," I say, "no, not really."

"I'm getting my MFA," Katie says. "It's only my first semester, but I'm really loving it." She reaches into a tote bag at her feet and digs through it ungracefully. I notice that the tote bears the name of the school where she must be getting her MFA; the same school from which I got mine not four years ago.

"That's cool," I say.

"It's really, um, scrappy and hands-off and self-directed? Like, I barely know any of my classmates and we only meet once a week, so all the work is on your own, and then you, like, come to class and share it and go back home. But, um, I think it's a good model, you know? Because they really want you to hustle and get out there and make your own connections and really live that New York writer life, like, right off the bat?" She pulls out a lavender Moleskine and opens to a new page. I watch her write ~* NYPL TALK *~ at the top.

When I first moved to New York, I was like Katie. I had big dreams but no friends, and this seemed like the great failure of my life. Desperate to find one friend, any friend, I would go out and tromp around the city in hopes of making the right kind of eye contact with the right person at the right moment. I would walk to the Meatpacking District every weekend and visit the same few stores, try on armfuls of clothing I couldn't afford, talk to the shopgirls, feel ignored when they ignored me, imagine that things were different, go home, hate myself, pick the edges of my fingernails bloody, cover the wounds in ointment and bandages, stress about infection, cry.

Now Katie turns to me. "Do you need a piece of paper?" she asks, still whispering loudly.

"No," I say.

The person behind me shushes us. I keep thinking: And this is my night off.

Over the course of the craft lecture, we're told that to enhance our manuscripts, we should change all our characters from people into cats, just to see what it brings out in our pages. Cats or dogs. We're told to freewrite with crayons held in our nondominant hands, so that as we're writing, we feel like children again, we unlock something new and old at once in ourselves and our work. We're told that even if other people—other writers—are talking about the things we're talking about or thinking about the things we're thinking about or writing about the things we're writing about, we shouldn't be intimidated. No one but us can write our version of the world.

I look over at Katie. Her face is happy in the glow of the stage lights. She's writing without looking down at her notebook. She believes. I want so badly to be moved by the famous author's words. I want to be nice to Katie, to show her a cool bar after this, or at least not to talk to her like she's diseased for being friendly. I want to live in someone else's brain.

"Under your seat," says the famous author, putting on a sneaky smile, "there's something I want you to reach for." Surprise: it's crayons. I hold them in my hands and stare. In my head I hear Poppy saying *Art is dead art is dead art is dead.*

Halfway through the talk, I spot an extremely of-the-moment actress sitting across the aisle. I hope Katie doesn't notice her. Katie seems like the kind of person who might ask me to take a picture of her with this famous woman after the lecture.

When the Q&A starts, I pull out my phone. Poppy has texted me lots of times to ask where I am.

shes foaming at the mouth

I think shes fuckign dying

like she's literally foaming at the mouth

ok wait google says that it could just be shes dehydrate,d

im going to give her some water

ok she's drinking she's like super thirsty

omg

i was like what am I going to do with this dog's dead

fuckign body lol

remember that urban legend about the guy with the

suitcase with the dead dog in it on the subway

and the other guy robs him thinking its electronics or

something

ok she had a bad poop just now (outside but she's fine

what do you want for dinner?

??

I text back that I'm just now seeing her texts, that I've been in a lecture, that I'll be home in an hour.

"Excuse me," says the person behind me, leaning up so that their chin is nearly on the back of my folding chair, "there's no recording allowed."

I turn around to face this person: a youngish man in a bad hat. He looks mean. "I'm not recording," I say.

"We're not supposed to have phones. They said at the beginning to silence our phones."

I hold my phone up. "I'm on silent."

"It's distracting."

I don't feel happy with my alone time. I don't feel like myself. I don't even feel there's a self to return to. I pick up my bag and leave.

"Bye," I hear Katie say. I look back at her and wave. The look on her face tells me she was hoping we'd become friends. I can see her mourning the end of the whole night she'd envisioned: she'd ask me if I wanted to grab a drink or a coffee sometime during the week, to talk about the lecture, because she's new to the city, because her program sucks, because she's just been through a breakup, because things were supposed to be one way and they're another, because she has a shelf of Moleskines waiting to be filled the way she's seen other, better writers on Instagram and Twitter post pictures of their shelves of Moleskines full up with their brilliance, because she can't keep going to these kinds of things and saying hi and meeting people like me, people who ruin the illusion that New Yorkers look out for one another, that it's not so hard to make a home here after all.

Back home, after the talk, I open my computer and sit down to write for the first time all year. I flip through a folder full of screenshots of the mommies, willing an intelligent thought about America to come to me. Not a single one does; I'm not surprised. I never really thought there'd be a project, a website, an essay about the Internet and femininity and identity and personhood and capitalism and nationalism and anti-Semitism. I just wanted an excuse to feel like the way I looked at the Internet was different than the way everyone else looked at the Internet; like the way I wasted my time was special.

There's never been a reality in which I could be a serious thinker, a serious writer. I'm a Floridian. I'm a consumer. I'll never blossom into the woman of ideas I like to imagine myself as late at night. It's not that art is dead. It's just that I'm not going to be one of the ones who makes it.

One Saturday, I wake up to find Amy Klobuchar sitting by the front door, licking it. When she sees me, she comes over and puts her head between my shins and whines.

"She wants to go out," I say in the direction of Poppy's room. There's no answer. "Poppy," I say, walking over to her door, twisting its doorknob, pushing it open. She's not in her room.

"You wanna go walkies?" I say to Amy.

Amy barks.

"Let's go walkies."

I dread solo walks with Amy Klobuchar. She's a difficult creature to manage. When anyone but Poppy walks her, she goes down the street tight with fear. Her posture shrinks, her tail curls beneath her, she whips her head around left-right-left-right-left-right; nearly everything she encounters outside is a threat to which she's compelled to respond inappropriately and with great randomosity. She leaps viciously at things like a toddler or an empty Cheetos bag floating on the wind; she whines in fear and skitters from pigeons, free sidewalk junk, bike locks. She nips at heels, strains to throw herself in front of moving cars, rushes at piles of trash, picks up rats in her mouth; to walk her is to near cardiac arrest. Several times on each block I have to smile at a well-meaning neighbor and say with smarm, *Sorry, she's not very friendly*, knowing this will only make them more determined to break through to her and thus prove themselves exceptional to themselves. Once she got a girl's finger. I treated it like a hit-and-run.

In my pocket, my phone buzzes: my mother. I hold it for a minute, deciding whether to answer. Amy yelps; down the block, the way we came, a man's dragging a garbage bin in from the curb. I pick Amy up, avoiding her ears, and sit with her on a weathered wooden bench outside of an annoying coffee shop. She struggles to get down, but I hold her fast.

I answer my mother's call, posing with Amy, squishing her face against mine for the camera. My mother's face oozes into an aggrieved moue.

"How could you let this happen?" she asks. "How could you let her adopt a dog."

"I didn't even know about it," I say. "I had no clue until I walked in the door and the dog was there. I had literally nothing to do with it." One day, I promise myself, I'll stop throwing Poppy under the bus. "But it's going fine. The dog's really sweet."

"This is clearly the decision of an insane person," my mother says. "You don't think this is an insane decision? She's going to kill that thing. She can't take care of an animal. She can't take care of herself. You're enabling her, you know, look at you, is she the one taking care of the dog? No, you're there with the dog. You're encouraging her to live in a way she isn't capable of. She doesn't know any better because she's fucking nuts, but you should."

"Poppy's fine," I say. "Everything's okay. She's really good with the dog, she picks up the shit and everything."

"Don't say 'shit' to your mother."

"I booked our Thanksgiving flights down." I hope this morsel will place me in the sun of my mother's love.

"You're not coming down here with that rat," my mother says.

"You can't really call her a rat," I say. "She's pretty big. She's, like, twenty pounds." Amy Klobuchar licks the phone screen. "See, she loves you."

"Ugh," my mother says. "All right, well. I'm heading out the door to Maxie's." Her brow girl. "Her son got a golf scholarship."

"Good for him." I yawn.

"Stop with the yawning," my mother says, yawning, "you're making me yawn."

"Sorry," I say.

"I'm concerned," my mother says. "I'm very concerned."

"Sorry. Everything's really okay," I say, less sure that it is than I was a few moments ago.

"Stop saying that. Everything is not okay. You live with a mental patient, you act like she's capable. She's not capable. You didn't live with her then, right after her bad time, you don't know how low she gets. I mean, the state of that *apartment* when we got her—you can't imagine it. You don't know how frightening this is for me. You can't *i-ma-gine*. The last four years I've been preparing to lose my child. Do you know the rates? The rates of suicide in people with Poppy's condition? Astronomical. Do you know how much *gray* matter she's lost? Do you know that I don't *fear* my child will kill herself, I *expect* my child will kill herself?" There's quiet. "Oh, shit," my mother says, "Now Roberta's calling me on the other line. Uncle Benny might have Alzheimer's, he had the doctor today, and I told her this morning: 'Call me if it's Alzheimer's.' Oh, Christ. Goodbye." The call ends.

"Hi," says a man in an apron who's come outside from the coffee shop. "Our patio seating is for customers. And we don't allow pets on our furniture. Can I ask you to hop inside and place an order if you'd like to sit here?" This guy has one of those Harry Potter tattoos on the back of his left hand.

"Sorry," I say, standing up. "Thank you."

"Thank *you*," the barista says.

The whole way back home, I imagine what Poppy would've said to him: *She's my service dog. I have a blood disorder. I'm schizophrenic. How dare you. Eat shit.* Anything. She's always saying anything.

The leaves are starting to turn. Hasidic boys come up to me each morning when I'm on my way to the train, asking me if I'm Jewish. I tell them I'm not, but they know I am, they must; I've noticed they're selective about whom they approach. I have the face. I can't hide from these boys: my people.

Poppy's birthday approaches. I ask her how she might like to spend it.

"Do we have to acknowledge it?" she asks, pressing the space bar on her computer. She's watching a bizarre children's YouTube video entitled *What Was 9/11?* "At home Mommy and Daddy always wanted to do something for me like take me out for shrimp and it was just always sad and terrible. All I ever want for my birthday is for the day to just go by. I was actually thinking about drinking some fucking bleach, but all you have is Mrs. Meyer's."

I blink.

"I'm joking," Poppy says, forgetting it's upsetting to joke about drinking bleach after trying to kill yourself.

"Fine," I say. "I just wanted to, like, order you dinner or take you out for a drink."

"I'm not drinking. And you don't eat the same kind of things I eat."

"You don't eat the things *I* eat, but whatever. Fine, we'll do nothing."

Poppy starts the video up again. "What *was* 9/11, am I right," she says.

My phone vibrates. I booked all of us manis with my nail girl for the day before thanksgiving. 6pm. Tell your sister. I send back the painted-nails emoji. She reacts to the emoji with a heart. I get a little surge. Also, she writes, will you need your father to do your face? His books are filling up.

I tell my mom I'm okay on injectables. The uncanny experience of my father shooting my face up with Botox or Kysse while his longtime PA, Puella, holds a blue vibrator against my face to distract me from the pain is one I don't think I can take right now.

That's your choice, she writes back. Just remember it only works when you keep it up consistently. Otherwise all your progress will be erased.

I consider this for a moment, remembering how out of practice I am when it comes to Pilates. ok, I write back, i'll go if you're going!

A flurry of smileys fills my screen.

"Mommy made us nail appointments for Thanksgiving," I say. "And Daddy's giving me fillers."

"Psycho," Poppy says. "It's always this compulsory femininity with her, I can't. I don't know why you play along, you always freak out and think you're dying when you get the lip bubbles." She's making late-night mung bean fettucine, getting up from the table to sample noodles every minute or so and see how they're cooking. "Have you actually spoken to Mommy lately? Like, on the phone?"

"Not really," I lie.

"She hasn't called you to ask about the dog situation?"

At the words "the" and "dog," Amy Klobuchar lifts her head and looks at us expectantly.

I don't answer. "Has she said anything to you about it?"

Poppy sighs. "She told me I was being a fucking idiot and that in three weeks the dog would be dead and I shouldn't call her crying when it happened."

I don't say anything. I feel miserable about having sent the nail emoji; more miserable about having failed to prepare Poppy for our mother's ire.

"It's just, like—any step I take to change or improve myself or my life or give myself things to be responsible for, she's basically like, *You're never going to be able to be responsible for it because you're a fuckup and I hate you.*"

"She doesn't hate you," I say. "She loves you so much that it's like horseshoe theory, it's so much that it comes back around the other way and she doesn't know how and she does it wrong. It's this contradictory thing."

"Well, she's not going to let me bring the dog for Thanksgiving, so I don't know why she's making me nail appointments. I'm not going anywhere without her," she says, nodding at Amy Klobuchar, who is staring at her own reflection in the floor mirror and growling mildly.

"She'll let you bring the dog, come on."

Amy Klobuchar, tired of listening to us talk about her, snorts, stretches, and goes to Poppy's room, where her bed is.

On my laptop, I navigate to Facebook, where I have a rare notification: Molly has posted in the high school reunion group. WE ARE 5 TICKETS AWAY. YOU WANTED A REUNION. WE PLANNED A REUNION. YOU WANTED IT ON NOVEMBER 29TH. WE PLANNED IT FOR THE 29TH. FOR THOSE OF YOU WHO RESPONDED "GOING," PLEASE BUY YOUR TICKETS. Then she proceeds to tag a slew of people's names, one right after the other. Someone laugh-reacts to the post. Someone comments the eyes-looking emoji. A boy who was rumored to have masturbated all over another guy's living room rug in seventh grade types *facepalm*. I click his picture. He's gotten hot. I wonder if the rug story was true.

Poppy tries to put her hair up, but she has no hair tie on her wrist. Hair still gathered in her hand, she heads for her room.

"Oh, fuck," I hear her say. Amy Klobuchar slinks as well as she can slink from Poppy's room toward the front door, her fluffy tail between her rear legs, her ears low.

"What," I shout.

"She peed her bed." Poppy walks out of the room. Her hair is down. Her face is blank. "All the websites say dogs never pee their own beds because it fouls their safest space."

"Well," I say, looking at Amy, who is now lying on the floor near the door with her head beneath the kitchen cart—her version of hiding—"I guess we got the one dog who wants to foul her safest space."

I get back on the apps, where I suffer a Catherine wheel of terrible conversations. Defaulting a picture of myself posing with Amy Klobuchar garners me more messages than I ever dreamed possible. Guys love to pretend they love dogs.

I break out my dead aunt's gold bracelet for drinks with a thirty-eight-year-old named Charlie. Predictably, he explains Bitcoin to me, then says things like *I'm allergic to cocaine* and *When I was living down in Panama.*

"Ha ha," I say to everything. I think of one of my mommies, whose youngest daughter uses one of those speech-to-text tablets to talk. She's always making her tablet go *Ha ha . . . Ha ha.*

"I'd love to take you to dinner sometime," Charlie says, "if you're around and I'm around."

"I'm going home for Thanksgiving," I say.

Charlie blinks. "That's, like, kind of far still."

I shrug. "It's coming up."

On another date, I sit freezing in Prospect Park with a guy in a tiny beanie. We talk about where we're from, then he throws a rock at a squirrel.

"Did you just throw a rock at that squirrel?" I ask.

"I didn't want it coming over here," he says.

"It wasn't coming over."

"It might have."

My teeth chatter. "Okay, I'm not going to lower my core temperature for someone who throws rocks at animals. I have a dog who I love very much." I stand up and wipe off my butt.

"You serious?" says tiny beanie.

"Yeah," I say.

"It was just a rock."

"It's psycho to throw a rock at an animal."

"Don't use ableist language with me, you don't know me. I could be *medically* psychotic and that could be really offensive to me."

Nothing gets me going like when a certain kind of person pretends to care about ableism. I stoop over him and make a scary face. "*I'm* medically psychotic," I shout.

Poppy is stoned and fretting about the future.

"I'm nowhere," she says. "I'm going nowhere. I'm probably in, like, the top two, maybe three, percent of people who have ever been alive on earth, ever, in terms of comfort and wealth, I have an education, I'm not riddled with the Black Death, there's clean water, there's plumbing, there's supermarkets, there's a map in my phone, it even rotates—and I'm just fucking nowhere, I'm making nothing of anything. And it's like: our great-grandparents fled Europe for what? So one day we could buy thirty-dollar tubes of organic aluminum-free deodorant and sit on our asses making *content*? Looking at this fucking flat-screen all day? Doing nothing?"

"You're not doing nothing," I tell her, but I know that, cosmically speaking, she's doing nothing, and that I am doing nothing, too. I gesture at the dog. "You're raising Amy Klobuchar. Every day she's getting better and better." I think of the notes Gage wrote to himself and hung on the mirror. I wonder if he's still making them.

"She's no fucking better," Poppy says. "She always has diarrhea, she eats vermin, she licks the walls everywhere, she tries to jump in front of every car that drives past on the street, basically, and one day she's gonna succeed, and then I'm going to have to, like, pay a huge fine for pet negligence. Her life is worthless. Our lives are worthless. Everything is worthless."

"I can't talk to you when you're like this," I say, "when you're so fucking negative about everything. I think you just want to come up with something to be scared of. Because things are going fine for you for once." But I have to admit Poppy's making some great points.

Somewhere else in the building, a baby starts to scream a raw scream that sounds just like a bobcat's; it's a scream of indignation, of fury; from the scream I can hear that the baby's tongue is sticking out; I can hear that the baby is launching all their misery at the person who brought them into our stinking world.

On Instagram, a picture of a swollen-looking toddler, its eyes red and shut up, the caption: HOURS after mmr sh0t!!!!!!!! A picture of a white woman sitting on a staircase holding her beautiful daughter: If I had been a slave and had met with the slave-traders who kidnapped me and even those who tortured me, I would kneel and kiss their hands, for if I did not, I would not be a Christian...Not that slavery is ever okay... A story featuring a woman in the back of a dark car, asking for prayers as she drives to a mountain in Utah to begin a hike up to the site where a flight carrying her grandparents crashed in the mid-'60s, leaving no survivors, and turning her young father parentless; the first time anyone in her family has seen the site, and she's streaming it live for as long as her LTE lets her. A graphic of many interlocking circles labeled things like *OFF-PLANET ANCIENT BUILDER RACE* and *EXTRATERRESTRIAL NORDICS* and *PINEAL GLAND* and *NASA COVERUPS* and *WAVE/PARTICLE DUALITY* and *TIBETAN DREAM YOGA* and *DEEP LUNAR MINING OPERATIONS*. A picture of a long-nosed Jew, its claws hugging the world: *ROTHSCHILDS → 1938 → OBAMA??????* A picture of lizard people. A story that's a poll: *do you believe there is a demonic realm?* You can choose yes or no. I choose yes. I see that everyone else who has voted has chosen yes, too.

remember how you said at least the hives weren't on my face, Poppy texts, ruining my scroll. I tap into Messages and feel my pupils shrink back to normal.

lol yeah, I write back.

WELL, she says, NOW THEYRE ON MY FACE

I hurry into the living room, where Poppy is sitting on the sofa in a big T-shirt, which I know means the hives have come back on her trunk as well. Her left eye is swollen nearly shut. Her top lip looks puffed and ducky. I tell her she looks "Jenneresque" and she starts to cry, loudly, even though I meant it as a silver-lining kind of thing. Amy Klobuchar, curled at Poppy's feet, lifts her head and howls.

"Shut up," we both tell the dog.

"Quiets," Poppy adds, a bit more nicely.

The dog looks miffed. She licks her genitals. This we allow.

"I don't know what I'm going to do," Poppy says. "I don't know how I'm going to live my whole life. Like, waking up every day, wondering where the fuck my hives are going to be next, checking in on all my thoughts, trying to make sure I feel like me, like I even know who *me* is." Poppy claws at her stomach. "I feel like whatever—whatever engine inside me, whatever engine is inside every human that lets us keep going, hoping we're gonna, you know, maybe experience one nice moment each day, get a raise, eat some candy, it takes so much for me to feel that? And I can't live like that, I can't let that be how my life goes forever. And it's not even, like—where they tell you that hardship makes you stronger—it's not, it's not *teaching* me anything about myself or, like, showing me something about my capacity for suffering, my capacity for grace. It's just making me physically miserable, and existentially miserable, and it's making me fucking fat."

"You're not fat," I say, a reflex.

"Shut the fuck up." Poppy cries for a minute. "Why me?" she says. "Why is having things wrong with me my whole deal? If I saw a character like me on TV, I'd think, That's fake, or, like, Look at that fucking Lyme-warrior-ass whatever. Why can't I just get better?"

I rub her back, making quiet shushing noises. "It's gonna be okay," I say, though I can't imagine how it could be.

"I thought of what I want to do for my birthday," she says.

"Yeah?"

She shows me her laptop. "They're not buried on *Long* Island," she says.

Amy Klobuchar is, luckily, small enough to fit inside our extra-large L.L.Bean tote, so we wrestle her into it and jostle her onto the subway, off the subway, onto the Staten Island Ferry, feed her secret treats throughout the ride, use our bodies to shield her from ferry personnel and passengers who look like they might narc on us.

"Who's my special baby?" Poppy keeps saying to the dog. "You're my special baby." Her eyebrow is raised off her face a good half inch by a hive the size of a grape.

On the other side of the river, Poppy checks her map, locating the cemetery. "Oh, yeah," she says. "We can walk this."

Forty minutes later, we're not much closer to where we need to be; I demand a cab. We hail one. Amy Klobuchar cries in the backseat.

"I never let this doggies in my car," says our driver over and over, though he drives us onward anyway.

"I'm surprised there's a Jewish cemetery out here," Poppy says. "You don't think of Staten Island as, like, a hub for Jews."

dont talk about being jewish in front of cab drivers, I text Poppy. didn't you come up with the no talking in ubers rule???

She reads the text and gives me a look. *Why?* she mouths at me.

Not three minutes later, we approach a light. A family of Jews is making their way through the crosswalk. The children are laughing and jumping; the mother, in a shiny wig, pushes a stroller. "These fucking Jews," says our cabbie.

See, I mouth.

Poppy is silent the rest of the drive. We watch the map to make sure we're headed in the right direction. When our blue dot seems close to the cemetery, Poppy texts me.

waht do i do about tipping, she writes.

what do you mean

ok so if i dont tip because of the jew comment then that just reinforces what this guy thinks about jews.,,,,... but how can i tip now????

Nonetheless, when the car pulls up to the curb at the cemetery gates, Poppy dutifully swipes her card, adds a huge tip, says "Thank you so much" as she pries open her door and squinches her way off the leather seat.

"She's not gonna shit in the cemetery, right?" I ask.

"She's not gonna shit in the cemetery," Poppy says, clearly struggling; Amy Klobuchar, nose to the ground, is pulling against the leash, sniffing in every direction; driven nuts, it seems, by the smell of the dead.

"Let me take her. If she shits, we're literally going to hell."

"I've got her," Poppy says. "There's no hell, by the way."

We split up. I start down one path and Poppy starts down another. The air is wet but biting, and when I wipe my nose, it's bleeding from the cold. I look at each tombstone, each bench, each arch, each slab in the ground, marveling at the names and their spooky old spellings: Faiwel, Herschel, Dwosza, Yitzchak, Reuven, Yetta, Leibel, Meyer, Szoszana. One woman, Gussie Turchin, has a ghostly rendering of her face sandblasted into her headstone. The right side of it is empty—presumably awaiting Mr. Turchin. Grandfathers, bubbes, dedushkas, Yiddishe mammes. Loving, devoted, beloved, all of them. There are two tiny headstones set into the grass, next to each other: *BABY,* says the first. *BABY,* says the second.

im ready to have a panic attack, I text Poppy after I spot the headstone of a man who was born in the same month of the same year as our father.

do you have any idea how many rebeccas there are here, she writes back.

lmaoooo, I respond.

i can see you, she writes. look up

When I look up from my phone, I spot the two of them in the near distance: Amy Klobuchar is, of course, hunched and shitting on a granite grave marker, in full view of God and the few other families here today.

"Can you help me," Poppy shouts, struggling to unwind a poop bag from the spool attached to Amy's leash. "It's the last one," she says, fishing it out; as soon as she has it, she drops it, and a big wind comes up and carries it away.

"Just leave the shit there," I whisper-yell, stomping over.

"We have to pick it up," Poppy says. "It's, like—right on top of a body here." She stoops and picks up a large leaf. "I can use this," she says.

"Don't use that," I say. "What are you gonna do with that? Drop it."

"It's my dog," Poppy says. "I'm responsible for her." She crouches down and uses the leaf to try to pick up the poop. The leaf falls apart in her hands.

"Jesus Christ," I say, stooping.

"It didn't get on me, it's not on me, it's fine."

I open up my bag and dig out a pack of tissues and some hand sanitizer. "Stop it, stop it," I say to Poppy, who's still trying to scoop the poop off the granite and into the grass. She has a very certain look in her eyes; it scares me. I ignore it, or try to. I grab her hands and squirt as much hand sanitizer as I can into them, then rip out a bunch of tissues and pile them in her palm. "Wipe," I say, like she's my child.

"Excuse me," says a little voice. We both turn toward it. A small Orthodox boy in a suit is coming toward us. He's carrying a lulav. "Excuse me," he says again in a thick Yiddish accent, "are you being Jewish?"

"No," we say at the same time.

We wander separately for one more hour, inspecting. My eyes hurt, my face hurts. Rebecca and Tuvia are nowhere.

"We should just go," I say to Poppy when we meet up again at a large dark obelisk in the middle of the field.

"But the directory *said*," Poppy whines. Her eyebrow hive is pushing her eyelid down, making her look sleepy. Amy Klobuchar is back in the tote bag now that we're about 60 percent sure she won't shit in it. Poppy's holding the straps up on her shoulder with both hands. Amy snaps at some new-falling rain. A shaky man in a kippah sits davening on a bench nearby, a small prayer book in his hands. "We came all this way."

"I'm just getting really cold," I say.

"Fine," Poppy says, hoisting Amy Klobuchar up higher onto

her shoulder. "We'll go. We'll go without having accomplished anything, without having found anything, without having even finished walking the cemetery, knowing that our great-grandparents' graves are definitively unquestionably here, knowing they left their homes, the homes of their ancestors, in the hopes that *we* could live, you know, these American lives, and now we're so—we're so *cold* that we can't even do them the one kindness of looking upon their resting place and thanking them. I'm sure on their journey across the fucking ocean they probably weren't as cold as we are right now."

I look at the ground, feeling bad.

"This was supposed to be my birthday celebration," Poppy says. She stares out at the cemetery. It's like she's trying to make her face extra wistful. I start laughing. She looks at me, furious.

"I'm sorry," I say, "I'm sorry, it's just you look like that meme, the one that goes, 'I enjoying mysekf by the lake when I remember instances of regret,' it's too much—you know this meme, right?"

"I don't know the meme," Poppy says.

"That's impossible," I say. "Everyone knows it." I open up my phone and look for the meme.

"Stop," Poppy says. She swats at my phone. "Stop."

"No, you have to see it—"

"This is not 'I enjoying myself by the lake,'" Poppy says.

"It's 'mysekf,'" I say.

She seems angry. "This is, like, real. This is real fucking human misery, this is my abject sadness at not being able to find a way to grieve, or it's—I don't know, not knowing what to grieve, it's not being able to want to be alive, it's, like, our people have been chased from every home they've ever known, and *I've* been chased from every home I've ever known," Poppy says, being in my estimation just a little dramatic, "I couldn't live in the moldy house, I couldn't live with Mommy and Daddy because they got sick of me, now you're sick of me, and I'm sick of you—"

"You're sick of *me*?" I ask. I can hear myself squeak.

"—You're always making fun of me, you're always making fun of *everyone,* you say horrible things and you don't even notice, it's so second-*nature* to you to just say whatever—you called Starlab *gay* once—to *me*—"

"I know, but it *is*—sometimes there's no other word—"

"You, like, transcribe conversations you overhear in public, and you screenshot every text you get so you can make fun of it later, and you get mad about hypothetical situations that don't exist, and you find an enemy everywhere you go, and you're always on your phone, you don't even fucking recycle, I can't take it anymore." Poppy stares at me.

"Am I like that?"

"*Yes*," Poppy says. "I mean, obviously my experience of you isn't you, and your idea of yourself isn't you, and the self isn't something that can ever be described by anyone, but."

"Okay," I say. "You're just talking to talk."

"I'm not. I'm talking to talk to my sister. And I'm not a meme, Jules, and your whole thing with being addicted to memes and the Internet and the mommies and all your miserable fucking irony is making me ill," Poppy says, and she walks away. Amy Klobuchar stares back at me from the tote with her tongue out. I'm alone with the shaky man on the bench, and he's staring at me, too. For a moment it's like he's an important respected distant relative of mine, and Poppy is my parent, and she has slapped me on the wrist in front of him.

"I'm sorry," I say to him.

The man nods at me. He forgives me my interruption, then takes up his prayer for his loved one, in the rain, alone, in the middle of a cold island.

The cabin air is dry and chemical. Everyone around us is watching *My 600-lb Life*. Poppy's head is back and her mouth is open and she's making throaty snores. Amy Klobuchar, in a purple vest from Amazon that says *SERVICE DOG DO NOT PET,* pants belly-up on Poppy's thighs. Valiantly I have taken the middle seat, leaving them the window. The guy to my left has his shoes and socks off. He's talking very loudly to the person across the aisle from him, ostensibly his buddy. They want to buy snack boxes, but they're arguing over who will be the one to pay. When Poppy and I argue about who's buying something, we're always begging the other person to pay, but these guys are ready to fistfight each other because they both so badly want to be the one to pay.

"I got it, I got it," says the guy across the aisle.

"Don't listena him, don't listena him," no shoes no socks says to the flight attendant, pushing his credit card up toward her face.

"Fuck you, it's forty bucks, you think I don't got forty bucks?"

"The day I ask you for money is the day I'm sucking your dick, all right? All right? The day I ask you for money is the day I'm sucking your dick."

The flight attendant takes no shoes no socks's credit card and slides it through the reader.

"Fuck you," his buddy tells him.

"Fuck you," says no shoes no socks.

The flight attendant hands them their snack boxes.

"Whadda we got," asks the buddy, opening his box. "Fuckin', cheese, fuckin'—crackers, here, we got—grapes—" He lifts a sad clump of grapes out of the box and pops one into his mouth.

"Pfft," says no shoes no socks, "fuck outta here." Then he pokes me in the arm. "You want my snack box?" he asks. "It's full of these bullshit snacks, but I just paid forty dollars for it so my buddy here could suck on some fuckin' grapes. Here, take it, Ionwannit."

"Are you guys from Long Island?" I ask, eyeing the fuckin' grapes for slime as he passes me the snack box.

"You fuckin' bet," says no shoes no socks. The teeny-tiny plane avatar on the flight-tracker screen before me tells me we have two hours and thirty-two minutes left to go.

Outside the chilly airport, the weather is wet and hot: Florida in November. Amy Klobuchar, nose to the ground, struggles against her harness. She finds a place to pee, but then a blue-haired, meth-skinny woman dressed in a unicorn-print pajama onesie yells at us—Amy Klobuchar is peeing in the smoking area.

"I'm gonna fricken do something if that dog pishes on my pajamas," the woman says, shaking out a Newport and pulling up her unicorn-horn-adorned hood. A massive guy standing near her is smoking with one hand and, with the other, using a Theragun to massage his body.

We make our way to the very back of the parking garage, following instructions our father has texted us. Amy Klobuchar sniffs the tires of every car she can. Soon we hear honks: our father in his brand-new Range Rover. When we walk up and open the doors, a Range Rover logo projects onto the ground via LEDs, and motorized steps fold out so we can haul ourselves into the car with ease. The front seat is more comfortable than my own mattress. Retreating home into the soulless hug of my parents' wealth—it always feels so good at first.

"My girls," our father says, leaning in for cheek kisses. His face looks tight, plasticized. He's been microneedling himself again.

Amy Klobuchar howls at him from the backseat, wagging her tail and spinning in circles, trying to get to him. Poppy lets her scrabble her way up to the front, where she lodges herself on his lap in the driver's seat.

"Holy shit," our father says, patting her flank. "Three legs."

On the drive, our father tells us all he's been up to lately. He's been getting back into weight lifting, he's been loving this great new Xbox game where you play as a fourteenth-century French orphan trying to survive the Black Death. "And I'm into crypto now," he adds.

"No," Poppy and I both groan.

"It's— No, listen, it's very lucrative, it's the currency of the people. It's doing very well. You two oughta each put about fifty thousand into it, see how you do."

"Daddy," I say, "we don't have fifty thousand dollars."

"Okay, well. Your mother's been doing a lot of research about, you know, the state of the world. And how bad things are, and how things could be close to some kind of big collapse."

"A *collapse*?" we both say.

"Whoa," our father says, "whoa, I said *could* be, could be. Anyway. She feels like maybe it's important for us to get our money out of the banks, maybe start looking into some, you know, alternative things. Frankly, I don't know what to do about some of it. Some of this new stuff, you've heard about this new stuff? But what can I say, I'm a feminist. I respect my wife. I'm not gonna stand in her way."

"What new stuff?" Poppy asks.

"Are you guys, like, buying gold bars?" I ask. "Are you *prepping*?"

"Your mother can tell you more."

Poppy and I look at each other.

Our father merges onto the Sawgrass Expressway, nearly hitting a big truck with an Oath Keepers sticker on one side of the back window and a Minnie Mouse sticker on the other. He drives over the rumble strips for a few seconds while Poppy and I squeal.

"God," Poppy says, "you're such a bad driver."

"There are no bad drivers," says our father, "just bad passengers."

We don't say anything.

"That's a metaphor," he continues. "For life."

When we walk in the front door of our childhood home, the first thing we hear is Christmas music. Poppy raises her brows at me, then goes to her room right away to drop her bags. She keeps Amy Klobuchar leashed and drags her along.

In the kitchen, my mother fusses with her iPad. "Fuck," she says. "Steve, how do I get Michael Bublé on here?"

"This fucking music," says our father.

"Hi," I say to her, kissing her cheek.

"So your sister's not going to bother to say hello?" my mother asks. Something animal inside me grows warm. Right away, Poppy's the bad one and I'm the good one.

"I missed you so much," I say, going in for the full hug, doing all I can to pull ahead.

"No no, watch out for my hair," says my mother, grabbing my arms and setting them back by my sides. "I just saw my hair girl today, what do you think?"

It looks unnatural and dated. "It looks beautiful."

"Ruth Ginsburg's in the hospital again," she says, as if she and Ruth Bader Ginsburg are close. "This could be it." Michael Bublé pours from the overhead speakers.

My father flips closed the case on my mother's iPad. "All right," he says. "I'm gonna visit the little boys' room."

"Thank you," says my mother, "for the announcement."

Poppy enters the room with Amy Klobuchar in her arms.

My mother looks at me. "You let her get a giant rat."

"God, stop saying that," Poppy says. "She's a collie mix."

"Corgi mix," I say.

"I think she's a collie."

"*I* think it's a pit bull. If it's not from a breeder, there's always pit in there," says our mother.

"Where's Pepper?" Poppy asks. Pepper is our parents' thirteen-year-old standard poodle. Who came from a breeder.

"I have her locked up safe in our room. I had no idea what kind of animal you'd be bringing into my house; I had to protect my Pepper." Pepper, like a sufferer of a Victorian malady, stays on a blanket in our mother's closet most of the time anyway.

"Okay, so I think Amy and Pepper should meet outside," Poppy says, "where it's neutral, so no one feels territorial and no one feels small."

"*Small?*" my mother says. "*Feels?*"

"Dogs have very real feelings," Poppy says.

"Look at you, the dog whisperer. If you stopped feeding her, she'd eat you."

"You think Pepper would eat you?" Poppy asks.

"If I stopped feeding her, yes," she says. "I'm under no illusions about me and Pepper."

I collect Pepper from my parents' bedroom. When I flip on

the closet light, she doesn't even lift her head; she just swivels her eyes at me. Her cataracts make them look like big wet Cinnabons. I scratch her behind the ears.

"You wouldn't eat anybody," I say. "Blink once if you wouldn't eat anybody." An old game I used to play with her: *Blink once if you're human, blink twice if you can understand me, blink three times if I'll get into Yale.*

Pepper, who's always liked me in a quiet way, looks at me now and blinks twice.

I leash her and pull her outside, where Poppy has brought Amy onto the grass. My mother slips on some flip-flops and follows me. Pepper and Amy spot each other. Amy barks.

"If she fucks with Pepper, I'm suing you," our mother shouts at Poppy.

"If Pepper fucks with Amy," Poppy shouts back, "I'm suing *you*."

Pepper yoinks herself away from me; her leash jumps from my hand. Amy bolts, too. They chase each other in circles, already friends.

Since I was last home almost a year ago, my childhood bedroom has been wallpapered, recarpeted, and, as Poppy warned me back in March, fitted with stage-bright LED high hats. When I flip on the light switch, the room seems to glow.

Disturbingly, there's a white WayLife-branded tote bag sitting on my bed. Inside are three mini-bottles of essential oils. On my bedside table, a diffuser pumps ylang-ylang or something into the air. The light at its base changes color gently, from pink to blue to green.

Get well with Wendy. Ring Around the Toesies. All those Instagram comments on the pages of women who use WayLife, sell it, swear by it, claim it was sent to them by Jesus himself to heal them, prosper them, anoint them. Oils are just a part of it. There's so much more; there has to be. Her temple. Her smoothies. Her getting my dad into crypto. What if she *is* buying up gold bars, storing drums of dried food in the garage, getting into flat-earth Reddit? What if she, too, believes humanity's being controlled by an off-planet ancient builder race?

My mother is a mommy.

For dinner we order in. When the food arrives, Poppy and I open up the boxes to find that every dish has meat in it.

"I told you I'm plant-based now," Poppy says to our mother.

"Did you?" she asks, taking a slice of sausage-topped pizza. "I can't really remember the last time you called, actually, so I certainly don't remember you saying anything about being plant-based. And even if you did, I have no idea what 'plant-based' could possibly mean. We all need meat, we all need iron. What we should all be eating, actually, is offal."

"What?" Poppy asks.

"Offal. Animal organs. We're animals, we need to eat other animals."

"Are you hearing this?" Poppy looks at me.

"Don't mock me to your sister right in front of me," says our mother. "Don't try to pull her into this."

Things are like this every time we're home. Poppy and our mother fight constantly, our mother antagonizing Poppy, Poppy antagonizing our mother, our father and me sitting quietly, looking at our devices.

When I was first with Gage, I told him how things often went at home, and he told me that if he had a family who talked to each other the way my family talked to each other, he'd simply never see them. The problem for me, however, is that when I'm home, I have access to a dishwasher, and a very large shower, and my parents pay for everything, and I always leave with new clothes and shoes and face injections. I'm very easily Stockholmed by any promises of money and comfort. Gage called me a champagne socialist unironically mid-breakup. *I never said I was a socialist,* I told him, even though we'd held a joint membership with the Democratic Socialists of America for two years. All our friends were getting engaged and I was obsessed with the sizes of everyone's rings. *That's a sixty-thousand-dollar ring,* I'd say, showing him a picture of a friend's ring. The implication was that I would never be happy until I, too, had a sixty-thousand-dollar ring. I can see now how that could kill a relationship. But maybe, it occurs to me, I never really wanted a big ring; maybe I don't really care about all the stupid material things I think I care about. Maybe I just want a life that looks more like my mother's so that I can have her approval.

"Am I even still *allowed* to say 'orphan'?" my mother's asking when I tune back in to the conversation, woozy with epiphanies.

Poppy picks at a wet side salad. "Of course you can say 'orphan.' It's a descriptor, it's not a slur. You can't say slurs."

"There are so many things I'm not allowed to say these days, or that you and your sister *tell* me I'm not allowed to say, I can't keep up. Everyone's so sensitive. Your generation. And what's with the tattoos?"

"We don't have tattoos," Poppy says.

"But your *generation* does," says our mother, like it's our fault that they do. Like we made our generation go out and get tattoos, just the two of us, alone.

"The other day," our father says, "I was asking Dr. Kang how he feels about the word 'Oriental,' and he said: *It's old-school. That's all. It's just old-school. It's not racist.*"

"Jesus Christ," Poppy says.

"Don't talk like that in front of me," says our mother. "Don't you dare take the Lord's name in vain in my house."

"We're Jewish," Poppy says.

"You really can't say 'Oriental,' Daddy," I tell my father.

"Dr. Kang said it's okay."

"He didn't say it's okay," Poppy says. "He was just trying not to tell you that you were being racist, because it's awkward, and because, as a person of color in the workplace—a workplace *you* control, where *you* employ him—he probably has to constantly defer to the racist things you and your patients say so that he's not fired or maligned or whatever."

"Wow," says my dad, looking at me. "*Maligned*. Guess I can't say 'Oriental.'"

"Are you selling WayLife?" I ask our mother.

She shrugs. "Maybe, why?"

"Because it's snake juice," I say. "For *Mormons*." Our mother hates Mormons, or claims to. She always used to say that they were gentiles who wanted to create for themselves the persecution the Jews felt so they could imagine themselves as special.

"Essential oils help a lot of people. They're helping me."

"How are they helping you?"

My mother looks at me. "Each oil helps me in a different way. I don't have to explain myself to you. I'm running my own business."

"But I bet you have to report to someone," I say. In the bathroom earlier, I googled a list of things to say when someone you love has gotten into a cult, things to say when someone you love has gotten into a conspiracy, things to say when someone you love has gotten into a pyramid scheme. "I bet you have to buy in. How much did you have to pay for all the stuff? Can I ask that, how much you had to pay?"

"The dog has to go out," says Poppy, standing up from her seat. "Amy," she calls, "wanna go walkies?"

I keep going. "I bet you had to buy in, and you had to buy it from some woman above you, and you have to pay it back by the end of next month, and you're trying to sell to your friends but not your *best* friends, because you're embarrassed, but no one's buying, and you're going to have to pay even more to catch up.

Has anyone mentioned anything about Holocaust denial, or the waters above the firmament, or tradfem stuff, or a mass globalist takeover, or intergalactic human trafficking rings run by the governor of California, or an ancient builder race—" I stop myself. Our mother is staring at me, her mouth hanging wide. This is the most I've ever said to her at once, probably, in the last five years.

"Take Pepper," she says, flicking her hand at me. "Get out of my *face*."

"I'll go too," says our father. "It's nice out."

"And I'll just sit here," our mother says, "alone, worrying about intergalactic trafficking. I mean, what is *wrong* with you? What do you *think* of me?"

"Sorry," I say.

"You should be. I'm your mother. If I want to believe in intergalactic trafficking, I'm allowed. If I want to believe in it, *your ass* should believe in it. Because I'm your mother."

On the walk, our father carries his phone as a flashlight and tells us about everything that's happened on the street in the last nine months. "Remember the Lowes? Their son got killed in their house, bad drug deal?"

"Yes," Poppy and I say together.

"Husband just died. Liver something. Real shame. Now Claudia's all alone in that big house." As we pass the Lowes', we see a very old pickup truck parked prominently in the driveway with a *FOR SALE* sign in the window.

"Just so sad. And over here," he says, pointing to a hideous wall of giant stacked rocks one neighbor has used to line their driveway, "we've got this monstrosity. I called the city five times, I wrote a letter, and guess what?"

"What?" we ask.

Our father smiles brightly. "They're making 'em take it down. Look." He points his phone at the far corner of the rock wall, where it's clear that some rocks have been removed from the top. "I did it."

Amy Klobuchar takes off barking, chasing something, probably a possum. Her leash slips out of Poppy's hand. "Shit," Poppy says.

"Wow," says my dad as Poppy clops down the road to catch up with the dog. "She can really still get some mileage on those things. The dog, I mean. On her three legs."

"You don't have to keep pointing out her number of legs," Poppy says.

"I don't think Mommy should be getting involved with the oils," I tell my dad.

"Oh, the oils are great," he says. "They really relax my mind. I put some here at bedtime," he says, tapping his temples.

"How do you feel about the deep state?" I ask.

"The what?" he says.

"Never mind," I say, and I leave it at that. Already I've said too much.

In the morning, the air-conditioning is out. The air in the house is still and wet. By noon, it's cooler outside than in.

"*Mi trabajo me está matando,*" our parents' housekeeper, Myrna, says into her phone. "Y *ahora han llegado las hijas.*"

Poppy and I look at each other. Silently we gather our laptops and our snacks and move to the patio.

"She says her job is killing her," Poppy whispers, "and now 'the daughters' are here."

"I can speak Spanish," I say. "You're not the only one who speaks Spanish."

Our mother pokes her head out onto the patio. The hair around her face is curled from the humidity. "The house is about to be listed," she says, "and we're going to have showings every week."

"We know," Poppy says.

"Don't interrupt me."

Poppy opens her computer.

"Don't ignore me."

Poppy closes her computer.

"You eat out here, you clean up and wipe the table when you're done. We need to sell this house. It's your father's re-tirement."

"Mommy," Poppy says, "how would us eating on the patio stop you from selling the house in two months?"

"Six weeks. And if the house looks like hoarders and pigs live here," our mother says, swanning back inside, "like I imagine your *apartment* does, I would think that might keep us from selling the house, wouldn't it?" We say nothing. "I'm going into the office in half an hour for some lasers. Jules, are you coming?"

"Um, I was thinking I might not want to?"

"We don't cancel doctors' appointments last-minute in this family."

"Well, it's Daddy, and it's not really a *medical* appointment—"

"Jules, let's go."

Through the big glass doors, Myrna looks at us. I give her a limp smile which she does not return.

On the door to my father's office, there's a shiny new sign: *GOLD AESTHETICS,* it says.

My mother greets all my father's employees with air kisses. She asks them how their children are, so on. One of them brings us some numbing cream in tiny glass pots.

"Ching ching," my mother says, cheers-ing the pots like we're celebrating.

"I don't think I need this," I say. The cream smells terrible, like Vicks.

"You always say that and you always regret not putting it on," my mother says, smearing the cream across her nasolabial folds. "I got him to pull out some extra syringes for you. Make sure you thank him. It's valuable."

"I don't want to do too much."

"No, it's gonna be just a zhuzh, right on your cheeks. Imagine how gorgeous your eyes will look, how fabulous. They're so small, like Nana's, you just need some help to make them pop. Your grandmother, her poor soul, my poor mommy," she says, "she never *had* that, she never had the *chance* to make her poor eyes pop. You can do this whenever you want. You should be coming home three times a year to do it. You should move home and work here, even better, and then you could be doing regular peels, and then you could meet someone interesting." She leans in close to whisper to me. "Wait till you see Puella. She goes to this trainer now, she doesn't eat anything. She looks like a concentration camp victim."

"Mommy," I say, "her family was in the Holocaust."

"No they weren't."

"Yes they were. In, like, Latvia. She told me once."

My mother sighs. "That's a shame. I'm gonna have to speak with her. She shouldn't be talking to patients about things like that."

On the wall nearby that leads down the hall to the exam rooms, I see that sometime in the year since I've been here, my father has hung statement art: three enormous hot-pink canvases that read *LASERS, BOTOX,* and *FILLER.*

In the exam room, Puella sweeps in wearing cool mulberry-colored scrubs; she's positively skeletal. I tell her she looks great.

"Ladies ladies ladies," she says, "my favorite ladies. Time for some zhuzhing from me and Dr. G., huh?" My mother is getting some sort of fat-removal thing done on the flesh beneath her chin. It involves her sucking on a tube of laughing gas while Puella aims lasers at different parts of her face and neck. I sit in the corner, wearing a sticky pair of yellow-tinted sunglasses, listening to my mother get high.

"And you should see this dog they brought home," she squeals. "It's got"—she sucks on the tube, laughing—"it's got three legs."

Puella laughs. I fill with rage.

When it's my turn, my mother sits in the corner, her face reddened. She comes down slowly, hissing through her teeth as her face burns more and more.

My father walks in. "My treasures," he says, kissing us both on the head.

"Long time no see," I say, and he laughs—it's so easy to make him laugh.

"Sit in the big chair," he commands, "and smile for me." I obey. "Oh, yeah. You're pulling up here where you're always pulling up. Puella," he says, motioning for her with two gloved fingers. She scampers up beside me with the vibrator and lays it on my cheek.

"I don't need the vibrator today, Puella," I say.

"No, feel how calming," Puella says.

My father hits me with two stinging jabs in the corners where my nose joins to my face. "Smile now?" I smile. "Gorgeous as always. No gum." He holds up a mirror so that I can see myself. I'm always shocked by how immediate the effect is, how quickly my face becomes new. Now, when I smile, it looks like I'm trying not to. "And we're doing cheeks, right, honey?" he asks, preparing a new needle.

"Um," I say, assuming he's talking to me.

"And lips?"

"Yes," my mother says. I can hear her texting.

My father sticks a cannula into my top lip. My eyes water from the pain. Puella wipes the tears away with a tissue. "God, I wish your sister would let me at her face just once," he says.

"I know," I say, feeling horrible. "She could be so pretty."

There's a new employee at the billing desk with a shiny gold name tag that reads *Amy*. "Amy," my mother says to her as we breeze out, "have you met my daughter? She just adopted a dog who's also named Amy. Isn't that funny?"

"That is funny," Amy says, staring at her computer screen.

"What kind of dog is she?" my mother asks me.

"Oh, we don't know for sure."

"She's some kind of pit bull with three legs."

"She looks like a corgi to me," I tell this new Amy, suddenly desperate for her to like a dog she's never met and never will. "And she's really sweet."

"All dogs are sweet until they maul someone," says my mother. "But I sincerely hope she doesn't maul *you*," she continues, donning her sunglasses with a little magic in her wrist, "considering your father's just put so much hard work into your face, and for *free*."

That night I stay in bed, my whole face pulsing and swollen. The air-conditioning still hasn't been fixed.

Around nine Poppy comes into my room, her eyebrows severe. "Someone died by jumping off the roof of our apartment building," she says.

"What?"

"Someone who lives in our building jumped off the roof into the courtyard and they're dead."

Amy Klobuchar bounds into the room and leaps onto my bed, exposing her belly for a pet.

"How do you know?" I ask, ignoring the dog.

"The building Facebook group. Someone posted and was like: *Why are there all these cops in the building?* and three people commented to be like: *Somebody jumped and was taken away in an ambulance but everyone on the sidewalk could see their whole body all fucked up, their head all exploded like a watermelon.*"

I pick up my phone and go to the Facebook page.

Hey y'all, recent events just have me thinking about how you really don't always know what others are going through, even you're neighbors. Just want to throw out there—if your going through a tough time and need a human to talk to, I'm always happy to hold space. Anywho, hope all y'all are doin well, the post says, and then there's a peace-sign emoji. Everything about it strikes me as fake, annoying, idiotic: the use of "human," the use of "y'all."

"It's so fucked up, isn't it?" Poppy's been reading over my shoulder. Her voice is soft, emotional. "Someone said it was a woman, but I don't know how you could possibly, like—determine that? From a crushed-watermelon body?"

"Clothes, maybe? Boobs? Or if she was pregnant?" This makes me think gaspingly of Nina. Nina the cool mommy. Nina, the one person I've met in recent memory I didn't hate on sight. Nina who played with her baby on the roof even though the super wouldn't like it. I read through the post again, scroll through the comments. Nothing points to Nina. Nothing points away from her. I try not to give the thought any more air. "Thank god we're not there right now," I say. "So much weird shit happens in that building. Do you think it's, like, that person would've rather died than live another minute in our building—"

Poppy gets up and walks away. At the door, she turns and starts walking back toward me. "You know," she says, "you need to learn some fucking empathy. How reductive to joke about this."

"You were kind of just joking about it—"

She ignores me. "People who kill themselves are at the very end of their pain. The terminus of their pain." I'm impressed by her use of "terminus." "Their pain is so huge, so real, so consuming that they can't see or feel anything but pain. They're on fire. How *dare* you. Whoever it was probably loved living in our fucking building." She's close enough to smack me, and she does.

"Get off of me," I say, shaking her away. "You're deranged."

Poppy goes quiet for a minute. "Being here's really hard on both of us, isn't it?"

"I'm not *doing* this, get out."

Poppy nods. "At least we're only here for a few days," she says. She looks at me. "Then maybe when we're back home, we'll be able to talk again."

In the morning the air is fixed, but the water's out.

"Motherfucker," says our mother, peering through the window of the cabana bathroom at the water tank in the yard, which is spilling gushes into the crabgrass.

"Motherfucker," she says again, struggling to reach the water-tank guy on her phone. "I'm going to divorce you," she says to our father, "keeping me in this house like this. I'm cooking Thanksgiving dinner for nine tomorrow. For *nine*. And for *your* family." Any time someone from our father's side of the family is involved, our mother points out that it's his family, not hers. "I need you girls to pick something up for me." She's texting. "It's some kind of water purifier. I'm sending you the address. Sunshine State Supply or something. It's in that shitty plaza with the Albertsons up near the bad mall. I reserved it under my name, and it's paid for. The guy's name is Stan. Pick it up by two. Don't flush anything." She swoops off to the grocery store with her phone to her ear, dialing and redialing the water-tank guy.

Sunshine State Preparedness Supplies. Hazmat suits and mini-grills hang in one window; in another is a rack of pamphlets whose covers read *Dare to Prepare!* and *Your Apocalyptic Pharmacy* and *Grow the Best Rhubarb* and *Survival Mom* and *Solving 9/11* and *The Infidel's Guide to Understanding Islam, ISIS, and the Quran*. A typewritten sign in the window reads *ARE YOU PREPARED FOR STHTF?* It's an acronym my mommies use a lot—it means *for shit to hit the fan*. There are a couple magazines—*Guns & Ammo, Backwoods Home*. One magazine has Anne Frank's face on it. It's just called *ANNE FRANK*.

LIFE IN THE SECRET ANNEX, says one headline.

WHO BETRAYED ANNE? says another.

THE DIARY—REIMAGINED

HER LASTING LEGACY!

"Look," I say, putting a finger on the glass.

Poppy swats at my hand. "What is it with you and Anne fucking Frank? Stop touching the glass."

Movement: an old white man with thick white hair and a thick white beard behind the counter waves at us. He looks like Tracy Letts. He's wearing a shop apron. This must be Stan. I wave back.

"This is South Florida," Poppy says. "It's not supposed to be like this here. This is, like, a place for luncheons and plastic surgery and bubbes and zaydes and pink tile."

"Soon everywhere's going to be like this," I say. "Wave." Poppy waves.

Inside there are shelves and shelves of gardening tools, gas masks, sacks of dehydrated potato flakes, canned meats, molasses; up at the counter, a case of knives and tough-looking lamps and watches; boxes and boxes of gleaming Berkey filters.

"Hello," says Stan, suddenly behind us.

Poppy and I both jump. "Hi," I say. "We're picking something up."

"When did you guys open?" Poppy asks.

Stan puts his hands on his hips and winks at the ceiling. "Let's see, five months ago?"

"Prime real estate here," Poppy says. "You get the mall people, you get the surgical center people, you get the Albertsons people."

Stan puts out his fist for a bump. "Right on," he says.

"How do you think the world's gonna end?" she asks, bumping him.

"The world *as we know it*," he corrects. "I could see a nuclear attack taking place high above ground level, taking out all the electric. I could see riots and looting, high-level Antifa stuff. I could see mass incapacitation of the population through the food supply."

"Antifa," Poppy says. "Interesting, interesting."

I poke her, very gentle. I want her to stop. I'm afraid to fuck around with these kinds of people; it's the first time I've been face-to-face with one, and I feel sweaty and terrified.

"When you say midair nuclear attack," Poppy starts, "are we talking—"

"We're picking something up," I say again. "It's under Wendy."

"Wendy!" says Stan. He goes for a box on the back counter: it's a giant Berkey. "Are you Wendy?" he asks, looking at me as he sets it down between us. He's attached carry handles made of plastic to the top of the box.

"Yes," I say for some reason.

And now Stan offers me his fist. "You're a smart woman, Wendy," he says.

When we get home, our mother's on the sofa with a blond woman. Amy Klobuchar sits prettily in front of them, panting with joy as the blond woman pets her head. Spread out across the coffee table are lots of different little WayLife packages. The room smells like pussy, but I know it's just the oils.

"Hi," says the blond woman. "Oh, you're looking so mature."

"You remember Belinda?" my mother asks. She has a very specific look on her face. "We were in the booster club," she offers, "at your school. Belinda Frangi."

Belinda Frangi. Of the dog-fucking Frangis. "Booster club," I say. "Right, boosters," I say again.

"Boosters. That's how we know each other." Belinda nods a lot, and gratefully.

"And now," my mother says, "Belinda's one of my WayLife colleagues. Isn't that funny?"

Poppy, carrying the Berkey, adjusts it up onto her hip. "Is she your boss?"

Belinda laughs. "There aren't any bosses in WayLife," she says, "but if there *were,* your mom would be *my* boss." Belinda reaches out to scratch one of Amy's ears.

"Oh, she has this thing with the ears—" Poppy starts, but Amy closes her eyes in pleasure at Belinda's touch.

"We're gonna put this down now," I say, hustling Poppy to the kitchen.

"Her son raped that little dog," Poppy mouths once we're alone.

"I know," I mouth back.

"You know?"

"Mommy called to tell me and she said—"

"Jason Frangi was why we needed the police. I mean, kind of, yeah. How could that woman ever touch a dog again?" Poppy whispers, unboxing the Berkey. "How could she even *look* at a dog? Is it bad that I don't want her touching *my* dog?"

"Life goes on," I say.

"I saw him once, in Publix, when I was still living here," Poppy says.

"What did he look like?"

Poppy lifts the shining hulking Berkey barrel into sight, setting it gently on the counter. "Like a guy who'd fuck his dog to death."

I nap until Belinda leaves. Once she's gone, I go back into the kitchen to find a snack. Poppy and my mother are sitting at the breakfast table by the window. Poppy's crying. When I walk in, the two of them look up at me, animal, afraid. Poppy gathers a pile of tissues sitting in front of her and holds them in her fist on the tabletop.

"What's going on?" I ask.

"We're just having a chat," my mother says. She puts her hand on top of Poppy's fist. "We're just crying it all out."

"You're not crying," I say.

"I was," my mother says, but it doesn't look like it to me.

I open the fridge and pull out a small cup of yogurt. I look at the expiration date; it's a week gone by.

"It's fine to eat," my mother says.

"Okay," I say.

"Eat it," says my mother.

"I'm eating it," I say. I peel back the foil; the yogurt inside is curdled and runny. I sniff it.

"Oh my god," Poppy says. "She's so anal."

My mother laughs. "Does she do this with you?"

"All the time," Poppy says. "I told her to see a therapist, but she won't."

My heart blackens. "I'm much better than I used to be," I say.

"Clearly," says my mother, gesturing at the yogurt.

I grab a spoon and shove a huge watery bite of yogurt into my mouth, staring at the both of them. I can't tolerate being ganged up on.

"Whoa," Poppy says. "Psycho."

"What are you guys *talking* about," I say through the yogurt.

My mother dusts dust that isn't on the table off the table. "It's none of your business," she says. "It's just between us."

I look at Poppy, desperate. But she's staring down at my mother's gorgeous bony hand atop her own.

I take the yogurt cup back to my room and throw it out in the bathroom trash. When I turn around, Poppy's standing there.

"We really were just talking about nothing," she says. "Seriously, nothing. I just cry so easy when I'm around her."

"You're icing me out."

"Your life is icing me out with her," Poppy says. "Have you ever heard the term 'triangulation'?"

"Shut the fuck up with triangulation," I say, pushing past her toward my bedroom. I shut the pocket door that connects to the bathroom and lock it and put my head against it. I'm breathing so hard. It's miserable to be on my mother's good side, miserable to be on her bad one; miserable to be Poppy's confidante, miserable to be a joke to her.

"I'm sorry," Poppy says. I don't answer her. "I knew you'd throw the yogurt out in here," she calls. I open the door. Poppy's putting the yogurt down the sink, rinsing out the plastic. I know she feels me watching her. She looks mild as Jesus. I close the door back up.

That night after all our nail appointments—my father, who buffs and gets a coat of clear once a month since he works with his hands, comes, too—we sit down as a family to eat a rotisserie chicken. Poppy eats some iceberg lettuce with olive oil.

"You know," our father says, sucking on a skinny brown bone, "one of my patients earlier today, I told her my girls were home for the holiday, and she asked about you two, and I told her you're living together in a converted Jewish hospital in Brooklyn, and she says, *In Crown Heights?* and I say, yes, in Crown Heights, and she says, *I trained at that hospital,* and she tells me when she was a girl, she lived with her family off Flatbush Avenue and she was a nurse at the hospital. Is that amazing or is that amazing?"

"Amazing," our mother says, "but maybe not in the way you're thinking."

"What do you mean by that," I say. The tone of my mother's voice makes my asshole clench.

"Amazing, astounding, appalling. That you're living in a dirty old *hospital*, alone, halfway across the country, in the most violent, polluted city in the world."

"It's not really across the country," says Poppy. "It's on the Eastern Seaboard." She picks at the salad she made for herself. "Belinda's nice."

"Belinda's wonderful," my mother says.

"Fucked up about her son," says Poppy.

Our mother shakes her head. "Let's not talk about it. It's not nice for the dinner table."

"I bet it's hard for her to, like, live a normal life."

"It's impossible."

"So shouldn't you, like—not be getting her into a pyramid scheme?"

"It's not a pyramid scheme, who do you think I am?"

"How'd *you* get into this?" I ask. "It's, like—essential oils, pyramid schemes, church—those things are—they're for goys, like how the army is for goys, being a cop is for goys—"

"Being a cop is for any American. Michael Levy's a cop, Joy's son, you know him."

"I've *met* him," I say, "but I don't *know* him. All those things are for goys. Not for us. I feel like I'm on glue around here."

"I bet you do know what it's like to be on glue," says my mother.

"You know, Jules," my father says, "you're being very narrow-minded. Moses consecrated the luchot with oils, it says so in Torah." He sips some water. "And listen, hey—you wanna talk Jews and pyramid schemes: Madoff."

"Madoff was running the scheme," Poppy says. "He wasn't a pawn in the scheme."

"What can I say, I'm not a normal Jew," says our mother. "And you know better than to talk like that, generalize like that, it's anti-Semitic. Jews aren't all the same."

"Yes, we are," Poppy and I say at the same time.

"I'm helping Belinda run her own business," our mother says. "I'm helping her make a future for herself. From the *ashes* of her former life."

"From the ashes of the shih tzu her son fucked until it died and then cut up into nuggets, maybe." Poppy eats more salad. "She has no future, Mommy. You're exploiting her."

"That's very harsh, Pauline," our father says to Poppy; she freezes at her full name, deployed only in times of great strain. "You've suffered setbacks, you've behaved in ways that, you know. That aren't good, that scare us. And yet the people who love you have always rooted for you to succeed."

"I got depressed and stopped taking care of myself, I didn't engage in bestiality and then dismember the animal I'd *engaged in bestiality* with."

"Um," I say.

"—And you guys have never rooted for me. And please don't call me Pauline." Poppy takes a big drink of wine.

"Selfish, spoiled girls," says our mother. "You judge and you judge."

"Girls? Girl," I say, pointing at Poppy. "I didn't do anything."

My father waggles his hand like: *You did a little*.

My mother continues. "Poppy, do you know that when I was pregnant with you, one of the early tests came back and said you had Down syndrome? *Down* syndrome? And I said I would keep you right away. Wanna talk about something Jews don't do, Jules? Keep babies with Down syndrome, show me a Jew who keeps a Down syndrome baby. Me? I didn't even think about it. I was ready to be burdened. I was ready to take it on. Your father over here said we should abort, but I insisted. One more test, one more test, let's just see. And thank God, because everything was fine, and here you are."

"Oh, yeah," Poppy says. "Everything turned out totally fine."

Our mother picks up her plate and stands above us all. "I'm inviting the Frangis to Thanksgiving," she says. "It's the right thing to do."

Poppy's eyes go huge. "Please say sike. We have *two* dogs here."

"Jason can't come," our mother says, "it's stipulated, or whatever, in his bond. He can't have any contact with animals. Are you crazy? I'm not talking about bringing a deviant here, into my home. I'm talking about his parents, his poor parents. Who have nowhere to go, Belinda told me today. Who didn't ask to be burdened. They shouldn't have to bear his shame, they shouldn't have to be pariahs."

"You can't say 'pariah' anymore," Poppy says.

"I just said it. And I'll say it again."

I pick at my chicken. "I think—even having just the two of them over seems like a social situation I can't handle. We don't need to be angels here."

"Are you about to tell me," our mother says, "that it's not very Jewish to do the right thing?"

"Exactly," I say. "We're exempt."

"You are such a bitch," my mother says, getting in my face. "Such bitches, both of you. I don't know who you are. Where did I go wrong? Where could I have gone wrong?"

Our mother puts her plate in the sink, then takes herself to bed. When someone's offended her, she loves to take herself to bed. She holds us so large in her mind. All she wanted to be her whole life was a mother of daughters, and she didn't find the ones she wanted in Poppy and me. Of course she sees us as alien, nefarious; of course she assumes the worst of us; of course she's become one of the mommies. She's been a conspiracy theorist as long as she's been our mother.

It's all so awful it could make me cry, and it does, and then I'm crying into my chicken.

"Oh, honey," my father says, "I thought rotisserie was one of your safe foods."

Well, posts Molly the organizer in the Facebook group for my high school reunion, it's canceled. I told you all that if no one bought tickets there would be no event. For those of you who did buy tickets, sorry. You'll be refunded through Eventbrite. Hope everyone has good Thanksgivings. Lots of people laugh-react to the post. Below it, there's a comment: lets do it Anyway!!!!!!!! shooters ft laud tn 9pm!!!!!!!!!! xoxoxoxoxo natania

Within minutes, Molly replies to Natania's comment. Just FYI everybody, Natania G.'s gathering will not be official or affiliated with Glades Prep in any way. This is important for reasons of legality and liability. Glades Prep nor its former class officers are not responsible in any way for any contingencies associated with this new and unsanctioned event. I click on Molly's profile, wondering briefly if she's a lawyer. She's not.

I convince myself that there's a version of me who decides to go to the mini-reunion for the die-hard reunion-cravers somewhere out there in the universe. Then I convince myself that that's the universe I'm in. I get dressed, put on a bracelet, drag a highlighter stick across my swollen cheekbones.

On the way down the hall, I stop in Poppy's room. She's on the floor in front of her bed, stroking Amy Klobuchar and watching what looks like *Deadliest Catch*.

"Is this *Deadliest Catch*?" I ask.

"No," Poppy says, "but it's like it, kind of." She looks up at me. "Why are you wearing that?"

"I'm going out," I say.

Poppy looks me up and down, very slowly. "No, you're not," she says.

I sit on the floor and show her Molly's post, then Natania's. "Why not," I say. "YOLO, whatever."

"You're telling me that in ten minutes you're gonna be, like, in the car driving to the beach to go do shots with Natania G., listening to Y100. Like, Rihanna's playing and you're driving out to drink with people you regularly recruit me to mock with you."

"Sure," I say.

"You haven't spoken to any of those people in ten years," Poppy says. "You're not going."

I look at the screen. A lobsterman has sustained a large wound. His forearm bleeds and bleeds. I sit down to watch his buddies wrap their dirty shirts around his hulking, hairy arm. "You're okay," they keep telling him, "you're okay."

Poppy and I sit on her bed, getting ready for company to come over the only way we know how: by hate-stalking each person due through our doors.

Our cousin David is a Realtor who sells multimillion-dollar mansions along the South Florida coast; he's rich, he loves America, he's never displayed an emotion in his life. His spotty Instagram is dotted with low-res photos of his most obnoxious listings. The numbers are surreal, practically unimaginable—$60 million for an empty lot on the Intracoastal—and my brain's about to overheat thinking about how much money he must have, about how set his children's futures are, about how, even though he's only eleven years older than I am, he's achieved a lifestyle I'll never know.

David's wife, Allyson, loves to post online about human trafficking. She's a rich shiksa—she has nothing to think about *but* human trafficking. The couple times a year we see her, Poppy and I try to goad her into talking about QAnon, but she never quite falls for it. She's always drinking Red Bull—*The mark of a true idiot,* Poppy has always said of Red Bull drinkers.

Allyson runs a concierge service called Glory Estate Staffing. All these women who don't have to work, out there working! She pairs butlers, valets, nannies, housekeepers, gardeners, and laundresses with rich families across South Florida. Her website is a frequent destination for Poppy and me; today we notice some changes. A banner featuring a picture of Allyson and her giant white veneers hovers over all; I truly believe, says new copy beneath it, that when our ambitions are aligned with our greater Purpose given to us from God, we can achieve just about anything. I am blessed and humbled to offer a trustworthy Platform for both Families and Candidates to find meaningful work and assistance. My Passion and my gifts from Him always move me forward.

"Why are half the nouns capitalized, like in German," I say.

"You know why," Poppy says.

Belinda, unsurprisingly, has zero social media—but when we search *jason frangi south florida dog murder* a slew of lurid articles appears. Someone's even started a Change.org petition called *DEATH PENALTY FOR JASON FRANGI*.

We must stand up for ANIMALS! They were not designed as sexual toys, says a comment from one signer.

HANG HIM FOR HIS HANEOUS CRIMES! says another.

"Does Florida even have the death penalty?" Poppy asks, so we search *florida death penalty*.

Why Florida Loves the Death Penalty, teases Vice.com.

At two o'clock, David and his family arrive. First through the door is our smallest cousin, Miles, who's dressed in a hot-dog costume. It's too big on him, and the bottom part of the hot dog drags a little bit on the ground. He's staring down into his iPad, his mouth open. Poor Miles. Allyson missed her window to get him a helmet when he needed one as a baby. Now the back of his head is as flat as the face of a cliff.

"Hi," we say, reaching out for hugs. He presses his face into our bellies stiffly, wordlessly.

"Whatcha watchin'?" I ask, twisting down to look at his iPad, trying to sound nice.

"YouTubers," he says, showing me. On the screen is a video called *DID YOU KNOW? In Your Lifetime You'll Probably Indirectly Cause the Death of Another Person*. A guy in a zany beanie stands in front of a whiteboard, moving his hands over a colorful graph. Amy Klobuchar rushes up to us and barks, ready to play. Miles, absorbed, startles and falls backward. Instantly, he's crying.

"She ruffed at me," he screams. "She ruffed at me and now I peed." Sure enough, some pee leaks from the hot-dog costume.

"Oh, honey," says Allyson, coming deerlike through the door on a pair of rhinestone-covered heels. "It's okay. It's okay." She smiles at us. Her veneers are glowing. I can see hate behind them, and ill will. "Nice dog," she says, her eyes bulging. They're always bulging. She hurries Miles toward the powder room and leaves him in there to clean himself up.

"I think she's wearing, like, fake super-blue contacts, don't you?" Poppy whispers as our cousin David comes through the door.

"'Sup," he says, fist-bumping me and holding out a bottle of wine. I know already that we won't talk all night, and that in a few hours, he'll fist-bump me again and say, *Later*; my entire life, this has been the fullest extent of our ability to interact. To think I had a little incest crush on him when I was small, before I knew what incest was.

Then come their daughters, Mia and Maggie, nine-year-old twins. They're in matching ripped jean shorts, choker necklaces, and cap-sleeve graphic tees that say SOCIAL BUTTERFLY.

"Kinda casual for a holiday," my mother says to no one in particular as she hugs the girls hello. Allyson passes her a bag of something.

"I can take that to the kitchen," I say, reaching for the bag, hoping to peek and see if Allyson and my mother are now exchanging oils or black-market virus samples or religious pamphlets, but my mother holds it firmly.

"I've got it," she says.

"Aunt Wendy, can I help you cook?" asks the helpful twin, Mia. The less helpful twin, Maggie, says nothing.

"You can help me with the sweet potatoes," our mother says, taking Mia's hand, "since your older cousins don't think they belong in the kitchen."

"Silly," Mia says, looking at Poppy and me, evil on her face.

"It *is* silly," our mother agrees, leading Mia away. "It's a young woman's job to help out on holidays. And you're a young woman now. But your cousins feel they're *exempt* from certain things." Allyson follows them.

"I'll help, too," Maggie says, but it's too late—she's stuck with us.

"How's school?" I ask stupidly.

"School can suck me," says Maggie, running for the kitchen.

In the living room, David tells my father about how much money he's making. Miles plops on the sofa with a new device. He starts up a game where he's shooting hookers. Poppy and I sit on either side of him and zone out, watching.

"Get her ass," Poppy says, reaching over and tapping a hooker in a white dress. Miles obliges and blows her away.

"Five me, five me," he says, reaching out his hand. Poppy high-fives him. "Yay," he says.

Mia and Maggie emerge from the kitchen holding either side of a large charcuterie board. Allyson and my mother follow them with plates and napkins. The four of them look like a painting or something. Our mother loves Allyson because, with Allyson, she can talk about Jesus. Allyson seems like the daughter she always wanted, and Allyson seems to know this, to draw some kind of wild energy from it. Maybe Allyson is the one who sold our mother the oils in the first place. Maybe Allyson is to our mother as our mother is to poor Belinda.

"Anyway," Allyson's saying, "I think they'll go to one in Maine instead."

"The girls aren't going back to camp next summer," our mother says, filling us in.

"Oh," Poppy says, "I thought they loved camp?"

"They do," Allyson says, "they do."

David walks over and picks up a whole thing of grapes off the cheese board. "Camp's letting transgenders in."

Allyson looks briefly at the ceiling.

"Oh, *transgenders,*" Poppy says, leaning forward for some crackers. "Yeah, can't have them there."

"Whoa whoa whoa," David says, looking offended, as if Poppy's the one saying something egregious. "I don't mean it like that."

"It would just be confusing," Allyson says, "especially for Miles, and *especially* because it's his first summer—"

"Imagine how confusing it's gotta be for the transgender kids, though, am I right?" Poppy says. She has on a kind of stand-up-comic voice. "They wanna go to camp, people don't want them in the camp, confusing!" She bites a cracker.

"I don't mean it like that," David says.

"I think it's fine," our mother says, "to keep the kids home until that camp figures things out."

"Maybe they should put a little oil on them," I say, "to wash them clean."

"What is it with you being down on my oils? They're for immune support," my mother says, "and *mindfulness,* and they're making me feel like an entrepreneur, and they're making me *money.*"

"You don't need money," I say. "You have plenty of money."

"No such thing as too much money, bro," David says, trying to fist-bump my mom.

"Poppy," she says, "do something with your dog." I realize very quickly that Amy Klobuchar has cornered Miles in our parents' sunken wet bar and has placed at his feet her favorite toy, a terrible dirty Lambchop with all her lashes torn off, and she is barking and whining, saying, *Let's play!* and Miles, we can see, has peed himself once again.

The front door opens.

"Knock knock," says Belinda. Amy rushes to greet her, her tongue flapping around in joy. Belinda stoops to hug Amy, nuzzling her face into Amy's neck. "You're the most beautiful widdle girl," she says. "The most beautiful widdle girl in the whole wide world."

Poppy eats another cracker. "So fucking tragic," she says to me. "You can tell the dog was her dog. You can tell it was some Oedipal thing."

Suddenly there's a finger pinching my ear.

"Ow," I say.

"Ow," Poppy says.

Our mother's got us both by our lobes. "Not one more fucking word," she says. She beams death at both of us. Then she puts on her best smile for Belinda and her husband, just like her Jesus would want her to.

At the end of the meal, our mother makes us all go around the table and say what we're thankful for. Maggie is thankful for Mia. Mia is thankful for our mother. Our mother is thankful for Mia but also for the rest of the family. Poppy is thankful for Miles. Miles is thankful for poop. On his second try, he is thankful for water. David is thankful for Allyson. Allyson is thankful for tequila and for God. I'm thankful, I tell everyone, that we're all safe and healthy. Belinda is thankful that our mother has hosted her at such a nice evening. Belinda's husband, Sal, is thankful for Belinda.

"No one's thankful for anything interesting," says my father. "I'm thankful for an election year next year." He raises his glass. So does everyone else except Allyson, even Miles, two-handed with his sippy cup.

"Oh," Allyson says, frowning into her potatoes.

"Oh?" my father says.

"It's just, it's been, you know. It's been a long few years. We don't need to get into it. We all know what each other thinks here."

My father puts on his amused face. "Not necessarily," he says, licking his lips. "What do you think, Allyson?"

Allyson looks at David as if for permission. But now he is looking at Allyson's potatoes. "It's just," she starts, "whatever kind of three years you think it's been for your side, imagine what kind of three years it's been for us. Between the lies, and the impeachment, and the constant fake news, the deep state—"

"The deep state?" Poppy asks.

"The deep state!" my father says, gesturing at me. "You were just telling me something about the deep state, weren't you?"

"I wasn't saying anything about the deep state," I say quietly.

"They've always been there," says Belinda's husband.

"And they always will be," says Belinda.

"When you say 'they,'" Poppy says, "you mean—"

Allyson tries to move on, going, "Either way, this election isn't up to any of us." I think I see her look at the ceiling, as if to imply that the election of the next president of these United States is up to God.

"It is up to us," Poppy says, "but hey, will you say more about the deep state?"

"It's the word of the week," our father says. "Phrase, phrase of the week. Everybody's sayin' it!"

Allyson shakes her head. "There's a lot of bad people out there."

"I agree," says our mother. "They're letting all the immigrants in so they can have their babies here for *free*. And the only one talking about it, I hate to say it, is Donald Trump."

"Who *are* you?" Poppy asks.

"Fuck Donald Trump!" scream Maggie and Mia, pumping their arms like they're krumping.

"They heard that on TikTok," David says.

In our parents' room, the dogs, excited by the twins' shouts, start to bark. Belinda and Miles both jump in their seats.

Allyson keeps talking. "I watched a documentary about George Soros last week, and, you know, it's everyone, it's a swamp, that's why they call it the swamp, they're all— I mean, have you heard about the emails, Podesta? How Podesta fathered Chester Bennington? Of Linking Park?"

"Linkin Park," Poppy says. She used to love Linkin Park.

"Have you heard about how Chester Bennington, through Linking Park, sowed demonic possession and discord among the youth of America in the guise of seductive music? I mean, it goes—it goes to the top. Or to the bottom. It's Democrats, it's Republicans, it's Christians, it's Jews, it's Epstein, it's all a cabal of pedophiles, and they traffic children through these tunnels, they send them back and forth between row houses on the Upper East Side, they send them to the set of the Ellen DeGeneres show—"

"What the fuck," says David.

"George *Soros*," says my father. "Come on, he's the oldest boogeyman in the book, he's the easiest target—you're smarter than that, Allyson—"

"Is she?" asks Poppy. "Because she calls them 'Linking Park.'"

"No," Allyson says, "I'm just saying—"

"Who are some of the bad Jews, Allyson?" Poppy asks. "Wanna name them? Like on a list?"

Allyson looks ready to answer, but David cuts her off. "Stop it, Allyson. Come on. My cousin's right. You're being friggin' stupid."

Everyone looks at their plates except Poppy, who's still looking at Allyson. "I still wanna hear about which Jews are the bad Jews. And I'm sure this whole family of Jews would also love to hear it."

My mother stands up. "Girls, help me clear," she says, meaning only me and Poppy. I stand and start to help.

"Stop it, Mom," Poppy says, staying planted in her seat. "Don't defend her just because you'd rather ally yourself with her, because it's more convenient, because you'd rather be someone else, because you'd rather have an easy daughter, because you'd rather, I don't know, tell yourself you're going to be saved. I'd call you a dummy, Allyson"—Poppy stands up and removes Allyson's plate from the table—"but what you really are is a fucking Nazi."

Allyson goes: "Excuse me?" Our mother tells Poppy to leave the table. David goes: "Whoa whoa whoa." Allyson says: "You know I'm married to a *Jew*."

"And you call him *a Jew*," Poppy says, "which proves my point."

"I am going," says Sal, standing up and touching his belly, "to go have a little me time."

Our father calls Poppy a troublemaker, then starts saying something about the Shoah, something about how one time he caught a rat in the pool skimmer and had to drown it and it was so terrible to take a life that he cried for days, something about how we don't understand the real Nazis' evil, how we don't call each other Nazis in our house. Our mother tells Poppy she's only doing the oils for her, to try to cure her hives, her depression. Poppy calls her a liar. Our mother calls Poppy ungrateful and tells her to go to her room. Poppy says she will; she's gonna go try to kill herself again. "Again?" three people say. "This is such a reality check," says Allyson, and she starts to cry. "Stop crying, Allyson," Poppy says, "no one feels bad for you." Maggie sees her mother crying and starts to cry herself. Mia cries, too. Maggie tells Mia to stop copying her and hits her. Mia bites Maggie. Everyone's chairs scrape back. It's time to separate the girls. I look down into my lap, fiddle with the hem of the tablecloth. It's embroidered with fat cornucopias, horns of plenty.

"Look at what you've done to us all," our mother says to Poppy. "You are the disappointment of my life."

Things don't get much better from there.

"Oh, I'm gonna miss you girls so much," our father says at the curb after a very quiet drive to the airport the next morning. He stoops to pat Amy Klobuchar. "And I'm gonna miss you, too."

"She'll miss you," Poppy says, scrolling on her phone, searching for our boarding passes.

"By the way," our father says, "the real Amy?"

"Yeah?" we say.

"I think she's gonna go all the way." He claps the side of Amy Klobuchar's flank in a rough, almost congratulatory way, a way that Poppy and I never pet her but a way that she seems to love. Her tongue hangs out and her eyes are heavy.

"*All* the way?" Poppy says, eyes bugging. "Like: to the White House?"

"All the way," he says. "She's the one." He smooches the dog on the snout, then stands up. "All righty, let me think, let me think, is there anything else I forgot to tell you while you were home?" He hugs us. "No, I can't remember anything. I guess we got it all. Safe flight." He kisses our heads, walks back around to the driver's side of the car, and gets in. Poppy and I struggle our bags up onto the sidewalk.

"Oh, no, wait, there was something," he says, rolling down the passenger-side window and shouting. "Patrick died. You remember

Patrick, right? The orthopedist in the office across the hall from me? Horrible. He was on his boat out in the Everglades and the gas tank exploded. He was all burned up, skin melting off the bone," he says, gesturing with his arms in a way that indicates skin melting off the bone. "And he still was able, I mean, miraculously, to paddle the boat back to—sort of down around where Homestead is, you know where—got some help, spent a week in the ICU. But it was too late, he died. Horrible."

"God," Poppy says. "We get it."

"Horrible."

"We know."

When we get to our gate and I look at my phone, I see that I've gotten a text from my mother.

I'm sorry things ended on that note.....Leave it to your sister to screw everything up. And WHY didn't you take the oils I left for you in your room????

the water you swim in, I write back, is the water you swim in

The celebrity cat Lil Bub has died. The end of the year is closing in. Poppy reports that earlier this evening she got her scarf stuck in the door of a C train that she thought for a minute she might like to board before deciding to step back and wait for the A.

"It was so intense," she says. "I literally could have died." She didn't die, though; she just lost the scarf. "I hope it didn't cause a track fire or anything."

"So you lost the scarf *I* lent you," I say, feeling like a fight, "because you got on the wrong train."

"I lost *a* scarf, my scarf, whatever."

"It was a scarf I lent you."

"Because you said it was ugly and you didn't know why you even bought it."

"Whatever," I say, "I'm busy, can you close my door?" I'm on my bed, in a towel, fathoms deep in the Instagram of the girl

Jon's now dating. Her name is Chelsie, she is twenty years old, and ten months ago, she was at the New York Botanical Garden to watch the corpse flower bloom.

Poppy huffs, steps out, shuts my door. Then she opens it again, startling me. I accidentally press the heart next to a comment comprised of beautiful florid emojis someone's left beneath a heavily filtered image of Chelsie and the flower.

"The point of the story," Poppy says, "is that I didn't want to die, I didn't let the train take me away. I could have died but I didn't, and I didn't even want to. I'm free. I like myself. I can take care of myself. I don't want to compromise myself or slight myself or get rid of myself. I'm new."

"One second," I say, hurrying to unheart my little heart. Before I can say anything else, she's shut the door again.

I google *corpse flower* and spend a few minutes reading about the plant's life cycle. If you are a corpse flower, you endure months and months of quiet nothing; then you're here, you're gorgeous, you smell like a dead animal, you are photographed by twenty-year-olds, you wither and die after one nothing day. It sounds to me like a life I'd like to live.

In the middle of the night, a scratch at my door. I twist the knob and see Amy Klobuchar.

"Okay," I say, and I get back into bed, patting the space next to me, assuring Amy she's welcome. She can never accept it on the first try, though. "Okay," I say again, "up up." Still, she stares and pants at me. "Come on," I say. "Come." Nothing. "*Okay*," I say, louder and happier. "Up ups. Come on. Come *on*. It's okay." She looks back toward the door. "You want back out?" I get up and open the door. She looks up at me, then at the bed. I close the door and walk back over to sit on the edge of the mattress. "Come *on*." I pat it hard, with both hands. "*Up*." Now she hops up. I check my phone for the time. By its light, I see that Amy's foaming at the mouth. "Holy shit," I say, and I rip myself out of bed, away from her, knocking stuff off my nightstand.

Poppy flips on my bedroom light. "What?" she's saying, "what?" Then she sees Amy. "Oh my god," she says, "again?" Greenish foam covers my pillows.

Giving Amy water doesn't help, so we summon a car and hurry her to the nearest all-night animal hospital, three neighborhoods over. Amy Klobuchar smiles a creepy smile the whole ride.

"What if she has rabies," I say quietly once we're in the waiting room.

Poppy scratches Amy's ear. "This is just like when you thought you had AIDS. How would she have gotten rabies?"

"Uh, the *sidewalk*," I say. "Or—you're always letting her drink out of those dirty little communal bowls in the park."

"Just because you have a thought," Poppy says, "doesn't mean it's real. Sometimes thoughts are just thoughts."

"Feelings are facts," I say back.

"Shut the fuck up, Jules."

Amy howls.

The vet, weary, tells us that sometimes animals can foam at

the mouth when they're dehydrated or overexcited or both. Amy Klobuchar's heavy tail thwonks against the metal examination table.

"We know," Poppy says, "but she did this a few months ago, too."

The vet gives Poppy a look. "Maybe you're consistently failing to give her enough water."

so fucked up, I write out in a tweet draft, that the only time i ever want a baby is the day i get my period

I look at it for a minute, decide it's not good enough.

the only time i feel ready to get pregnant is the day before i get my period

That's not right, either, because it's not that I want the pregnancy but that in the moments just before my period starts, I feel overwhelmed by and deeply desirous of the idea of a baby that's mine, a friend I made for myself.

I consult Poppy. "Do you ever want a baby right when your period hits?" I ask her, standing in the doorway to her room.

"I don't think I *actually* want a baby, like, ever," she says, "but also, yeah, basically every month around my period I want one."

Amy Klobuchar sidles up to me and sticks her nose in my crotch. I scratch her behind the ears.

"I, like, really want a baby right now. In a way that feels real."

"You don't want a baby," Poppy says. "You shouldn't have a baby." I'm not quite sure what she means by that last part, but she says it so easily that it must be true.

"I shouldn't have a baby," I repeat.

"Have you spoken to Mommy or Daddy since we got back?" Poppy asks.

"Not at all." I don't tell Poppy that two days ago, our mother texted me to say that if Poppy wanted to remain in the will, she'd better send every person present at Thanksgiving dinner, including the children and the Frangis, personalized handwritten apologies before the end of the month.

"Do you think she'll ever speak to me again?"

I shrug. "Life is long."

"I didn't do anything that bad."

"I think calling someone a Nazi at dinner isn't great."

"It isn't *great*, sure, but I can come back from it, right?"

"You can come back from anything," I say, meaning it.

"I can come back from anything," Poppy repeats. She doesn't mean it. Her face falls into a cry. "Fuck," she says, wiping away a set of huge tears. "Why do we need her so much? Why do *I* feel like I need her so much?"

"Because all anyone wants is to be mothered. Taken care of," I say.

Poppy sniffles. "Is that what you learned about America this year? From your mommies?"

"No," I say. "It's what I learned about you, and it's what I learned about me."

Poppy buys Amy Klobuchar a special foam mat, embedded in which are several buttons she's labeled things like *Play*, *Outside*,

Love You, *Speak*, and *Pew-Pews*. She's recorded herself intoning the attendant command for each button; when the dog presses down on them Poppy's voice warbles out, distorted and mechanical.

"Finn recommended it," Poppy says. "They said that learning words can be very therapeutic for dogs like Amy."

"What does that mean?" I ask.

"This is Finn's life's work," Poppy says. "Dogs can learn around a hundred and sixty-five words, usually." She presses the *Love You* button. "Love you," says the mat. Poppy gives Amy Klobuchar a hug and tells her she loves her. "I'm teaching her that when she presses the *Love You* button, I'll give her a hug, which is a sign of love." Over Poppy's shoulder, Amy tilts her head at the floor, then looks at me.

"Dogs don't like hugs," I say. "And that seems like a lot for her to put together." Just last week, we caught Amy Klobuchar softly growling at something under the couch; it was a pair of slippers. If there's a dog who can learn a hundred and sixty-five words, it isn't her.

Poppy releases Amy. "You have this overall energy lately of—of just wanting to shut me down."

"I don't want to shut you down."

"It's a button. It's cute. You don't have to be mean about it. Are there any buttons you'd like to add? There are still like five extra in there. You could make one that says 'Jules' so she could learn your name, you could make one that says 'Snack' so she could ask for a snack—"

"I just don't think dogs like hugs that much, I read about

it somewhere. They like eye contact better." I press the *Love You* button. The mat tells Amy it loves her. I snap my fingers in her face to get her attention and look her in the eyes for a long time. She opens her mouth and starts panting. "Look," I say. "She loves it. What makes you think she knows your name but not mine?"

"Panting can signal distress," Poppy says. She picks up Amy and the mat and takes them into her room. From the living room, I hear the mat's uncanny, servile voice repeating: *Love You. Love You. Love You.*

On Twitter I learn that a White House official is dating a mean girl Poppy and I went to middle school with, Lainey Kolski. Now she has a high-profile position on the Hill.

A photo of her from an event in D.C. is making the rounds on social media. In middle school, I remember, she repeatedly called Poppy *dyke* and *President of the Junior Lesbians,* making fun of Poppy's high-ranking role within our school's chapter of the South Florida Junior Thespians.

The dress she is wearing in the photo is sequined and shiny, designed to be KiraKiraed. I remember she played golf and she was good at it. She looks exactly the same as she did when we were children. I wish I'd hit her then.

I text Poppy the picture. She ignores it and instead sends me an Instagram message: i shouldn't be encouraging you lmao but this came up on my discover page........

She's sent a post from an account called jennybaby_flatearth. It's a picture of Frodo holding the earth.

One lie to rule them all.............., says the caption. Instant follow. I scroll through the rest of jennybaby's feed; obviously she's a boymom of four, and obviously she lives in a suburb of Las Vegas. An image of an astronaut floating in space, working on a satellite. Which of these best describes nasa??? A) LIARS b) ACTORS c) FREEMASONS d) ALL OF THE ABOVE!!!!!!!!!! An image of a girl in a pinafore standing over a well: anyone who studies this stuff, illuminati, federal reserve, hollywood, freemasons, zionism, elite, transhumanism, fake jews, fake global earth....... all of it. Anyone that goes realy deep finds god, the bible and jesus christ. It's all about him. it's a war on HIM.

Finally Poppy reacts to my text: lainey looks like her soul has completely rotted. I look at the photo again. I wish Poppy was right, but the world isn't like that. She looks amazing.

One of the Leighs sends me a text.

i saw a play last night that made me think of you!!!!

omg, I write back, what was it!

it was this play about orpheus and eurydice, she writes, and eurydice dies and goes to the underworld and her father is there and she's confused and she's like: where's my room!! and he's like: there are no rooms in the underworld!! but he gets some string and he builds her this little room out of string. and i was so moved to see it!! because it made me think of you!! and poppy!! and of how you have built her a room of string this year!! and I know it's been a long time since we have seen each other and there is much to say and i know you have been busy with her and i just wanted to say that i see you and i see your room of string! that you have built so lovingly!!

I haven't built Poppy a room of string, I don't think. I haven't built Poppy shit—she's still sleeping on the air mattress, and it's not just because she's too lazy to build a real bed. She feels unwanted, and I have made her feel that way. I press the heart-react button on Leigh's message. Then I go into Poppy's room and put together the bed. The whole time I keep thinking that when she comes home, she'll be so happy. But she doesn't come home until after I'm asleep; in the morning, she's gone before I'm awake.

um, I text her, where are you? you didn't say anything about the bed

Poppy writes me back an hour later: i told you i would rather do a return and get the money.

i built you a room of string!!!!!!!!!!!! I type, delete, type again, send. Poppy doesn't respond.

My only goal for the year was to be able to touch my toes by the end of it. Last December I saw a post somewhere about how stretching for just two minutes a day would change your life. But now a whole year's gone by and I haven't stretched two minutes a day and I haven't changed my life.

At a Pilates class, I struggle through a routine everyone around me seems to know well. One woman is so confident and experienced that she's chewing gum. During an exercise involving a bar and some springs, the instructor comes up to me and touches my back. He says, "Imagine your spine is a sleeve of Oreos. Now imagine those Oreos slowly becoming Double Stuf Oreos. Lengthen. Lengthen for me, lengthen lengthen lengthen. Knit those ribs. Knit those *ribs*. Now imagine your Double Stuf spine resting against a pane of thin glass. Very thin, very delicate, like a stained-glass window. Yes. And lengthen. And lengthen. And lengthen. And *knit*."

At the end of class I thank the instructor for the visual metaphors, telling him how helpful they were.

"What brought you to the mat today?" he asks.

"Um," I say, "I want to be able to touch my toes."

"You know," he says, "not all of us are built to touch our toes. Some of us will never touch our toes. And that's okay!"

"Also I'm trying to lose a little weight," I say.

He scrunches his face. "Pilates isn't really a weight-loss tool," he says. "Pilates is more about creating stability."

"I would love some stability, too. I'm always so, like," and here I make a face suggesting I'm someone with a lack of stability.

The instructor nods. "We can help you create some physical stability for sure."

I nod back.

"Remember to wipe down your equipment," the instructor says, handing me a wipe.

On the way home from class, I call my mother. Bad as things are, I can't help but miss her. I tell her about Pilates, about Lainey, about wanting a baby whenever I'm on my period.

"No matter how badly you think you want a baby, don't have one. I'm saying ever. Parenting isn't for the faint of heart. It's a miserable job."

"You think I'm faint of heart?" I ask.

"I'm putting in my latkes order at the good deli tomorrow, and I need to know—are you coming for the holidays? We can do stone crabs on New Year's if you stay through New Year's."

I'm shocked. "Do you really want us to come? For that long?"

"Oh, your sister isn't invited. I can't have that behavior in my house. Not when I need the good energy for selling it. But I saw your Instagram story the other day—honey—you're a little uneven, your smile on the left side is pulling up a little high still. You need to come in and see your father. I don't want you walking around like that. I'll pay for the plane ticket."

Faint of heart, inflexible, incompetent, uneven—

"I have to go," I say.

"Are you coming home or not? The flights are only getting pricier—I'll pay for it, I'm telling you, but I don't want to spend more than I have to here—"

"I have to *go*," I say again.

"Are you being robbed? You sound scared. I heard about that girl who just got killed in the park. Are you in the park? Is it dark there yet? Of course it's dark there. Are you in the park after *dark*?"

"I'm in a different borough than that. I'm not being robbed."

"Don't lie to me, I can hear it in your voice that you're scared."

"I'm a little scared, but just about life."

"Say *I love you* if you're being robbed. Say, uh, *I don't love you* if you're not being robbed."

"I don't love you." I hang up.

At the end of the workday on the Friday before Christmas, Emily Slacks me to ask if I have some time after lunch to chat.

It's budget cuts, it's restructuring, it's big changes coming from the top, changes that are unwanted but necessary; it's nothing, of course, nothing to do with my high-quality work or my fun personality. Now, as if I'm in an episode of television or something, I'm walking through the Flower District with a box of my desk stuff: an ugly prayer plant, a pretty prayer plant I got after growing resentful of the first one, my backup keyboard, a hardcover of *The Last Samurai,* which I kept on my desk to intimidate my coworkers.

fired lmao, I text Poppy. She doesn't write back. I cycle through some reasons why: She doesn't like me anymore. She's moving out. She's about to have another depressive episode. She's fucking the dog trainer.

"You're a fuckin' junkie," a guy who seems like a junkie is screaming at no one. Everything is covered in pretty lights. Flurries that look more like nuclear fallout than snow are coming down all around. It feels like a great time to buy something, but I'm not near any good shops. And everyone who passes is staring at my box, knowing exactly what it is. At the next trash can, I unpack the important stuff into my tote and toss everything else. I step to the curb and then realize: I don't need anything, actually. My possessions are holding me back. I dump the rest, even the keyboard. Enlightenment is the release from the pull of possessions. It's all going to be different now. The whole walk to the train, I catalog the things I have at home that I hate: weird brown shirtdress, purple IKEA mirror from three versions of myself ago, pretentious art books stacked high on an ugly decorative chair. I'm getting rid of it all.

are you having sex with the hot dog trainer rn or something lmao, I text Poppy. Immediately I regret it. Would it be so bad if she were? If she had someone else? If she had a little fun?

The subway car I step onto is empty except for a lone man: it's a bad sign, but I ignore it and stretch out on a bench, sitting sideways with my feet up. I put on my headphones and open Instagram. One of my mommies has posted a very long story. "I want to share a prayer right now," she says to her camera, messing with the front pieces of her hair. "Because through prayer there are a lot of revelations, beauty, downloads, connection, creation that can be born." Now she's on a new slide. She's put on a golden glitter filter that makes her face sparkle. "So I'm going to say a prayer, because one of my followers messaged me asking how to pray. So I'm going to show her. First, close your eyes and start to just think about things that you might wanna ask for." She closes her eyes, which makes the filter go away. "So for instance I pray that my follower who is seeking a deeper connection to holy sources, the higher power, Christ, Christ consciousness—instill in her clarity, progress, determination, patience, hope, light, essence, enthusiasm—fill my heart and body and mind with your spirit to guide me, to walk the path in this life that you have put me here to do, please fill me with that clarity, that light, the connection—" The filter switches. Now the mommy's head is ringed in pink blossoms. "Please transform all of my doubts into faith and fierce love. And to all of my friends and followers, online and off, I hope they have the will and the strength to confide in you, Lord, and I hope you'll please fill them with their own strength and belief and faith that anything is possible and that they can find a better day and know all of the goodness and abundance that is here on this planet for them to receive." The filter switches: big kitten ears and silly wet kitten eyes. "Amen." The mommy's kitten nose twitches. "So there you have it," she says, "that's how you pray! You just close your eyes and let in the light and recite what you receive, and if you just open your mouth and speak what it is that you pray for, you connect with something bigger than yourself and you find peace."

Weirdly, I'm emotional. It feels like this mommy has just prayed over me; like maybe she's made it so everything will be okay.

Poppy writes back: idk what the fuck you're talking about.

The man sitting at the other end of the train stands up and walks toward me, preparing to get off at the stop we're sliding into. He stands at the door closest to me and holds on to the pole just over my head, like a threat. I look up and see him staring at my feet.

"That's disgusting," he tells me as the doors open. "People sit on those seats."

"You're disgusting," I say. He steps off the train. I feel extremely proud of myself for about a minute before I realize that I've had almost this exact interaction before, years ago, on a different train, with a different man.

"You could go back to BookSmarts," Poppy tells me over dinner. "They have a lot more money now. I don't know how things were when you were there, but they seem different. I could talk to them for you."

"I could talk to them, I worked there first."

"But you don't work there *now*."

I reach over and grab Poppy's hair and pull.

"What the fuck," she says, "let go."

Amy Klobuchar, tail wagging, runs over and jumps up to lick my wrist. *Get her!*

"I was kidding," Poppy says, "I was kidding, ow, let go of me."

I know she wasn't kidding, but I let go anyway.

"You need to chill out," Poppy says. "You got laid off, it's not the end of the world. You have savings, you're, like—you know, healthy. You're fine. You'll find another job."

"Every problem you have is the biggest thing in the fucking world, and then I have one problem, and you tell me to be like: whatever."

"No, that's what you fucking do to *me*."

"Stop saying *fuck* just because I'm saying *fuck*," I say, and then I stand up and leave the table and take myself to bed.

In the morning, though, I do email BookSmarts. I tell them that I'm unfulfilled in my new role, that it's not challenging me, and that I'd love it if we could have a discussion soon about me coming back to my old role. *My* coming back to my old role? *Me* coming back to my old role. I tell them that I understand if there aren't any opportunities available at the moment, but that I'm hopeful I'll be able to return and keep shaping the future of e-learning.

Minutes later, my old boss, who's always online on the weekends, emails me back. Sure, he says. Contract, W-4, I-9 attached. And they are. So I fill them out and sign them, quick quick, and send them right over with lots of thank-yous and questions about when I'll get access to Slack back, when I should start, given the holidays.

Honestly if you could go into the drive this weekend and get some work done on *Far from the Madding Crowd* that would be awesome. Want to publish before 24th. Thx.

The twenty-fourth is Tuesday. I flip through some old emails, find some old links, reinstall the BookSmarts Google Drive on my computer. I open up the *Far from the Madding Crowd* file. Fifty pages of work. Due in days. Hours, when I think about it. I look out the living room window. A pigeon is flinging itself over and over against the mesh netting that hangs from the scaffolding, flying higher and higher, desperate for a place to rest.

I email my boss one more time. Actually, I say, this was a bad idea. I don't want to do BookSmarts again. I'm sorry. I'm in a very strange place right now and there is a lot going on in my personal life. Really sorry again for the confusion. He doesn't email me back, which feels right. Next I email Emily. I thank her for the opportunity to have been a small part of something so big and amazing. I wish her a warm and restful holiday season. I ask her if there's any way she could keep me on in some sort of freelance capacity. I tell her I'll write anything. Minutes later, a response—my heart pops. But it's just Emily's OOO wishing *me* a restful and warm holiday season. I can't even think of original words. At least, I tell myself, I put them in the better-sounding order.

I call my father. "Hi, Daddy," I say.

"Hello, sweetheart," he says. "How's my best girl?"

"Um," I say. "I lost my job. Right before Christmas. And Hanukkah." I try to make myself cry.

"Oh, honey," he says. "But you're such a good little worker, what happened?"

"I know," I say. "I worked so hard, I don't know, I don't know what happened."

"Hang on," he says. "What?" In the background, I hear my mother. "It's Juju," he says to her. "She got let go."

"No—" I say, willing him not to tell her anything else, but it's too late.

"You tell that—" I hear my mother say. Then I hear some rustling. "Give me the phone," she says. "Give me the phone." Then she has the phone. "You have the *audacity*," she screams, "the *audacity* to call and ask for *money*?"

"I wasn't asking for money," I say, though the truth is I just hadn't gotten that far. "I was just sharing."

"Sharing my ass," she says. "You're shit out of fucking luck. You want money, you earn money."

"But you have two *Range* Rovers," I say, breaking, straining. I feel foamy, like Amy. "I just need a little—in years and years I've never asked—remember how scared you were that I was getting robbed? I've kind of gotten *robbed* here."

In the other room, Amy is playing with her mat. *Love You. Love You. Love You.*

"I've never liked you living there. You've never thrived. You wasted your time with that bozo asshole, you work shitty jobs, enough. It's enough. You want money from us, you come home and work in the office. Act like you deserve it. Your poor father. He was so excited to get a call from you. His face, you should've seen it. Lit up like an angel. You scavenger. I have nothing to say to you." There's quiet, but we're still connected. More rustling: incredibly, she seems to be passing the phone back to my dad.

"Well," he says. "You heard her."

"I did," I say.

There's a silence. Then: "So, any big plans for the weekend, angel pie?"

"I wouldn't say you debased yourself," Poppy's saying, "that's a little strong—" Amy Klobuchar sticks her head out of her L.L.Bean bag and whines. Poppy pushes her head back into the canvas and holds it closed. Amy cries some sharp, high yowls. "This is for your own good," Poppy says to her. "You're going to Montauk. Do you know how lucky you are, you come live with us and we take you to fucking Montauk? You could've wound up in, like, Illinois or something. In Queens."

We're on the platform at Atlantic, hurrying toward the train that will take us east. Last night, as the fake-ass specter of Hanukkah dropped over us like cloth and Monday threatened near, Poppy decided that even though the compulsory Christianization of the month of December is a profound threat not just to the nation but to the world, we should get away for Christmas. To the Hamptons. On her. She googled *room of string* and conceded that I have indeed made her a room of string; that I have made my home her home at great personal sacrifice; that we deserve to create our own traditions; that a trip to the beach will help me clear my head and get ready to search for work in the early days of the new year. I texted my mother that I wouldn't be coming home, that I wouldn't go anywhere Poppy wasn't welcome, now or ever. I haven't heard from her since. I'm on a crying jag and I can't stop. Doom is in the air. I'm Jell-O.

"I keep humiliating myself," I tell Poppy, "in front of so many people in so many ways in such a short amount of time. I'm nothing. I have nothing." A balayaged girl wearing a puffer vest and wheeling an immaculately clean Away suitcase stares at me as she hustles past.

"I personally don't care about this aspect of crying publicly," Poppy says, "but you're making a little bit of a scene."

On the train I scroll Instagram, fighting against the poor phone service. My mother has posted an image of a new shipment of oils. *Contact me for an Amazing Opportunity!* says the caption; the words are bookended by emojis of sparkles and American flags. It's so stupid I can't bear it.

"I'm not going to be able to find a new job and I'm not going to be able to pay rent and she's gonna make me move home and work at the office during the day and package her little snake juices at night," I weep, holding my phone up to Poppy's face. "I'm gonna have to be her mommy accomplice."

Poppy's asleep.

Wake up, I think.

Instead, she reaches over and holds my hand. I can see a fresh hive—Poppy's first in months—peeking out from under her sleeve.

From the Montauk station we call a car to drive us to our surf shack. The Uber takes twenty-seven minutes to arrive and costs us nearly sixty dollars. At the house, we follow the instructions that were emailed to us and locate the lockbox around the side, near the outdoor shower. There's of course a terrible moment when the lockbox isn't working and our Uber driver has pulled away already, and we have all these bags that are full of electronics and wine and our dog, and we think we won't have a way of getting in, and our phones have no service, and we feel cursed. But after we each try the box twice, it pops open—seemingly because we've broken it—and we let ourselves in. The house smells like a hotel, a little bleachy, but it's clean and pretty and there's expensive-looking wood flooring. Immediately Amy Klobuchar squats and pees. Thank god there's no rug.

"Are you feeling safe now that you've done that?" Poppy asks the dog as she slams around looking for a paper towel and some cleaning spray. "Are you feeling in control, you feel like you own things now? Idiot." She sounds like our mother.

Amy Klobuchar, excited by all the movement, pants and wags. I pet her.

"Don't pet her," Poppy says, more like Wendy every second. "She'll think you're praising her."

"But I love her," I say.

"It's not love to do things that confuse the things you love," she says.

It's cold and gray out, which makes sense, because it is winter, and winter comes even here. Poppy wants to stay inside and get high and listen to music.

"I'm gonna go into town," I say, "to East Hampton." This morning I followed lots of little shops and cafés on Instagram. I want to smell whatever candles they have burning, touch clothes I can't afford, pick out something I only half want to take home as a souvenir. All the things I already do almost every weekend in Brooklyn, except I'll be doing it somewhere nicer than Brooklyn. But when I pull out my phone to call another Uber, I see that prices are surging, that it'll take the car another twenty minutes to arrive, half an hour to get to East Hampton, half an hour to get back. It occurs to me that it's the offseason. Probably very little is open, even with the holidays. Probably whatever shopkeepers I encounter will be bitter townies, angry about having to work, ruining the enchantment for me.

"Actually," I say after staring at Uber for several moments, "I'm gonna stay."

"Yeah, it's miserable out," Poppy says. "Just stay here, get every second's worth outta this place."

"That makes it sound like we're too poor to be here. We're not poor."

Poppy looks at the ceiling. "I didn't mean it like that, I meant it to be encouraging. Like, it's too gross to do what you wanna do, so you should really try to enjoy doing something else."

"You didn't mean it that way."

Poppy blinks at me. "Okay, when do you want to do Hanukkah presents?" she asks.

I didn't get her a present. I thought we were doing a kind of restorative ironic pagan solstice mental health thing; I thought we were divesting from all religion, ignoring the clamor of capitalism, bringing a tough year to a quiet end.

"Um," I say. "Tomorrow night?" In my mind I'm scrambling as to how I can get Poppy a present on Christmas Eve Eve, in a resort town, when I don't have a car, and when I've just told her I don't feel like going out. "I'm gonna lay down," I say.

"*Lie* down," Poppy says.

On the bed, I open my computer and search for something for Poppy. Soon it becomes clear that there's no way to find her a beautiful handmade object that will ship, somehow, in the next three hours. A trip to town suddenly seems worth it.

"I'm gonna go, I think," I say, and I call a car.

"Well, then, I wanna go, too."

I look at the dog. "We shouldn't leave Amy here."

"She'll be fine, we leave her all the time."

"But this is a strange place. She's scared. She already peed the floor."

"Here," Poppy says, tossing some of Amy's toys into the bathroom. "We'll just keep her in there with some water. There's a skylight. We'll be back before it's time for her to eat."

"You always want to do everything I do," I say, hoping this piece of cruelty will make her cry so she lets me go into town alone.

Poppy focuses very deeply on buttoning her coat.

In the first couple of stores, I try to pay attention to what Poppy picks up and looks at. But everything she likes is so ugly. Men's short-sleeve collared shirts, brown planters with gray boob shapes all over, a many-hued beanie. Gifts, I remind myself as I watch Poppy pocket a small wooden spoon in a fancy dry-goods shop, are not about the giver.

The bookstore is open, a safe bet; but the whole time we're browsing the shelves, Poppy's whispering about how weird the store's stock is and how she can't find any of the books she's been thinking about trying to read. But then on a new-releases table I spot a modern retelling of *Little Women,* its colorful cover advertising a hip-looking cartoon version of a girl who's clearly, cringingly supposed to be a millennial Jo March.

"Okay, let's go," Poppy says. "I want a snack." On the way in, she spied a bakery across the street.

"You go over," I say, "I wanna look a little more."

After Poppy's been gone a couple minutes, I pick up the book and bring it to the counter. As a compulsion, I buy a tote, too, and ask the person behind the register to gift-wrap it all together.

"Is it good?" I ask the gift-wrapper on duty.

She looks at the front of the book, then the back of the book, then the front again, then the back inside flap. "I've never even heard of this book," she says. "But I guess if you really like *Little Women*, then, yeah. It'll be good."

When I join Poppy at the bakery, she's writing in a notebook.

"What are you doing?" I ask.

She blinks up at me. "Writing some poetry." She slides the notebook to me so I can read.

The water at the mouth
of the stream is both salt
and not even now all I want
is a day out sick recumbent
in bed, warm
cup in hand
the sea is a wild and terrible
place
sharks have many rows
of teeth and every time
they lose one there is
already
another on the way

"This doesn't make any sense," I say. "Are you feeling too sad again?" I touch her forehead like I'm reading for a fever.

"I'm fine," she says, swatting me away. "Poetry doesn't have to make sense. I thought it was pretty good. Like, the break here, between 'warm' and 'cup'—"

"I wouldn't get into writing if I were you," I say, looking out at the street. "It's all bullshit."

Poppy closes her notebook.

"I'm sorry," I say. "I'm really doom-pilled right now. I don't like myself. I don't like anything. I don't like my body, I don't like what I eat, I don't like buying things, I don't like reading things, I don't like working, I don't like writing, I don't like New York, I don't like it *here*—"

"You have to stop," Poppy says. "You're out of control. Are *you* feeling *too sad?*"

Across the street, someone's getting proposed to near the Lululemon.

"Like that," I say. "Don't you hate that? Doesn't that make you wanna—wanna just freak out?"

Poppy looks at the engaged couple. The girl is holding one hand over her mouth and looking at the other hand, the hand that now has on it a glinting ring I can see all the way from where I sit, while her boyfriend photographs her. "I feel nothing about that," Poppy says. "They seem happy. I'd love to be that happy."

My tongue feels like it's swelling.

On Christmas Eve, we wake up to a thump at the door. Packages abandoned on the front step. They're for the owners of the surf shack.

"They're from *Barneys*," I say. "These could be, like, some of the last packages from Barneys ever."

"Ooh," Poppy says. "What's Barneys?"

I go into the kitchen and get some scissors. "Should I do it?" I ask, putting on an excited face as I look back and forth between the scissors and the packages.

"No," Poppy says, "absolutely not."

"I'm gonna do it," I say, and I slam the scissors through the soft heart of the packing tape.

Inside the first package, there's a wide-rimmed black hat. Poppy puts it on her head. "Look," she says. "I'm in the 'Formation' video."

"No," I say, "you're not," and I take the hat off her head and put it on my own. I open the second box. Inside, there's a bottle of D.S. & Durga. "You can have this one," I say.

"I can't use this," Poppy says, "because of my hives. You take it." She hands me the perfume.

"I don't want it," I say. It's Debaser. Years ago in a store in Greenpoint I tried on some Debaser, and it was so beautiful I kept smelling my own wrist the whole way home on the subway, and I got in a mood for days because I couldn't justify buying it. And then I got this complex about D.S. & Durga being so expensive, and it filled me with so much rage and sadness, and I got a bad feeling when I walked by a bottle in public or when I thought I could smell someone wearing it. I yearned for it and I hated it; there were times I could've bought it and didn't and was proud of myself and mad at myself and existential about the beauty of want, about the smallness of objects, and I told myself that I was stronger than want, stronger than objects.

I let Poppy pass me the bottle anyway; in exchange I give her back the hat. I uncap the perfume and spray myself. It's not as nice-smelling as I remember.

"We should take the boxes home with us," Poppy says, placing the ravaged packages in the bedroom, "so they can't ever trace it."

Poppy wears the hat for the rest of the afternoon. When we take Amy Klobuchar for her suppertime walk, Poppy even hands me her phone and asks if I'll take a picture of her. Poppy never asks to be photographed. She often cringes about how she *hates to be perceived*, borrowing the obnoxious linguistic tic of the masses. She has a scant presence on social media, few images of herself on her phone at all anymore. But something about this hat!

She posts the picture I take of her, behatted and walking down the middle of the road, dead yellow grass on either side of the blacktop, to her long-dormant Instagram. When we get back to the house and start cooking, the expensive ingredients we bought during our trip to town yesterday roasting and sizzling, I notice she's checking her phone a lot. It should make me feel good; anything Poppy cares about should be a victory, a blessing. But the idea of Poppy caring about likes makes me feel dead inside. Caring about the cruel void of the Internet, the expressions of self that are shelved there, the ineffable contours of memes and memes of memes and memes of memes of memes—that was always my thing. Poppy's somehow too good for it, and not good enough.

After dinner, presents. I open what Poppy got for me: it's a line drawing of the Jewish hospital building, in the early 1900s, framed in warm teak. Model T–looking cars flank the road; an old man in a long black coat and big black hat walks up Classon Avenue.

"I didn't draw it myself," she says. "I commissioned it. I found this old picture, and I just wanted to share it with you." She smiles.

I lean forward and grab Poppy, hold her, crying a little, feeling like shit for making her feel so unwelcome, for making her feel like she's not part of my life, for making her every day harder and less fun, for never having built her the room of string. At the same time, I have a nasty thought: she's doing all this so I'll feel guilty, so I'll never make her leave; so she can drive me out one day, so she can replace me, so she can have my life.

"Stop stroking my hair," Poppy says, "oh my god, it's just a drawing. Are you okay?"

"I got you a shitty book," I say, shoving my present into Poppy's lap. "I didn't think of anything good. I got it so last-minute. I should've just told you I didn't have anything. You thought so hard."

"We can trade responsibility, you know," Poppy says, "like, over time, who gets the thoughtful gift and who gets the not thoughtful gift. We have our whole lives. We don't have to always be perfect. God, stop *crying*."

Poppy opens her present. Her face, in the firelight, looks happy and excited. She tears the paper off and sees the cover.

"*March Girls,*" she says, and smiles. The smile is real. "Do you really think I'm Jo?"

I feel nothing when it comes to *Little Women,* but if I had to pick a little woman to be, *I'd* be Jo. And Poppy, obviously, would be Beth. But I pretend I don't think this, and I smile, too, and I nod, and I tell her what a Jo I think she is.

The next morning I wake up to find that my vasectomy-reversal mommy has made a decision: Summer will be the name of her and her hubby's miracle baby.

the best christmas gift of all is coming next month!!!!
now let's narrow down a middle name mamas!!!! here are
some of my favs, my indecisive self just can't pick!
Summer Jaye
Summer Rae
Summer Rayne
Summer Grace
Summer Faith
Summer Fayth

"If it's coming next month," Poppy observes after I show her the list, "then it's not really a Christmas gift? Is it?"

"It's not," I agree, laughing. "You can't call something a Christmas gift if it doesn't come at Christmas." I love feeling better than the mommies. I love feeling better than anyone. I scroll a little longer, standing there in front of Poppy; our mother has posted twice. One square: a picture of last night's menorah, three candles lit. The caption: Lonely Chanukah Last Night. Parenting Is not for the Faint of Heart. Blue-heart emoji, white-heart emoji, tearful-face emoji. She's sharing with her Instagram audience of forty-seven people exactly what she said to me the other week. She's making it seem like Poppy and I have both died, or we're somehow both in the hospital at the same time. Her second-most-recent post, from earlier in the week: a meme of a vintage cartoon housewife cooking; above her stove, text reads: *FOR THOSE WHO LIKE TO STIR THE POT... YOU SHOULD KNOW WHAT YOU'RE COOKING BEFORE YOU GET BURNED*. She's captioned the post with her signature angry-face bleepy-mouths. I assume it's directed at me.

"Look what I found," Poppy says, turning her laptop around. It's a big beautiful shelving unit sold by some modular furniture start-up. "I was thinking we could get it for that little nook in the kitchen where we have the bar cart and the littler shelf, and we could just scoot those things around, and that way there'd be more space for all the, like, plates and glasses and appliances and stuff. You know, open storage, which is classy, and then there's more room in the cabinets for food. There's just not enough space, I've noticed lately, and I'm always so frustrated, looking for spots to put things where they won't all topple over."

I swallow. "Yeah."

"And look, you can get all these color combos, and it's all held together with these brackets? I think we should order it now, like, *to*day, and that way it'll get there not that long after we get back, and we can start the year off all fresh and organized, like spring cleaning but early?"

A little cloud moves through my head. "You want to stay? Like, into next year?"

"Well, yeah," Poppy says, "ideally. I mean, it feels like we're in a rhythm now, like we've figured out some space and boundaries and stuff." To me, this doesn't sound exactly true. "You're renewing the lease next month anyway, right? Like, you haven't mentioned not renewing, you haven't mentioned wanting another—another place, a different situation."

"Yeah, I guess," I say, realizing I haven't.

Poppy puts the laptop aside. "Well, what else were you thinking? You really want to move all your stuff? I mean, it's a pretty great setup   "

"No, I know, it is. I just feel itchy."

Poppy flips her hair part from one side to the other and fluffs it. She's getting angry. "Itchy?"

"Just, like, I don't know. Do I really want to stay in New York forever?"

"Not forever, we're just talking about another year."

"Right, right, but it's, like, every year that I stay is a year I stay. You know? And if I can't get a new job, I'm not even going to be able to afford it, so."

"Mm-hmm," Poppy says. "And where are you feeling itchy for?"

"I don't know, I was thinking, like, Portland or something.

Somewhere in Oregon. What's that place with that college, Eugene? Somewhere with a saner cost of living."

Poppy blinks. "You've never once in your life mentioned cost of living. Or wanting to live in Eugene, *Oregon*." She looks down at her laptop. "You're just trying to blow me off and get me to move out so that you can decide you don't actually want to move to, like, Eugene," she says, putting "Eugene" in air quotes, "and then you can just live alone, and be alone, and die alone."

"I'm not," I say. "But it's, like—you know how you're a different person when you're around your family than you are around other people? Or even, like, just around yourself? I've been the person I am around my family for nearly a *year*. And you never even set up that bed I got you, the little-sister bed, so I had to do it, and it didn't even mean anything to you. It's like you don't care about closeness, permanence, whatever. You wanna be here when it suits you and not when it doesn't."

"Those aren't related. You always do this," Poppy says. "You're so emotional, so—so, like: you're my best friend, then you just fucking ruin it with excuses. You're so full of shit. If this were, like, a relationship, it would be an abusive relationship."

Poppy's words dry my mouth out. One time when I was little, I remember, my mother told me she loved me so much she wished she could marry me. "If this *was*. If this *was* a relationship," I say.

"I'm pretty fucking sure it's 'were.'"

"It's 'was.' Plus, what a weird thing to say. What a completely fucking insane thing to say, If this was a relationship."

"*Were* a relationship."

"I can't build my whole life around my sister," I say finally. As soon as I do, I wonder why I can't.

Poppy's face tightens. She tucks her bottom lip into her mouth, and I know I've fucked up. "Why not?" she asks. "Tell me." Her voice is needful. "Why not?"

I don't want to think about the answer. I make myself cold. "This is just like when we were little. Like how we used to take all our baths together, way too late into life, and then when we were, like, eleven—or when I was eleven—I wanted to start taking showers instead of baths, and also I had started getting pubic hair. So I told you we couldn't take baths together anymore because I was taking showers from now on. And you had such a fit, and you would come into the bathroom when I was showering and take off all your clothes and get in and sit on the floor of the tub and wash yourself in the floor-of-the-tub water." I remember looking down at little Poppy, her little square face, her little wet bangs, her little bony body in the corner of the shower, I remember kicking water at her, I remember saying, *You love my dirty shower water,* I remember the bath toys she'd bring in and line up on the edge of the tub, I remember slapping them off, calling them babyish, calling Poppy a baby, screaming at the top of my lungs for her to get out, turning the water as cold as it would go, suffering just so I could make her suffer. I realize I'm crying.

"This isn't the same," Poppy says. She's crying, too. "Back then you moved on to showers. You changed. But right now you haven't. You haven't moved on to anything. You just don't want me with you."

"It's because you're *keeping* me from changing. You're in the way, you're always in my way." I say it even though it isn't true. I say it even though it's clearer now than ever that I'm the one in Poppy's way.

Poppy puts her face in her hands. "Fuck," she says. Her shoulders shake. "I am, I am. I'm sorry, I'm such a fucking— And this trip, it's just like: we're doing all the same things here we do in Brooklyn, I'm shoplifting, you're being insane, I wanted to pretend, but we don't work together—"

"Don't cry," I say, "I didn't mean it, I promise." It's the same thing I used to say after I'd slugged Poppy in childhood, or bitten her, or nearly drowned her in the pool or made her weep or made her scream. Now we're hugging. "I take it back, you can stay," I say. "We can figure it out. You can stay, you and the dog, we can keep things how they are, it's fine, it'll be fine." The words feel like bullshit. I stop crying pretty quickly, but Poppy keeps going for a while.

"I don't know if you can take it back," she tells me.

Outside it's snowing. I wrap her in a hug. "I can, I do, I just did."

"I'm so sad," Poppy says into my shoulder. "Life is so hard."

"Life isn't that hard." I hold her close. "But it's a little hard."

We take a walk on the beach, our chins tucked into our jackets against the cold so that we're each staring at our own feet. To our left are some huge sandy dunes, almost cliffs; to our right is the water. Amy Klobuchar barks at every wave.

"*Water*," Poppy says to her, pointing at the water. "That's just water."

We're not saying anything much to each other. It feels terrible. "What was your favorite part of the year," I ask.

Poppy turns around to face me and walks backward for a few steps, looking at me with pain. "I don't know," she says. "Probably just walking in the park with Amy."

"I meant your favorite part of the year with *me*," I say.

Poppy looks out at the ocean like she's in a movie. "I think you were right before. Maybe it's not the best idea for me to keep living with you. I'm in your space, I'm in your shit."

Now my throat is getting tight. "No," I say, "it's okay. You're not, I told you I didn't mean it."

"It's okay, it's okay if you meant it. I'm giving you an out. I get it. We'll decide later," Poppy says, patting my shoulder. "But you're right, I think. Kind of. It might be time for a change." I know what she's doing—trying to make it so I'm the weepy one, so I'm the one who's begging her to stay. I'm not going to let her. Poppy and Amy walk on, so I follow them, thinking of what I can say to turn things my way again.

"I don't know," Poppy says, "I guess just all the nothing stuff was fun. Watching movies, grocery shopping, whatever." She's lying. We both know it. "What was your favorite part of the year with me?" She's challenging me. She's using her challenging voice.

"Um," I say. Before I can come up with an answer, we spot something in the distance, on the sand. "What is that?" Poppy says. "Is it a cat?" We get nearer to the something, which is still and small and white.

"Oh," Poppy says, when we're right up near it. "It's a skull?"

"It's a jaw," I say, because it is a jaw. "Pick it up."

"I don't wanna touch it," Poppy says. "You think I wanna touch an animal part that came out of the filthy sea?" Amy Klobuchar barks at the jaw, then drops into the stance that means she's asking it to play with her. "I actually think it's one of those big horseshoe-crab things."

"Do they have horseshoe crabs here?" I ask, taking a picture of the jaw with my phone.

"What are we looking at?" someone asks. It's a man. I turn around, a little scared that I didn't sense him coming toward us from the dunes. He's dressed well, in a big nice mackintosh coat and sandy Bean boots. He has a dog with him, too: a huge silky orange retriever holding a big piece of driftwood in its mouth.

"We don't know, actually," I tell him. "I say it's a jaw, she thinks it's a crab."

"I said it might be a crab," Poppy says. "I didn't say I think it's a crab."

The man's golden sniffs Amy Klobuchar's butt. Amy Klobuchar sniffs the golden's butt. "This is Portnoy," the man says.

"This is Amy Klobuchar," Poppy says. I'm embarrassed she's given out the dog's full name. Mostly, to strangers, we just call her Amy; her full name is ours, a special inside joke.

The man laughs. "All right, *Let's get to work.*" The way he says "work" is really mean. He's making fun of Amy Klobuchar. "I don't come across a lot of Klobuchar stans, I think her campaign's kind of fucked. It's sad for her."

Poppy blinks at him. "I think she's going all the way."

He laughs. "You guys from New York?"

"Yeah, we're from New York," Poppy says. It sounds like she's still trying it out. "We're just here for the holidays, Airbnbing, you know."

"Nice, nice," says the man, and he looks at the piece of bone in the sand. "You know, I'm out here all the time, my fiancée's family's got a place, so I'm usually pretty good at this kind of thing, but I gotta say, I can't tell what this is."

We all look at the thing that only I know is a jaw. "It's a jaw," I say. "Look." I reach down and pick it up. It's cold and slimy. I hold it in my open palms between the three of us so we can get a better look.

"I can't believe you touched it," Poppy says.

"*I* can't believe I touched it," I say.

"You know what," the man says, "I think it might actually be a—" but he doesn't get to finish his sentence, because Amy Klobuchar makes a snarl, the snarl she makes when she's excited and scared, and the golden pulls its lips back over its teeth, dropping the driftwood, and at first I think they're just playing, because sometimes it takes time to get used to a new friend; then the golden lunges to bite. But Amy is smaller and quicker, and she is first, and she gets the nape of the golden's neck, hard, between her teeth, and she's growling and growling, and I can't believe it's happening.

"Oh," says the man.

"Amy," says Poppy, "Amy, no—" as if "no," the command Amy is worst at listening to out of all her commands, will save us in this moment. "Off," Poppy says, "off!" and she reaches out with her hands, but she's afraid to get too close, and now the golden starts crying.

"Get off of him," says the man, kind of reaching for Amy but unable, for some reason, to grab her, "get off of him," and he drags the second "him" out for many seconds, it's the worst thing I've ever heard, and then Poppy says one last thing, in a peppy screechy voice, "Amy, *pew-pews,* Amy," she's even making the finger guns, and immediately Amy releases Portnoy, her tail is wagging, she turns to face us, she drops to the ground, her belly to the sky, she's smiling, her mouth is clean, a miracle; somehow she hasn't drawn blood.

"Jesus Christ," Poppy says. "Thank fucking god, I'm so sorry."

The man is crouched down, inspecting Portnoy's scruff. "You're okay, boy," he says, "you're okay." The golden is panting. It shakes its head. It looks at the water. Then it looks at Amy. Then it goes for her in one quick bolt, pinning her to the sand.

Amy's cry is worse than the golden's was. All I can say is "Oh, holy shit, holy shit," and now finally the man is man enough to reach out and grab Portnoy by the collar, but Portnoy's mouth is much bigger than Amy's, and Amy's throat is much smaller than Portnoy's, and that's how Portnoy has her, by the throat, and he will not let her go, and then he starts to jerk his head, and he lifts her off the ground, and he's worrying her back and forth, there's blood, the man still has his dog's collar, and he, too, is being jerked back and forth by his big dog's strong neck, and Poppy is saying *Please stop* over and over again, saying it in the way that someone being held down on a metal table and rapidly fucked with a kitchen knife might say *Please stop,* and Portnoy is growling like a mountain lion, growling like I've never heard an animal growl before, and then he stops shaking, but he will not release her; he spins in circles with her, wagging his tail.

"Drop it," says the man. "Drop it right now."

Portnoy looks up at the man with sweet eyes and lowers Amy onto the sand. Astoundingly, she's alive; she skitters away, sneezing, into Poppy's arms, spattering her blood all over. I'm thinking: Gross gross gross gross gross.

Things are quiet for a minute. Amy lies down. Poppy pets her soft triangle ears and says her name over and over. Amy's whining, panting. She keeps sneezing and trying to shake her head like she has something in her ear. Part of the flesh below it seems to be missing, but there's too much blood to tell. I'm aware of seconds passing. Portnoy drops into a playtime stance and barks like: *That was great!*

"Portnoy," says the man in the voice of a parent. Then he looks at us. "I would say I'm sorry, but, uh, that would be admitting fault, and my fiancée's a lawyer, and that's something I've been advised never to do in an accident, uh, or an accident-adjacent situation, so, uh."

Portnoy barks again, then sits in the sand and wags his tail. He's smiling, and his mouth is covered in Amy's blood. The man squinches his nose, takes a step back, twists Portnoy's leash tight in his hand. He's looking at the ground. "I'm, uh. Again, I legally shouldn't say I'm sorry here. She looks pretty okay, actually. You're okay, aren't you, Amy Klobuchar?"

Amy Klobuchar is panting harder now. Frothy pink blood is coming out of her mouth. Her eyes are half-shut, the way they are when she's falling asleep. She doesn't look pretty okay.

I don't have any sense of what to do. I can only think of what I'd do if I'd just been in a car accident. "Should we exchange information?" I ask. My voice sounds like it's been screaming, but I don't remember screaming.

The man won't look up from the ground. I follow his gaze; his eyes are locked on the jaw, which I've apparently dropped back on the sand. "I have to go," he says, "I just wanna—I have to—there's a vet I know out here, actually, uh, and he's—he's a great dude—" His dog barks at him, happy. He pets him. "Why don't you *stay,*" he says to me and Poppy, as if we, too, are dogs, "stay *right* where you are, I'm gonna—I'm gonna go get this guy's, uh—card—" and he stumbles back up the beach, over the dunes, pulling Portnoy, who runs and barks and leaps.

"He'll come right back," I say. "He'll come right back and help us— Is she—she's okay, right?"

In answer, Poppy leans over and throws up on the sand.

"Shit," I say, "Poppy, gross."

Poppy finishes puking. "I can't—" she says. She retches once more, but nothing comes up. "I couldn't help it." She spits a couple of times. "Holy shit," she says, looking at me, her eyes bright and weird. "It really does happen."

In the distance, at the top of the cliff where the parking lot is, there's the sound of a car starting. We both turn toward it.

"He's not coming back," Poppy says. She stands up and starts moving toward the parking lot. "Stay with her, don't let anything happen to her, put pressure on that—on that one spot."

"I don't want to," I say. I look at Amy. She looks at me. She looks like herself but very tired. I feel my stomach shiver and I look at the ground. "I can't look at her for too long, it'll make me sick, I'm afraid of throwing up, *you* just threw up, you know that's why I have my food issues, I can't stay with her."

Poppy lets out a mean laugh. "Fine," she says. "I'll take her." She unzips her jacket and makes space inside for Amy. "Come on, Amy," she says in a very sweet voice. She reaches down to scoop Amy up. Amy snarls low and bares her teeth and lets out a little bark. She puts her ears down. She shrinks away. She looks at us with big angry eyes. "Amy, come," Poppy says again, opening her arms and reaching for Amy's collar, and Amy wraps her teeth around Poppy's jacketed arm. She growls the way she growls when she's playing with one of her favorite toys, and then she lets go, and she runs away down the beach, leaking blood. She hooks a left and climbs a dune.

"Fuck," Poppy says.

"Fuck," I say.

"Sh—oh, fuck. Jesus. Okay, come on," Poppy says, starting up toward the lot after Amy. "This is not good, this is not good, there's the road up there—"

"Hang on," I say. "I need a minute here." I look down. The jaw's still there.

"You can't have a minute," Poppy says. Her face is crumpled. "This is— We have to go, we have to find her, we have to call a car, we have to get a vet—"

Poppy's very worked up. I know she's right to be. I hardly feel anything, though, but tired. Dropping off some groceries one morning, my mother found her own mother dead in her condo. She told me in the weeks after that it was the only thing she'd ever feared her whole life, the thing she'd feared more than anything else: finding her mother dead on the floor. When it was happening, though—when she was moving through the horror of shaking her mother, of staring into her mother's dead gray face, of calling for help, of waiting for help beside the body, of watching the body being carried away—it was just what was happening. She had total clarity. It didn't feel that bad. It just felt like the next part of her life; like nothing, she said; like picking up dry cleaning.

Poppy zips her jacket back up. "Fine. You need a minute, you can have your minute." She turns away from me and walks up the dune, hands in her pockets.

"Okay," I say, just standing. "I'll be here."

When she's gotten a little ways away, she turns back and looks at me.

"What?" I call.

She doesn't answer; she just turns around and keeps walking.

I sit on the sand next to the big splotch of Amy's blood. For a while I look out at the sea. The jawbone is next to me, and I kick it into the waves. I look at my phone. I think about calling the cops, but then I remember how Poppy feels about the carceral state. I think about calling my mother. I think about calling Gage. I have terrible service this close to the water. I open my secret Instagram; the images won't load, but I can at least read some captions.

Capitalism married with Judeo/Christian Values is a VERY GOOD THING! American Capitalism is NOT A BAD WORD! It's a beautiful word. Own it. Create your dream ring with an eco-friendly, affordable, lab-grown REAL diamond. when i was only 11.....i had emergency brain surgery.......i could not appear in the dance competition i had trained so hard for...... it was devastating......but recently through this community of #girlbosses i have come to realize...... that if i hadn't suffered then....... i never would have one day found my way to this path and journey of healing my body by healing my gut #guthealing #guthealth. It's a Christmas miracle, y'all: my chapbook FALLWATER is forthcoming from White Rabbit Press 5/16/20. Can't wait to share these poems with my favorite folx. If you and your fam aren't wearing matching Christmas jammies, what are ya even doing? Mom lyfe best lyfe!! BABY NUMBER SEVEN.........IT'S A GIRL!!!!!!! Is this even real?? Head to the YouTube link in my bio to watch the full gender reveal with our families! My kids will never eat a HAPPY MEAL. Depending on where you are in your journey in the matrix you may or may not be ready for this but they have found HUMAN DNA in MCD*NALDS MEAT which makes you wonder how they are disposing of all the children they use for the harvesting of adr3nochrome........to all our followers: a calm and bright christmas from the starbabies at starlab hq. scroll to see what cosmic gifts your sign will unwrap this year: YESHUA WAS NOT BORN ON THIS DAY!!!!!!!!! CHRISTMAS IS AN ABOMINATION OF PAGAN SUN WORSHIP IT IS NOT ABOUT OUR

MESSIAH Our society hates children. From pedophilia to abortion to gender experimentation and mutilation, children are placed on the altar of adult depravity every day in this country. My only solace is a holy, just God who will one day pour out His wrath. There's a version of me who throws her phone in the ocean, but it's not this one.

Suddenly my feet are wet. "Fuck," I say. A wave's coming in, and I'm so lost I haven't even noticed. Now the toes of my boots are full of water, and the ocean has, very cinematically, brought the jawbone back to me. It gleams at my side, wet and sinister. I pick it up again, even though I don't want to. I stroke one of its many teeth. I remember a story from Hebrew school. *With an ass's jaw,* Samson said, *I've killed and I've killed.*

I could sit forever, but I shouldn't. I put the jaw in my pocket and look over my shoulder toward the dunes. Something dark comes into view then: someone is coming down the beach from far away, but I can't see who it is. They wave their arms over their head at me. I wrap my hand around the jaw. Whoever it is, they're coming closer. I can't tell if it's Poppy. I can't tell if it's the guy with the dog. I can't tell if it's just a stranger. I suppose it doesn't matter. I've looked at them; I'm still looking at them. It's too late, now, for me to get up and leave. It's too late to pretend that I don't know they're there.

ACKNOWLEDGMENTS

Thanks to Monika Woods for her sharp guidance, and to Bryan Woods, Becca Schuh, Renée Jarvis, and the whole team at Triangle House for their dedication and friendship. Thank you to Emily Polson for seeing all this project could be, and to everyone at Scribner for showing such care and attentiveness toward it. For their encouragement and enthusiasm when I most needed it, many thanks to my writing group: Maddie Crum, Jessie Shabin, Ariel Courage, Erika Recordon, James Chrisman, Andrew Blevins, and especially Michelle Lyn King, who's been there for everything. Thank you to friends who were generous with their readership and their advice throughout the writing of this book: Claire Luchette, Claire Carusillo, Kelsey McKinney, Alana Grambush, Taylor Lannamann, and David Burr Gerrard. Thank you to Don and Sue Tanner for the enormity of their love and support. Thanks to Jess Tanner for coming to stay, and stay, and stay. To Rocky, for being so bad. And to Sasha Fletcher, for his good eye and his wild heart.

ABOUT THE AUTHOR

Alexandra Tanner is a Brooklyn-based writer and editor. She is a graduate of the MFA program at The New School and a recipient of fellowships from MacDowell, The Center for Fiction, and Spruceton Inn's Artist Residency. Her writing has appeared in *Granta*, the *New York Times Book Review*, *The Baffler*, *Los Angeles Review of Books*, and *Jewish Currents*, among other outlets. *Worry* is her first novel.

WORRY

A NOVEL

ALEXANDRA TANNER

*This reading group guide for **Worry** includes an introduction, discussion questions, and ideas for enhancing your book club. The suggested questions are intended to help your reading group find new and interesting angles and topics for your discussion. We hope that these ideas will enrich your conversation and increase your enjoyment of the book.*

INTRODUCTION

Worry follows Jules and Poppy Gold, twenty-something sisters-turned-roommates living together in 2019 Brooklyn for the first time since childhood. While relearning how to cohabitate, the sisters navigate internet addiction, the pressures of work, a slew of physical and mental illnesses, secular Jewish identity amid a rising tide of online and offline antisemitism, the adoption of a maladjusted dog named Amy Klobuchar, and their mother's descent into right-wing conspiracy theories over the course of a tumultuous year. When a Thanksgiving trip home ends in shambles, Jules and Poppy are forced to confront not only the current state of their relationship, but also what the future holds for them—as individuals and as sisters.

TOPICS & QUESTIONS FOR DISCUSSION

1. From mommy bloggers to tradfems to anti-vaxxers to flat-earthers, Jules engages with a very specific kind of online community. How would you characterize these influencers and why do you think she is obsessed with them?

2. The vagaries of sisterhood are a major preoccupation of the novel. Tanner writes, "[Poppy] won't let me in. I wish I could claw her face off, get to her soul, understand who she is, feel safe in thinking I know her. . . . If I were still writing, I'd write a shitty short story about us . . . and in it there'd be a sentence like: *Having a sister is looking in a cheap mirror: what's there is you, but unfamiliar and ugly for it*" (page 165). How does this help you better understand the Gold sisters? Would Poppy describe Jules the same way? If you have a sibling, does this thought resonate with your own experience of that relationship?

3. Poppy's recurring, debilitating hives are an ongoing source of strife, but they also bring the sisters together. Consider these flare-ups—do you think they have a symbolic quality? How do the sisters' struggles with mental health also impact their relationship?

4. Another theme in the novel is a deep sense of disconnection with those around us, and Tanner often dramatizes this via the texting habits of her characters. For example, when we see Jules composing and sending texts, there is often a marked difference between how she's feeling and what she ends up saying. Why do you think this is? At points in the novel, Jules and Poppy get into major arguments that only end or resolve over text messages. What do you make of this?

5. Discuss the entrance of Amy Klobuchar into the sisters' lives. How do the circumstances of her adoption and subsequent presence impact their relationship? Consider this exchange between Poppy and Jules after Amy pees her bed: "'All the websites say dogs never pee their own beds because it fouls their safest space.' 'Well,' I say, looking at Amy . . . 'I guess we got the one dog who wants to foul her safest space'" (page 188). Do you think Jules and Poppy are each other's safest space? Why do they so often "foul" this space with petty cruelties?

6. After attending a performance of a Greek tragedy that has been updated with references to social media, Poppy "whines

about the state of the American theater, trying to put words to the reason why the play was so intensely bad. *We hate big ideas and big emotions. The Greeks felt but we don't feel. We have TV in our hands. Art is dead.* . . . Poppy's ideas about dead art, to me, are just as numbing as the ideas in the play . . . Dead art is everywhere. Dead art is my life" (pages 64–65). Discuss this sentiment, which comes up throughout the novel. To what extent do you agree with Poppy? To what extent do you empathize with Jules? What do you think Jules means when she says "Dead art is my life"?

7. Consider the role of work in the novel. What do Jules's experiences at BookSmarts and Starlab tell us about her? What about Poppy's experiences at the private school where she works? Discuss the multi-level marketing schemes Jules's mommies are caught up in, and her comment "All these women who don't have to work, out there working!" (page 234). What do you think drives the mommies to participate in these schemes?

8. A residual source of tension between the sisters is the expensive, nonreturnable bed Jules unwittingly bought for Poppy while high on sedatives. Poppy refuses to use it, opting instead for an old air mattress. How does the bed reflect larger issues in Poppy's own life and her relationship with Jules? What problems of her own is Jules projecting onto Poppy?

9. Discuss the ways Jules and Poppy's secular Jewish identity is explored in the novel. Revisit the SodaStream argument (pages 15–17) and the sisters' search for their great-grandparents' graves (pages 194–200). How do these scenes speak to each other, and what do you think Tanner is trying to illustrate? What was your response to the moments of antisemitism the sisters face, online and off?

10. Consider Poppy's declaration that "Love isn't really part of my worldview" (page 108) and Jules's subsequent insistence that their views on love are not as different as Poppy would like to think: "You're queer, it's not like we live on different planets. . . . We're, like, literally the same person" (page 109). How much do you think their worldviews and experiences actually differ? To what extent does Jules give space to Poppy's queerness?

11. How does the sisters' disastrous Thanksgiving trip help us better understand them, both as individuals and in their relationships with one another and the rest of their family?

12. Discuss the sisters' often antagonistic relationship with their mother, Wendy. Consider this line from Poppy and Jules's reply on page 251: "'Why do we need her so much? Why do *I* feel like I need her so much?' 'Because all anyone wants is to be mothered. Taken care of.'" What other examples of mothering do we see in the book?

13. What was your reaction to the final scene of the novel and its ambiguous ending? What purpose do you think it served, and why do you think this is the note that the novel ended on?

14. The novel ends in late 2019 with 2020 looming large on the horizon. What do you think the new year—and the COVID-19 pandemic—holds for these characters?

15. In his essay "Worrying and Its Discontents," psychoanalyst Adam Phillips wrote this about a young patient: "For this boy, worrying could be a form of emotional constipation, an unproductive mental process that got him nowhere; and this was part of its value to him." In what ways does this quote explain Jules and Poppy's preoccupations? Does worry have any value to you?

16. Discuss the book's title. What did it mean to you before you started the novel? What does it mean to you now?

ENHANCE YOUR BOOK CLUB

1. Have everyone in your group share a kind of content or content creator that they feel compelled by despite not identifying or agreeing with it or them. What do each of you find compelling about it or them? What drives you to look, and continue looking, even if you don't like what you see?

2. Read another novel that's concerned with internet culture, such as Patricia Lockwood's *No One Is Talking About This* or Lauren Oyler's *Fake Accounts*. How is the internet and the main characters' relationship with it portrayed differently between these books?

3. Bring a favorite meme to share with the group, in the spirit of this moment from the novel: "'Memes don't *matter*, Poppy,' I shout. Now I'm crying. Of course memes matter" (page 40).

4. Try writing a BookSmarts page for *Worry*, either individually or as a group.

What is *Worry* about?

Worry is about two sisters in their twenties, Jules and Poppy, who spend a deranged year living together in Brooklyn for the first time since childhood. It begins in 2019, and Poppy's been living at home in Florida for a few years, dealing with chronic hives, depression, and parents who make her feel like an embarrassment; Jules is fresh off a big breakup, working at a job she hates, and she wants to be around someone who's doing worse than she is, so she lets Poppy come stay in her spare bedroom and try to get herself on-track. They become intruders in each other's lives: confronting how different they've become, trying to remeet one another, struggling to find compassion for each other. At the same time, they're getting into sloppy fights at Target, doing too many drugs, stealing each other's clothes and jobs and privacy, having huge ego death meltdowns. It's a slice-of-life story about two people trying to care for each other, and wrecking each other, and learning almost nothing in the process. And then, at the end, being like: "We made it. Time to crush 2020."

Talk a little bit about Jules and Poppy—who are they, and what do they mean to each other? How are their views of sisterhood and its responsibilities different?

Poppy's very sensitive, very earnest; I feel like she loves *Hamilton*. But she also really wants to die. She has this massive anger. Jules is neurotically self-absorbed, but deeply observant—she's not very intellectual at all, but I think she has this image of herself as, like, a girl who's too smart for her own good. Poppy has intense convictions about community and family and the work of "emotional labor," but they're a little performative. And Jules is way more barbed—she's only looking out for herself a lot of the time and she doesn't have the energy to pretend otherwise. I think there's a real sense of care between them, but there's also this more narcissistic awareness of being each other's mirrors: they project themselves onto one another, which I think is unavoidable between sisters.

What made you want to write a novel about sisterhood?

In 2016, my younger sibling and I lived together for six months in a two-hundred-square-foot studio—they were in New York for an internship and the apartment they were supposed to stay in was full of mold and they were breaking out in hives, so they came to sleep on my floor. The living space was so narrow that I had a daybed with a trundle instead of a bed-bed. We slept literally on top of each other. We fought every day. Physically. A nightmare.

A few years ago, though, I realized I was looking back on our time living together with real fondness, and I called my sibling and I was like, "I think I want to write about this—remember how fun it was?" And they were like, "That was the worst time of my fucking life. But I loved how often we ate at Buvette." Feeling tender and wistful about the most miserable things you've been through together—that's siblinghood, to me.

Did writing *Worry* teach you anything about being a sister?
The book draws so much on the dynamic I have with my younger sibling, and while Jules and Poppy are ultimately pretty different from us, it was so emotional to put the broader contours of our relationship on the page, to reencounter us in that way. It made me feel more protective of what we have, more grateful for the experience of being known so completely by someone. I've revised my understanding of what it is to be a sister over the last few years in all these different ways and it feels like a much more expansive role to me now. Sisters are often pressured to relate to each other in terms of this shared experience of gender, to have that be the focal point of the relationship, and that can feel so limiting and infuriating. When I look at the book now, I see echoes of that driving Jules and Poppy. There's something really feral and in-stinctual about how they are with each other, almost like they're very small children. Writing *Worry* taught me a lot about how to carry a sibling relationship beyond the structures of family and gender and distance, and about what it is to give siblinghood the space it deserves in your life.

Jules and Poppy are Jewish but they have a complicated relationship to religion—how did Judaism and other Jewish stories shape the novel's tone and outlook? What did it mean to you to write a Jewish book?

To me, the big questions in Judaism really parallel some of the big questions in writing, especially when you're writing from life: What are our responsibilities to our families and our communities? What are our responsibilities to our traditions, especially ones that maybe don't work so well for us anymore; to memories of the past, and memories of suffering? It takes the fullness of a lifetime and a lot of mistakes to arrive anywhere with questions that large. I wanted *Worry* to reflect that, the way my favorite contemporary Jewish stories do—whether it's something like *Uncut Gems* that captures that freneticism of feeling trapped between tradition and ambition, or Lexi Freiman's *Inappropriation*, which was a huge touchpoint in terms of my developing a sense of humor when it comes to feeling othered and insufficient and somehow behind everyone else; feeling uncertain about or annoyed with what it means to be a Jew. I wanted *Worry* to take on the bleakness and absurdity of it all.

How did Jules's internet mommies become such a huge part of the novel?

I knew I wanted to write something where I could transcribe the internet really closely, where I could explore what was so maddening and inane about "content." I'd been following a ton of mommy bloggers because I thought they were fun to look at, but as we got deeper into 2019 and into 2020, the lid kind of blew off and suddenly all these things converged on their corner of the internet: QAnon stuff, white nationalist stuff, performance-of-self stuff, MLM girlboss stuff. The mommies were my gateway to hell. It felt like they might make Jules even more insane and furious than they made me, so they became her way in too.

Poppy struggles with depression and mysterious hives; Jules is a hypochondriac with an emergent eating disorder; their dog, Amy Klobuchar, has lost a leg—how do illnesses, disabilities, and disorders shape the world of the book?
I think when you're living with any kind of illness—or when someone you love is—there's this desire to attach a certain kind of arc or a narrative to it: this is happening for a reason, this will teach me something about myself, this will make me stronger. "We tell ourselves stories in order to live," or whatever. But there's already so much, societally speaking, telling us that illness and disability is something we invent or bring upon ourselves or should be more capable of buckling up and riding out, and I think the need to give illness a structure comes in part from the shame of that. *Worry* explores the compulsion to make suffering feel instructive, useful, or fortifying, and shows how damaging that can be.

I'm starting to understand why you titled your debut novel *Worry*. Can you talk a little more about your inspiration?
Maybe nine or ten months into writing the book, I saw someone

tweet about this tertiary, more archaic definition of "worry" as a verb—"to slay, kill, or injure by biting and shaking the throat (as a dog or wolf does)." I thought immediately about Jules and Poppy's rescue dog Amy Klobuchar, and about her bad behavior. Seeing the word in that new context, it became this prismatic thing where it worked on every level: there was this new, feral dimension; there was the metaphor for Jules and Poppy's relationship, how "worrying" something is this repetitious act of trying to smooth something over, but ultimately messing with it so much that you wear it down; and of course there was the anxiety angle, that Seinfeldian sense of all these irritating ruminations and interactions becoming more and more intolerable. As a title, it just captured everything. And over the years I've been sitting with it, it's kind of started to feel like an imperative, too; the world's coming apart and it's, like, the president's getting Juvéderm? We *should* be worried.